Everybody Knows This Is Nowhere

ALSO BY JOHN MCFETRIDGE

Dirty Sweet

EVERYBODY KNOWS THIS IS NOWHERE

JOHN MCFETRIDGE

Harcourt, Inc.

Orlando   Austin   New York   San Diego   London

For Laurie, always

Requests for permission to make copies of any part of the
work should be submitted online at www.harcourt.com/contact
or mailed to the following address: Permissions Department,
Houghton Mifflin Harcourt Publishing Company,
6277 Sea Harbor Drive, Orlando, Florida 32887-6777.

www.HarcourtBooks.com

Published in Canada by ECW Press

Library of Congress Cataloging-in-Publication Data
McFetridge, John, 1959–
Everybody knows this is nowhere/John McFetridge.—1st U.S. ed.
p.   cm.
1. Detectives—Ontario—Toronto—Fiction.   2. Drug dealers—Fiction.
3. Toronto (Ont.)—Fiction.   I. Title.
PR9199.4.M426E84   2007
813'.6—dc22   2007034009
ISBN 978-0-15-101442-2

Text set in Sabon

Printed in the United States of America
First U.S. edition
K J I H G F E D C B A

KELLI COULDN'T BELIEVE THIS GUY, sitting there in his BMW X3, trying to talk her down from a hundred.

"And no condom."

Yeah, right. As if. That didn't worry her, she'd slip it on, he'd never know, but seventy-five bucks for a blow job. No way.

"A hundred."

It was warm in the Beamer, cold on the sidewalk. She'd been out almost an hour, it was after ten and this guy was the first conversation she'd had. Drizzling, cold for the beginning of October. It was only going to get worse.

The guy looked in his wallet and said, "I've got four twenties, you want them or not?" He held out the bills and she got in the car.

The door closed so quiet and solid.

Shit, Kelli wondered, how the hell did I end up here? "Pull into the alley, there beside the apartment building, go around back."

Twenty-five storeys high, concrete and steel, an instant slum when it was built in the seventies and it hadn't aged well. It would have blocked Parkdale's view of Lake Ontario if the raised six-lane expressway getting everybody with money out of town hadn't already.

Kelli relaxed. She'd seen the inside of a lot of Beamers and Mercs and, hell, even Land Rovers since coming to Toronto a month back. She looked at the guy, cheapskate biz boy in his thirties, and thought he wasn't so bad, really, just acting tough. It was always good to get the first one of the night out of the way.

She looked up and saw a man's face, floating, hanging in the sky. He looked her right in the eye.

Then he smashed into the windshield.

The cheapskate screamed like a girl.

And Kelli just stared at the face on the spiderweb of broken glass. The blood and bits of brain and bone. He must have fallen the full twenty-five floors.

A YOUNG CHINESE COP jumped out of the first car to show up, red lights spinning. He walked around the X3 and looked inside. Kelli said hi, and waved at him.

The shock had worn off pretty fast and now she was just taking everything in. The guy, the customer in the driver's seat, had tried to get her to leave, telling her she didn't need to stick around, he wouldn't tell anyone she was here.

Yeah, right. She wasn't going to miss this. This was the most exciting thing that had happened to her. Probably ever, if she thought about it.

The young cop, Cheung, spoke into the radio clipped to his collar, then signalled the guy to roll down the window.

Kelli watched him not knowing what to do. He'd need to turn on the engine to get the electric windows working and he didn't know if he was allowed to do that. He held his hands up, waved them around for a second, and then started the car.

Cheung jumped back.

The guy jumped.

Then he pressed the button and the window rolled down.

Cheung said, "Don't move."

Kelli laughed.

Twenty minutes later, after more and more cop cars and ambulances showed up, Kelli and Mark Lawson, that was the cheapskate's name, were standing with the rest of the crowd on Close Avenue. A young, dark-skinned female cop stood beside them, making sure they didn't go anywhere. Kelli sure didn't want to, all this excitement, but Lawson would have left his sixty-thousand-dollar car and taken off in a second. The dark-skinned cop was small but Kelli knew her type and knew she was plenty tough enough.

The cop with the small woman cop, a fat white guy in his fifties who'd been driving, was pissed off. He didn't even get out of the patrol car until the whole place was taped off. They closed off Close Avenue completely south of Queen. This time of night there was only traffic coming and going from the apartment building; the only other place on the block was an elementary school and across the street was the back end of the rehab centre. It was only a block over from Jameson, an exit from the Gardiner Expressway, and had its own little hooker stroll.

A dozen uniform cops ran around and a couple of ambulance guys stood by their rig smoking cigarettes. The body was still on the hood of the Beamer.

Then the detectives arrived.

The first one, the one leading the way, Kelli thought might have been Latin American; he was a big guy, dark skinned, broad shouldered, clean shaven, with short black hair like a crewcut, but there was something about him not really Latino. She wasn't sure. She watched him get out of the driver's side of the Crown Vic and take in the whole scene.

The other detective, a white guy in his late forties or early fifties, came around the car from the passenger side. The white guy looked less sure of himself, had less swagger. Kelli thought maybe he just got out of bed.

The fat cop, the pissed-off one, said, "Hey, Armstrong," so Kelli was pretty sure the big dark-skinned guy wasn't Latino. He didn't say anything so the uniform cop pointed at her and the cheapskate and said, "Mr. Suburbs here was picking himself up a drive-through BJ and before he could get around back Mohammed took a swan dive onto the hood of the Beamer."

Armstrong said, "You sure he wasn't pushed?"

"Who gives a shit, he's dead."

"Yeah." The rain was starting to come down heavier, half snow now. Armstrong said, "He have any ID?"

"I'm not sticking my hand in that shit."

Kelli watched Armstrong look around. She liked the way he looked, the way he took everything in and was clearly in charge but not bossing people around. She thought he might be South Asian, as they seemed to say in Toronto, but he was so big, square-shouldered.

The uniform though, he wanted to be in on everything, just not have to do any work. Kelli'd met plenty of guys like him. He said, "Hey, is he back?"

Armstrong said, "Who?"

"Him. Bergeron." Motioning to the other detective, who was talking to the young Chinese cop.

"What about him?"

"Is he back?"

"Back where?"

The fat cop had started out pissed off and now he was shaking his head and rolling his eyes, like talking to a kid. "Detective Bergeron, right over there, is he back at work?"

Armstrong walked past the uniform and said, "No, Brewski, he's not back at work, he just likes getting up in the middle of the fucking night to come down here and talk to you."

Kelli almost laughed out loud but the uniform cop was so pissed off now and she figured she might have to deal with him later.

She hoped she'd have to deal with this Armstrong.

The uniform cop waited till he was out of earshot, then said, "Why don't you go back to the fucking reserve, Tonto," and Kelli realized, yeah, that's it, he's Native.

ARMSTRONG SAID, "So what's the matter, you couldn't manage the X5?" and the guy, Lawson, said, no, that's not it at all, he just really only needed the six cylinders and Armstrong said, "Yeah, okay, whatever. So, you were just driving down the street and this guy hit your windshield?"

"Yeah."

They were standing under the awning in front of the apartment building. There was a small convenience store in the lobby selling cigarettes and lottery tickets, a crowd of at least twenty people standing around. Armstrong looked at them, the potential witnesses, and didn't think he saw a single one who had English as a first language.

He said to Anjilvel, the young female cop, "How about getting these folks some coffee? You want a coffee?"

Kelli said, yeah, sure, but Lawson said no.

"Donut?"

Kelli said, yeah, okay, and Lawson said, no thanks. Armstrong said, "Okay, why don't you get us a couple of coffees. And not that Coffee Style crap, go on up to the Tim's. Couple of double doubles."

Anjilvel ran off looking quite determined and Armstrong said, "We really appreciate you sticking around."

Lawson grumbled and stared at the cracked concrete.

Kelli said, "Hey, don't mention it."

"It's a real shocking thing to see."

"Yeah."

"Did you see him coming?"

Lawson said no, kept staring at the concrete, but Kelli nodded, said, yeah, she did.

"How did he look?"

Kelli didn't say anything, and Lawson said, "It was just a split second."

"Yeah?"

Kelli said, "He kind of smiled."

Armstrong looked right at her and said, "Smiled?"

She said, yeah. "He looked peaceful."

Lawson grunted, that smirking kind of disbelief and dismissal. Very biz boy.

Armstrong ignored him though, and said to Kelli, "Not freaked out? Not waving his arms around and screaming?"

"No, definitely not."

"Okay, that's something. Thanks."

EVERYBODY KNOWS THIS IS NOWHERE

Armstrong walked back into the street, to the X3 with the body still crashed through the windshield. Two men were getting out of a blue van with Toronto Police Forensics Support written on the side of it.

Bergeron flipped his cellphone shut and said to Armstrong, "That was Nichols."

"Let me guess. He's detained and won't be coming down." Inspector Alistair Nichols, head of the Homicide Squad, their boss.

"Right."

"Got nothing to do with it being freezing cold, raining, and Parkdale in the middle of the night."

"Not a thing. But he does want us to be absolutely certain this isn't a suicide before we get too involved."

One of the forensics guys backed into them while taking pictures and said, "I thought when these guys committed suicide they strapped bombs to themselves and went looking for crowds. Shouldn't he be up at Bathurst and Steeles?"

Armstrong said, "So, Cruickshank, it's not suicide?"

"I have no idea." He kept walking around the SUV taking pictures.

The other forensics guy, also white and in his fifties, put a big yellow ruler on what was left of the hood.

Armstrong said, "Come on guys, on TV they could tell us how much this guy weighed just looking at him, they'd measure the wind speed or something and the angle of the fall and tell us exactly what balcony he came off."

Cruickshank stopped taking pictures and said, "Well on TV they have limitless budgets for every crime scene, they have state-of-the-art equipment, they have ten people working on every case." He stopped, really just to get his breath, and Bergeron said, "Ed, it's okay, he's just yanking your chain."

Cruickshank said, yeah, right, I know. "Every goddamned time." The Toronto Forensics Scene of Crime team was made up of police officers. Some civilians worked in fingerprint analysis and identification. On minor crimes evidence was collected by SOCO, Scene of Crime Officers—regular uniform cops who'd taken a few extra courses. But all major crimes were handled by FIS cops, Forensic Identification Services. They didn't know if this was a major crime yet. Or a crime, but a dead body meant Homicide detectives took charge.

Bergeron said to Cruikshank, "Whatever you can tell us will be greatly appreciated." Then, walking away, he said to Armstrong, "You on the rag tonight, or what?"

"What?"

"Well, first Brewski."

Armstrong looked at the uniformed cop sitting in the squad car drinking from the Coffee Style paper cup and nodded. "Yeah, I don't know. That guy, he just taps my bitch bone."

"Anything else going on?"

"No, I'm fine." He looked at Bergeron and thought, man, I should be the one helping you out, first day back at work and you've got to be here.

"I CAN'T BELIEVE the crazy motherfucker jumped," Sharon said. She was back in her apartment on the second floor, smoking a cigarette and talking on her cell. "He was screaming and crying, then he walked out onto the balcony and jumped."

"Holy shit."

"Zahra said he was talking about going back."

Bobbi said, "What, back to Iraq?"

"Iran."

"Whatever. What for?"

"She said he kept saying, back home, back home."

Bobbi said shit. "She must have freaked."

"We all did. Me and Zahra and Katayun. I got them calmed down." Talking on a cell she didn't say she got them out of the grow rooms and back into their apartment, but Bobbi knew.

Sharon said, "So, don't come over here tonight, okay."

"Mom? Some credit."

"Right, okay. How'd it go tonight?"

"Okay. Fine."

"No one there?"

"Not him."

"Okay, good." Sharon was looking out the window. Cops everywhere, ambulances, crime scene guys taking pictures. She was hoping they didn't have the same kind of high-tech shit the ones on TV did. She doubted it.

Bobbi said, "How'd he find her?"

"I don't know. I think he saw her in No Frills and followed her. I don't think today, it might have been last week and he's been following her. Her and Katie."

"Shit. It's a good thing you were in the building."

Sharon said, these cops don't care about that. "It's a whole different department, corrections, not even cops."

"Still."

Yeah, still. She turned the EM on her ankle, the ugly grey electronic monitoring device, and took a deep drag on her cigarette. "Okay, good. You going home?"

"I'm going to Becca's. She's been asking for more, says she can move a lot more."

"Be careful. And then home."

"Mom, I know, okay?"

Sharon said yeah, okay, but told her to be careful again. Twenty-one years old, like all kids, thinks she knows everything.

Sharon took a good look at the street. She could tell the detectives who were in charge easy, the white guy in the wrinkled coat, looked to be fifty, and the big dark-skinned guy. She couldn't tell what he was, East Indian, Latino, something, wearing a thousand-dollar suit and nice-looking leather shoes in the freezing rain and slush. She hoped he caught pneumonia. He looked like he enjoyed his work and was good at it.

The last thing she needed.

The crime scene guys also seemed to be enjoying themselves. She wondered if there was any way they could tell what balcony Ku went off. Or if they might think he went off the roof. She tried to remember, was that door to the roof still broken from the party the punk kids had when they threw the pumpkins?

Shit, she hoped so.

THE DOOR WAS BUSTED, couldn't even stay shut. Armstrong pushed it and looked out.

Bergeron was right behind him singing "Up on the Roof."

The snow was coming down hard now, covered everything.

"Should we let Cruickshank up here first?"

Armstrong said, yeah, probably, and walked out anyway.

At the edge they looked over. Twenty-five storeys, didn't sound like much compared to the big office towers, fifty-five, sixty, or the stuff in New York, eighty or a hundred, but looking down, it was plenty far.

Bergeron said, he could have easily walked out here and jumped off.

"Yeah, he could have."

There were a lot of plastic lawn chairs lying around and one of those clay fireplaces with the chimney.

Bergeron said, there've been a few parties up here, and Armstrong said, yeah, and with Hallowe'en coming up there'll be more pumpkins tossed.

They could see the roofs of every apartment building on the next street over, Jameson, and most of those had furniture on them. Some of them had mattresses.

Parkdale spread out to the north and west.

Bergeron said, "It's a shame."

"What?"

"Look at all these old buildings, this neighbourhood. These were big family homes when they were built, mansions."

"So?"

"The way they're falling apart, now they're all rooming houses. All these new ones, these apartment buildings, they're crap the day they go up."

Armstrong said, "Yeah?"

"Changes, that's all."

"It's what happens. You know, down by the lake here, before there was Fort York, there used to be an Indian village. That's too long ago for anybody to be nostalgic about though."

Bergeron said, "Yeah, I guess so."

"You can't win. Now the place is getting gentrified, the yuppies moving in, and people hate that too. Maybe they're just reclaiming their old neighbourhood."

"Maybe."

So close to the expressway, six lanes of constant traffic— night and day—cut Parkdale off from the lake. The lake so huge you couldn't even see the other side. Buffalo and upstate New York.

Armstrong said, "This seem like a lot of vents?"

Bergeron looked where he was pointing and said, yeah, it does.

"HEY, DETECTIVE PRICE, Detective McKeon." Armstrong nodded, businesslike, at the two getting out of their car.

Bergeron said, "Hey, Andre; hi, Maureen."

Price, a bald black guy wearing sunglasses, looking as cool as Armstrong, said, "Didn't Vice just do a john sweep here last week?"

"A hundred and forty-one picked up. You should have seen the undercover work, fishnets and minis."

McKeon said she could imagine.

"We should put out a calendar," Armstrong said. "Show those firemen."

Bergeron asked McKeon how long she'd been back.

"Makes a week tonight. You?"

"This is it."

"Great start."

"How is the little guy?"

"He's great. Be seven months tomorrow."

"And you're on nights right away."

She looked at him, like, you too. "Where the action is."

Bergeron said, yeah. "You got somebody flexible watching him?"

McKeon nodded. "MoGib's taking some time off."

Armstrong said, "What, giving up on Hollywood?"

She said, yeah, and Price snorted. She said, what, and he said, you know.

"Tell me."

"You know."

"Why don't you tell me?"

"He's never going back to work," Price said. McKeon's husband, Morton, worked in the movie business as a location manager. That's how they met, she was working as a weapons specialist on some Hollywood blockbuster with Vin Diesel or The Rock or someone. But MoGib, he hated it.

"Wouldn't be the worst thing," Bergeron said.

Price didn't look convinced. He said, "Anyway, you think this guy was pushed, you think it's a homicide?"

"Don't know yet."

"Going to be a nightmare trying to get statements."

Armstrong said, "Like always. Least they haven't started throwing shit at us."

McKeon said, "Last week, up on Finch, after that little kid got hit in the driveby, guy threw a beer bottle, hit O'Brien right in the head."

Bergeron said, "Holy shit. She okay?"

"Yeah, had her hair in a bun, it bounced right off. She was pissed though, must have broken four noses looking for the asshole."

Anjilvel came back with two coffees and some donuts and Price said, "That's all you got, two?" She stood there like a deer in the headlights.

Armstrong said, "Figured you'd want some kind of extra-hot, all-foam, no-fat latte. Isn't a Starbucks for miles."

"Sure there is," Price said. "New one up on Queen, where all the art galleries are opening up."

Anjilvel looked like she was ready to run again. Armstrong took a coffee and walked with her towards the building. He said, "This is good, thanks. Can you do me a favour, find the super, bring him out here. And get a list of who lives in the apartments on the top floor facing the street. Say, top two floors?"

She ran off and Armstrong took the other coffee to Kelli and the biz boy.

Right away the guy said, "When can I go?"

"Any time now. We'll take your car up to our lab, 5050 Jane."

"Shit. When can I get it back?"

"Won't be soon."

The guy said, "Because this guy isn't a priority, right," and motioned towards the body on the hood of his car.

Armstrong said, "Well, you know how it is."

Yeah, he knew. Used to be thirty murders a year in Toronto, almost all of them drunks killing their wives. Then, almost overnight, it became a big American city, four million people, most of them born in some other country all coming to Toronto to make money. Any way they could. Fighting for territory, shooting each other with guns they rented for the weekend. This guy probably wouldn't be the only dead body tonight.

Kelli blew on the coffee through the little hole she'd peeled back in the plastic lid and said, "So, did he jump?"

"Don't know."

She said, "That look on his face."

Armstrong said, "Yeah." Then to the biz boy, "Might want to think about that X5 now."

BERGERON TOLD THEM about the vents and Price said, "Whole top floor?"

"Lot of it. Armstrong says you know someone in narco."

Price said, yeah, and looked sideways at McKeon like a guilty husband; something passed between them.

She rolled her eyes and said, "Guy who was up for my mat leave."

Armstrong stepped up beside them sipping his coffee and said, "Yeah, Low. You guys were the bargain-basement duo, Low Price."

Price said, "Fucking Levine. It's Loewen. He's working with Burroughs."

"Shit." Armstrong shook his head. "Guy's got some career path, from Price to Burroughs."

"He must be that guy," Bergeron said, "arrested the mayor's wife."

Price said he'd call him.

Anjilvel came back with a guy in his fifties: white, unshaven, and maybe from a little closer to the Middle East than Europe. He really didn't want to be outside, standing there in his parka and toque shivering.

Armstrong was wearing an expensive grey suit, a fresh white shirt, and Bergeron had a ten-year-old overcoat, hanging open over his Sears blue suit, like it wasn't snowing or raining or freezing.

Armstrong asked the guy what his name was and he said, "Maurice."

"Okay, Maurice, I want you to take a look at a guy and tell me if he lives in this building."

"Oh no, I can't do that."

Armstrong couldn't tell what kind of accent the guy had. He said, "Just have a look, see if you know him."

"Oh no, I can't."

Armstrong pulled him by the arm to the X3 and held on to him while the guy looked at the street.

"Oh no."

One of the forensics guys held up the dead guy's head enough to see his face. It was bashed in pretty good and covered with blood and one eye was gone.

Armstrong said, "Just have a quick look here, Maurice," and pulled his arm.

Maurice looked at the dead guy. He looked at him for a few seconds, took a good look, then shook his head.

"I don't know him."

Armstrong glanced at Bergeron. He was looking back, thinking the same thing.

This guy expected to see someone else on the hood of the car.

"Are you sure?"

"Yes, I'm sure. He does not live in the building. Never been here before."

"Okay, thanks a lot."

Armstrong let go of him and Maurice walked away. Anjilvel was right there, leading him back into the building.

Armstrong said, "Wasn't who he thought it was."

"No," Bergeron said. "Not like he's going to tell us who he was expecting."

The forensics guys started to pack up then. Cruickshank said they had another homicide to get to, a homeless guy beaten to death under the Gardiner. "Over by the SkyDome. Found him in a garbage bin."

"You mean the Rogers Centre, now."

Cruickshank said he had trouble keeping up with sports. "We're pretty busy, you know."

Armstrong said, "So what can you tell us here?"

"He's definitely dead."

"Thanks."

"You'll get a report."

"But no ID," Bergeron said.

"Nothing on him?"

"Not a thing."

"Well, that's something right there."

Cruickshank said, "Maybe for you detectives." Then he said, "Zinardi and Faulks are going to finish off here. Be nice."

The place was still taped off, but the crowd had mostly gone to bed, or gone somewhere.

Price flipped his phone shut. "Loewen said Burroughs wants to meet up, have a chat. I told him that hotel on Lakeshore, used to have the medieval show."

"Medieval Times? That's still open."

"No, the other one, what was it called?"

McKeon said, "His Majesty's Feast."

Armstrong said, "Oh yeah. I knew a serving wench there. Nice outfits."

McKeon said, "It's a hotel now, whole thing's been renovated. You practically hit it going by on the Gardiner. It's over there, you can almost see it from here."

They gave themselves half an hour. Armstrong and Bergeron went to check with the uniforms doing the canvassing, and Price said he hoped Levine and O'Brien caught the beaten-to-death homeless man. "See what kind of nicknames he comes up with there."

CHAPTER **2**

BOBBI, LIGHTING A CIGARETTE with one hand and looking at her Blackberry in the other, bombed across town in her cherry red Mini Cooper. The big Canadian flag on top just the right colour. She'd thought about changing the maple leaf in the middle to a marijuana leaf, like the kids had on their Ts, but decided not to. Maybe she was growing up. From Parkdale to Queen's Quay in ten minutes. From one world to another. She pulled up in front of the condo building, right in front of the NO PARKING sign, and got out. The snow was still coming down and she pulled her short fur coat around herself. Skin-tight faded Levis, black leather belt with double rivet holes all the way around, black ankle boots, and the fur coat. Short red hair getting covered in snow.

She waved at the doorman, a young guy sitting behind the desk, and he waved back and buzzed her in.

She said, "Where's Jerry?" and the young guy said he didn't come out nights like this anymore.

"Don't blame him."

She pressed the elevator button and the young doorman asked if she was going to see Rebecca.

"Yeah."

The elevator doors opened.

"Someone's up there already."

Bobbi held up the Blackberry and said, "On his way down." She smiled as the elevator doors closed, thinking, is it everybody's fucking business?

In the hallway on the fifteenth floor she watched the door to Rebecca's condo open and a guy come out. Younger than she expected, maybe twenty-five, only a few years older than she was, but not looking like a kid. He said thanks to Rebecca, and see you again, and good night, and turned and walked away without looking back. Bobbi thought all Becca's clients were older guys; two-fifty an hour is a lot for a kid unless he's living off Daddy's money. Plenty of those, but she didn't think this was one of them. Just something about his attitude, confident, not showy.

As he passed he said, "Hi," and Bobbi thought close up he was definitely not some rich kid, too rough around the edges, but he cleaned up good. She watched him get on the elevator.

Becca said, "Pick your tongue up off the floor, bitch."

"Fuck you."

Inside the condo they were giggling schoolgirls.

"Who was that?"

Becca walked across the living room, a bistro table and two chairs by the counter to the kitchen, and sat down on the white leather sectional in front of the open laptop on the coffee table.

"Never met him before, found me on my web page."

Bobbi sat down on the sectional and put her feet up on the coffee table, hooking the skinny heels of her boots on the edge. She said, "So how come he's seeing a hooker?"

"We say SP, now, service provider."

Becca typed on the laptop and the music changed from the grungy alt rock to Jann Arden. There wasn't a stereo in sight, just a couple of speakers on a wall unit and a flat-screen plasma TV. There was a plastic Ziploc bag of weed on the coffee table. Becca got out her smokes, Benson & Hedges 100's, from underneath the table, opened the pack, and took out rolling paper.

Bobbi said, "Did he want the full GFU?"

Becca crumpled some of the dope between her fingers, letting it fall onto the paper, and said, "GFE, it's Girl Friend Experience. Means they get to hug and kiss and cuddle."

"Yuck."

"Hey, now they all want the PSE, the Porn Star Experience, all facials and anal."

"Gross."

"There's a line on a Springsteen album, two hundred straight up, two-fifty up the ass, have you heard it?" She licked the edge of the paper and rolled the joint closed.

"I guess that's American dollars, eh? No, but my mom's got it."

Becca lit the joint and leaned back into the leather couch, holding it deep in her lungs, closing her eyes, before slowly letting it out towards the ceiling.

She passed it to Bobbi, who took a hit. Then she leaned back too, her head on the couch cushion, and closed her eyes. "So what did Boston Rob want?"

"Decent guy, straight fuck. Very good. Said he was only in

town for a couple of days. Mostly he wanted to sell me some homegrown."

Bobbi said, "Hey, that's my job."

Becca held up the joint. "It's pretty good."

Bobbi sat up. "It is good. He say what it is?"

"He said BC Bud, but don't they all?"

"This might really be, though."

"Says he's got lots more."

"Who the hell is he?"

"No idea."

"He just waltzes in here and tries to sell you?"

Becca stood up, her Lululemon yoga pants slung low, barely coming to her hips and her baby T tight across her expensive boob job. "I told you I could use more, lots of the guys want to buy. I offered him some, that's when he gave me this. He was nice about it. You want something to drink?"

Becca went into the kitchenette and Bobbi said, sure, mineral water.

"Perrier or Evian?"

"Perrier."

Bobbi picked up the baggie, must have been half an ounce. Too many seeds and stems, she figured whoever harvested didn't really know what they were doing. With so many grow rooms popping up it didn't surprise her, couldn't turn on the radio without hearing another ad for another homegrown supplies store, hydroponic or magic crops or whatever they were calling them, but usually for boomers in the burbs or kids. Not many try to stick their nose up and make a profit.

Well, Bobbi, thought, lots do but they get smacked down pretty fast.

Becca came back into the room with two little bottles and handed one to Bobbi, saying, "You're not worried about the competition?"

"I'm not."

Becca said, "You know, I'm still looking for a duo partner."

"Oh yeah, GFE or PSE?"

Becca sat down on the couch and played with the laptop some more. It had a purple cover on it with big yellow flowers, the same as her Beetle. "Here, she's okay with it, but she'll only touch the client, not me." She turned the laptop so Bobbi could see the web page.

"Looks good." Tiggy, Le Tigre. A girl in a tiger suit, looked to be about thirty with long black hair, nice body. "What's wrong with that?"

"They all want a show."

"No thanks." She kept looking at the web page and said, "What are the tributes?"

"The payments. The rates. Some girls say donation."

"It really is the information highway, isn't it?"

"Want to see my reviews?"

Another web page, this one the Toronto Hobbyist Review Board. Bobbi said, "Hobbyist?"

"What they call it now, the regulars. Look at this, I've been in the hobby for five years, I'm new to the hobby, I'm coming back to the hobby."

"And they review you?"

"Yeah, you get a good review, you're booked for weeks, months."

"What happens if you get a bad review?"

Becca said, "How the fuck would I know," and laughed.

"Is it like writers on Amazon, do you post your own reviews?"

"That's a good idea."

Bobbi took a hit on the joint and said, "He say how much he had?"

"I would have figured he's got a room in his parents' basement, but something about the guy, I don't know."

"Yeah, a little too confident."

Becca finished the joint and put the roach in the big glass ashtray on the coffee table. "Sometimes I get a guy in his twenties, usually his daddy's got money, you know? He's trying so hard to be cool, not to be nervous. This guy, he's really actually not nervous."

Yeah, Bobbi thought, but is he really cool?

"Well, he keeps trying to sell like this and Nugs'll find out. If he doesn't get nervous then he's too stupid to live."

"He didn't seem stupid."

Bobbi opened her purse, her Prada, and pulled out a silver Starbucks travel mug. She unscrewed the lid and took out another Ziploc bag full of weed, twice as much as the free sample Becca's guy had left. She said, "You still need this?"

"Course. And more."

Becca paid up, handing over half the money she just earned, and Bobbi stood up and started for the door.

Becca said, "You sure about the duo? Easy money."

Bobbi said, thanks for the offer, but no. "I'm working my ass off with this." She put the Starbucks travel mug back in her purse.

"Okay, see you next time."

"Yeah."

Bobbi opened the door and stopped. She turned around and looked back into the apartment, like a page from a magazine, everything in place and no mess. No pictures, just artwork looked like it came with the carpets and couch. She said, "Is that guy coming back?"

"He didn't make an appointment. Not yet anyway." She was opening up Bobbi's baggie, rolling another joint.

"Okay, thanks."

Becca said, "Hey, remember. Party like a rock star."

"Play like an all-star."

"Fuck like a porn star." She laughed and shook her head and concentrated on the joint.

Bobbi left thinking about the guy though. Maybe she should try to get hold of him. Give him the heads up about moving into Toronto, not the nicest town since the bikers took over.

THEY WERE STANDING in the parking lot of the Sheraton Four Points on Lakeshore, across the expressway from their crime scene. Loewen and Burroughs were already there and Price and McKeon pulled up right behind Armstrong and Bergeron. The restaurant in the lobby wasn't open but Armstrong said they should get some coffee.

Bergeron said to him, "How do you sleep, man?" and Armstrong said, "Sleep is for losers."

When they'd convinced the manager to let them in and put on a pot of coffee, they got settled at a table in the middle of the place. Armstrong said, "So, it's four apartments at least."

"At least." Burroughs asked the manager if he could fry him a couple of eggs, and the guy said it was four thirty, the cook wouldn't be in for another half hour and Burroughs said to the guy, "Yeah, but you know how to fry a couple of eggs and put some bread in the toaster, don't you?"

"Cruickshank's guys will be done by the time the sun comes up," Bergeron said. "Doesn't look like our guy has anything to do with it."

"I wouldn't think he does," Burroughs said, like he already knew everything. Sitting there, four thirty in the morning, his hair perfectly combed, his face freshly shaved, like he was happy to be there.

Even if the others did like their jobs, they didn't like to let it show.

Armstrong said, "Why not?"

"You said he was a camel jockey, right? Not VC."

"VC?"

"Cong, Viet Cong, Vietnamese. The guys who run the grow houses in town."

Like he was talking to an idiot. Armstrong looked at Bergeron and saw he was thinking the same thing: this guy has seen too many Rambo movies. VC. Shit.

Armstrong said, "So, you want to go in then?"

"No, we're going to sit on it," Burroughs said. "What the fuck's the use of a few hundred plants in Parkdale? This isn't Homicide, you know, we don't just bust down doors and drag out drunken husbands."

Armstrong said, "Right."

"You're going to see some actual police work here. This is what happens when you go up against professional criminals."

Price said, "Right, big time, international crime, right here in Parkdale."

"Don't know where it's going to lead," Burroughs said. "That's why we have to follow."

The manager brought out a dozen pieces of toast on a plate and put them in the middle of the table.

Burroughs said, "You just go about your business like you didn't even notice the rooms, we'll take it from here."

Price was looking at Loewen, who hadn't said a word. He still didn't say anything. Ten years younger than the other detectives at the table, poor Loewen was just trying to get ahead.

Armstrong said, "We still need to canvass the building."

Burroughs spread peanut butter on a piece of toast and said, "Oh yeah, you'll get plenty from those people. What kind of translation budget have you got?"

"Enough."

"What about helmets and body armour?"

Armstrong said, "We're fine."

Burroughs shrugged, he didn't really care. He said, "Wait'll we see how many more rooms are running in there. Last thing any of those people want to do is talk to cops."

Armstrong knew he was right. He still didn't want to let him be right so easy but he couldn't keep going with it. He said, "So you're just going to watch the building?"

Burroughs said, "Already happening."

"Can you tell how many rooms there are?"

"Not yet."

McKeon, who'd been watching but not saying anything, took out a piece of paper and said, "The uniform got us a list of tenants from the super. None of them look Vietnamese."

"So," Burroughs said, "we couldn't use that anyway." He glanced at Armstrong and said, "That'd be racial profiling, we'd never get a warrant, never get into court. Anything we'd get'd be tainted."

"Never mind he's Vietnamese, what if the same guy rents ten apartments in the one building?"

Burroughs started to laugh a little and said, speaking of profiling, did you hear what happened last week?

No one asked him, but he told them anyway. "Guys at 51 had a guy in the tank we wanted to talk to." He looked sideways at Loewen, who wasn't smiling, and kept going. "We asked them, could they soften him up for us, you know, prepare him for the interview." That'd been all over the papers since the Americans got caught with their pants down in Iraq—or with the prisoners' pants down, softening them up for interrogation. "So, we go down to Cherry Beach where they're working him over." He stopped and took a sip of coffee and a bite of toast. "And they're really working him over, pounding the crap out of him, shoving his face in dog shit, I mean, he's softened up."

He stopped, everyone waiting.

"And I say, what the fuck are you doing, and the guys from 51 say, what? And I say I told you the Indian, and they say, yeah."

Looking around the table, Burroughs shook his head, still smiling, said, "So I told them, not the fucking Tonto, the Paki. They had the wrong guy."

He still waited for the laugh and then said, "The wrong kind of Indian, they had the wrong Indian."

Price said, we get it, Burroughs, we get it. "No profiling."

"Yeah, well, fuck that. You just write up your IR's, call it a suicide, call it a failed attempt at flight, I don't give a shit, just stay out of our way."

ARMSTRONG AND BERGERON stood in the parking lot after the others had left. The sun was coming up on the lake, beautiful in the early morning, blue and pink and red, the water still. Not much traffic on Lakeshore but they could already hear the steady hum on the Gardiner right behind them.

Bergeron said, "So, what have we got?" He watched Armstrong think about it and he liked that. Bergeron'd known about Armstrong before he went off on leave, everyone knew about the Native guy working Homicide, some kind of affirmative action thing, but he'd never worked with him. So far so good.

Armstrong said, "You want I can drop you off somewhere, or did you park at College Street?"

"You just going to write this up?"

"Call it a failed attempt at flight?"

Bergeron said, "Up to you."

"It may be your first day back, but you still got the rank."

"You don't mind doing the grunt work?" Bergeron said.

"It needs to be done."

They walked towards the Crown Vic, the only car left in the parking lot in front of the hotel door, Bergeron saying, "Yeah, but is that all you want to do?" And again Armstrong was thinking about it. Bergeron said, "It's okay with Nichols, we want to write it up John Doe suicide."

Armstrong said, "Yeah," but he didn't say okay.

Bergeron said, "What?"

Armstrong said it was nothing.

"No," Bergeron said, "you're thinking about something," and he was glad to see it. He was thinking maybe this Native guy wasn't just a token. "What Burroughs said? Piss you off?"

"Yeah."

"But that's not it," Bergeron said.

"Maybe not."

"So what is it?"

Armstrong said, "What the girl said, the hooker."

"The way the guy looked?"

"The look on his face. She said he looked peaceful."

"Isn't that the way a suicide should look?"

Armstrong turned around and leaned back against the car. He really wasn't sure. He kicked the ground a little. "I don't know, guy walks up on the roof, takes a dive? No note, no scene, not telling the world who he's pissed off at."

"Happens all the time."

"I guess I just don't want to write it off right away." Armstrong shrugged, like he wasn't going to push it but it bothered him. "I'd like to find out where he lived, where he came from, what he left behind. Why he was so happy to go."

"How come he wasn't the guy the super was expecting."

"How come he was expecting it to be someone. I mean, the grow rooms, sure, but there's something else going on here."

"You know," Bergeron said, "that building looked familiar to me. Now I remember, it was all over the news after 9/11. One of the terrorists lived there for a while."

"Oh yeah. Nice quiet guy, never bothered anyone."

"Had a few meetings with his friends."

Armstrong said that was old news now.

Bergeron said it wasn't like that war was over.

"So you want to keep looking? Work it a while?"

Bergeron said, "Sounds reasonable."

"You think Nichols'll give us some time?"

Bergeron looked at Armstrong and said, "Everyone's still

walking on eggshells around me. Let me take that." Might as well make it work for him.

Armstrong said, that'd be good, maybe just a couple days, till something else came up. "Unless you want to go get statements from a lot of homeless guys under the Gardiner?"

Bergeron said, not really, no, and he was starting to like this Armstrong, thinking maybe he was just a good copper.

CHAPTER **3**

GORD BERGERON, FIFTY-THREE YEARS OLD. French-Canadian father and Scottish mother. Grew up in Sudbury, but he always said Copper Creek so people who knew would know his old man worked in the mine, got his hands dirty. Turned eighteen in 1972, the world was upside down, the sixties finally arrived in Canada. He'd had his share of trouble with local cops, spent a few nights in jail, and saw enough to know that those guys were having all the fun—driving the fast cars, carrying the guns, doing what they wanted, not taking shit from anyone. Sudbury wasn't going to hold him but he didn't know where to go. He drifted down to Toronto, into Yorkville like everyone else, but the hippies didn't appeal to him, too much talk and no one really doing anything. He loved the music though: Joni Mitchell and her "Big Yellow Taxi," Neil Young singing "Cinnamon Girl," and Mr. Soul and The Band backing up Dylan. There were some great festivals in Toronto then, he saw John Lennon and the Plastic Ono Band and The Doors at Varsity Stadium. And some crazy guy in makeup named Alice Cooper chopping up watermelons with an axe.

A few years of it though, and it was the end of an era. Jimi was dead, Janis, Morrison. Altamont put a knife in it. Yorkville went from free love and coffeehouses to all business. You could feel it. Bergeron felt it but didn't like his choices—go back up north, or get a suit and tie and start selling something. To him, going into an office was the same as going down into the pit.

He liked cars though, and cop cars were fast and could go wherever they wanted. No sitting in an office, something different every day. He liked it right away.

Met his wife, Linda, in the emergency room of the Wellesley Hospital a few years later. She was a nurse, putting fifteen stitches in his arm and taping him up. She said to him, "I'm supposed to tell you to take it easy for a few days, but you're going right back out there now, aren't you?" Two o'clock in the morning, stinking August heat wave.

He said, "Yeah, and you're still working here."

"Where the action is."

They got married that October.

Two kids a few years later. Gregory, now twenty-one at Queens in Kingston, no idea what he was going to do, and Amanda he'd just dropped off in Montreal for her first year at Concordia, some kind of arts program.

Linda gone a year now. The kids were barely teenagers when she had the first breast removed. She seemed to make a full recovery, you'd never know what she'd been through, but she stopped talking about the trips they were going to take when the kids were out of the house. Less than a year after her second breast was removed she fell in the backyard and thought she'd broken a rib. They found cancer in her bones. It was pretty quick after that.

Now Bergeron was standing in the kitchen of the empty house waiting for Armstrong, thinking how Amanda was right, he needed to be busy. Glad to be back at work, back in Homicide. He'd been at a desk for a couple of years, practically part-time while Linda was sick.

The car pulled up in front and he got in.

Armstrong said, "Little change of plans, we're going down to Coxwell and Dundas."

"What for?"

It was dinnertime. They'd worked till eight that morning on the jumper—or whatever he was—and then crashed. They weren't going to get a coroner's report on the guy for a few days, but the fingerprints and DNA samples would be run through the system.

"Missing person," Armstrong said, and turned onto the Don Valley Parkway heading south into the city.

Bergeron said that wasn't really their department and Armstrong pointed at the laptop mounted on the dashboard.

Bergeron said, "Ten years old."

The neighbourhood Bergeron lived in, had lived in since he and Linda gave up their apartment downtown when Greg was born, was like most neighbourhoods in Toronto, named for its location: Don Mills and the 401. The 401, the six-lane highway that was supposed to go across the top of Toronto when it was built in the sixties, now practically cut through the middle of it—the middle of the suburbia that just seemed to keep sprawling north, turning Toronto into the fourth largest metropolitan area in North America.

Armstrong said the ten-year-old girl went to the store for her mother, never came back. That was a couple of hours ago. "Levine and O'Brien are working it. They figure, you know, a kid, stranger abduction, we don't find her in the first twenty-four hours . . ."

Bergeron said, yeah, he knew. Over 90 percent of stranger-abduction kids that aren't found in the first twenty-four hours are never found or are found dead.

"They think she's still around?"

Traffic heading for the city centre was light and Armstrong weaved through it. The Don Valley Parkway followed the Don River, but you couldn't really see the water from the road. It really was down in a valley and then there was a city sticking out from all the trees.

"This new Amber Alert, we got on it right away."

The snow from yesterday was all gone and now it was sunny and hot. Everywhere Bergeron had ever been in his life had the same expression: if you don't like the weather, wait five minutes. He looked out the window at the sun hitting the big downtown buildings and said, "Big difference from yesterday," and Armstrong said, yeah. Bergeron said, "Welcome to . . ." and stopped. He looked at Armstrong.

Armstrong said, "You can call it Indian summer."

"I didn't know."

"I don't know where it comes from. It might be like Indian giver, like the way Greenland is all ice and Iceland is all green."

Bergeron said, "What?"

"You know, call it Indian giver, when we're the ones took the beads and got little pieces of shitty land, and whenever they wanted it back they took it. So Indian giver means taking something back you gave, people think it's what Indians did, not the other way around."

"You telling me Iceland is the greener one?"

Armstrong said, yeah. "But I don't know about Indian summer, maybe because it's like a fake summer, like a promise that's not kept."

"But we can say that?"

"You can say it to me. I got some cousins I don't know about." Armstrong looked sideways at Bergeron and said, "I go by people one at a time. You're not a racist."

"How do you know? Maybe I'm just better at it, more subtle."

Armstrong turned off the expressway, took the Bloor/Danforth exit and headed east for a block, then south on Broadview through the other Chinatown, which was mostly Vietnamese.

"Maybe. But I doubt it."

Bergeron was glad to hear it, but he wasn't sure if it's really what Armstrong thought or just his way of getting people off guard.

They turned onto Dundas Street, old wooden houses, some renovated, some falling apart, brand-new infill places and apartment buildings. For a few blocks Dundas was lined with garages and the backs of houses. Toronto grew up so fast in the last forty years there was no time to plan, it was all over the place.

Dundas and Coxwell, 55 Division, had within its borders million-dollar homes in the Beaches neighbourhood and the most public housing units in the city.

They didn't mix well.

THE COPS STOOD AROUND the reception desk and Levine gave them the story.

The girl, Bronwyn Miles, left her mother's house on Ashdale and walked to the store on Gerrard. The storekeeper, Rapinder

Singh, knew her. "He says she left at five after four. He's sure of the time. She had a litre of milk and a loaf of bread. She was fifteen cents short, but he gave her a stick of cherry licorice anyway."

Detective Ray Dhaliwal shook his head and said, "Immigrants."

Levine said, "Her mother called at four thirty. This would be the route she took." He pointed it out on the big map behind the duty sergeant's desk. "We've been calling friends and talking to neighbours and no one saw anything. If she didn't get into a car, then she's somewhere along this route."

He stopped talking and looked around the room at all the detectives, Homicide and some Intelligence guys, men and women all looking pretty much the same, middle-aged, could be middle management.

He said, "We figured if we could get the most experienced detectives out, going door to door as quietly as possible, if she's still around, we won't spook anyone."

"We supposed to be Jehovah's Witnesses?"

There was a little laughter, but not much. They all knew what he meant. They wouldn't spook anyone who might still have the little girl alive.

The 55 Division head, Keddy, stepped up from where he was leaning on the desk and said, "Okay, you all got your maps, you know your streets, let's get to it."

As the detectives started wandering out, Armstrong went up to Levine and said, "Teddy, it's cool."

"I talked to the mother," Levine said. "I just got a feeling, you know, that this kid isn't fooling around."

Bergeron stepped up to them.

Armstrong said, yeah, okay. "Hey, police work is teamwork, right?"

Bergeron and Levine looked at each other and then they nodded.

EAST OF COXWELL it was The Beaches. Or The Beach; the people there never could agree because there were so many new ones moving in. Once upon a time it was all working class, clapboard duplexes, and old cottages barely winterized, but then the racetrack closed down and the smell of horseshit went away. A new housing development went in that people made fun of; called it Pleasantville, but spent over half a million bucks for a three-bedroom. The rest of the neighbourhood gentrified pretty fast.

But west of Coxwell, towards downtown, it was a border stronger than Checkpoint Charlie ever was. Rooming houses, renos that never saw a building permit, falling-apart row apartments. It might be next in line for gentrification but it hadn't started yet.

The north end, Gerrard Street, was the India Bazaar. American cities might be melting pots, but in Canada ethnic groups are slow to mix. Little Italy, Greektown on the Danforth, Chinatown, Polish Roncesvalles, the India Bazaar—sociologists could call it a mosaic all they want, the city's officers could see it was still people living separate. And for a few blocks between the yuppie Beaches, the India Bazaar, and trendy Riverdale, there was the white-trash area nobody had bothered to name.

Bergeron and Armstrong knocked on doors for a couple of blocks. Half the houses they went to had been divided into apartments and no one knew their neighbours.

It was dark then, after ten o'clock.

They were close to Gerrard, walking out of a house, when Bergeron looked down the side.

He said, "That another door?"

Between the two houses was a walkway, crammed with bicycle frames and blue boxes no one ever put recycling out in. There was a small backyard and then the alley.

The gate from the alley was open.

Armstrong said, "Maybe," and walked along the side of the house. He passed a basement window, closed and frosted glass, but he tilted his head and looked at Bergeron.

Bergeron said, "Water running. Like a bathtub."

Armstrong knocked on the side door of the house. It was a step below ground level. Would never pass a current building code.

No one answered.

He knocked again.

Nothing.

Bergeron said, try again.

Armstrong knocked harder and said, "Hey, buddy, you home?"

The door opened a crack. A guy looked out. He didn't say anything.

Armstrong said, "Hey, man, how you doing?"

The guy, a white guy maybe in his mid-thirties, clean-shaven, short hair, didn't look drunk or stoned, looked at Armstrong and said, "Okay."

Armstrong said, "Got hot all of a sudden, didn't it? I'm dressed for fall and here it is, Indian summer." He never took his eyes off the guy.

The guy said, "Yeah." He was at least a head shorter than Armstrong.

Armstrong said, "Hey, maybe you could get me a glass of water, man, this heat, you know?"

The guy said no. "I don't have any."

"You don't have any water? Come on, man, I'm stinking here."

"No, sorry," the guy said, and started to close the door.

Armstrong pushed it open, knocked the guy backwards, and walked in.

"Come on, be a pal." He walked down a short hallway past the closed bathroom door to the kitchen at the back of the basement apartment.

The tub was filling up.

The guy followed him all the way to the kitchen saying, "Please, don't come in my house, please don't."

Armstrong got to the sink in the kitchen and turned on the cold water. He opened cupboards looking for a glass.

The guy said, "Who are you? Get out of my house."

The water in the tub turned off.

Bergeron said, "I got her," and the guy turned to run but Armstrong grabbed his arm and twisted. It snapped.

Armstrong slammed him to the floor and Bergeron came out of the bathroom with the girl in his arms, naked and soaking wet. He said, "Jesus Christ, she's still alive," and put her down on the kitchen floor.

The guy screamed and yelled and cried. Armstrong slammed his face into the floor and then dragged him outside and got on his radio.

Cop cars and ambulances were there in less than two minutes.

———

THEY WERE EATING chicken tikka masala, samosas, and pakoras, and drinking pints of Smithwick's at a place on Gerrard. The owner kept the buffet going after closing, till there were only the Homicide cops left.

Louise O'Brien, Levine's partner, was happily drunk. She was smiling and swaying slowly back and forth on her chair. She looked at Armstrong and said, "You win some and you lose some. We don't win like this very often."

Armstrong said, no, not often.

Usually the best Homicide can do is celebrate catching a killer, telling the victim's family who did it, listen to TV reporters go on about some closure crap no one ever gets.

It's not often they get to see a little girl taken to the hospital with her mother, knowing she'll be going home soon.

Andre Price said, "Now, if the asshole would just plead guilty and save us all a trial."

O'Brien said, "Come on, Andre, he's going to be on TV, that'll get him the best lawyers there are. Probably Mitchell Fucking Morrison."

A groan around the table.

Ray Dhaliwal said, "With the cast on his arm and that black eye, playing the victim. You should have broken his fucking neck."

Maureen McKeon, just back from her maternity leave, hung up her cellphone and stood up. She said to her partner, "Come on, Andre, we gotta go."

"What is it?"

"Drive-by, looks like one victim."

Price said, "Gangbangers?"

Everyone else was listening now, watching them.

McKeon said, "Ice cream shop, white guy."

"In a drive-by?" Price wasn't the only one surprised.

"What they said." McKeon had her coat on and was getting out her wallet, dropping a twenty on the table.

Price stood up and looked around, saying, "I have to use my Interac card."

McKeon dropped a couple more twenties on the table and said, forget it.

"Anybody else?"

The rest of the guys all said to have a good time.

"Yeah, right."

They had one last round, enjoying it while they could.

CHAPTER **4**

Bobbi got back to her mom's place in the middle of the afternoon, much nicer day, the snow stopped and the rain. The sun might even come out.

Sharon was watching a show called *Eye for an Eye* where people tell their problems to a judge calling himself Extreme Akim who doles out weirdo punishments. "Look at this," Sharon said, "I can't believe these people. They're fighting over custody of a dog, calling each other lousy parents."

"Be glad it's a dog," Bobbi said. "Won't be long till real custody gets settled on TV by a judge with a baseball bat."

"Yeah," Sharon said, "but he'll still make one of them crawl through the park on a leash."

"We can only hope."

Sharon asked if she'd had lunch yet and Bobbi said she just had breakfast. She stayed at Randy's, of course, after a long night. She made deliveries to four escorts, the Brass Rail, the House of Lancaster, and a couple of massage parlours. "Maybe a coffee."

"You see that stuff in the paper about the rub and tugs? The big exposé?"

"Margo says it's the best advertising they've had in years. She said it's like a how-to for newbies, listed all the services, all the prices. She said business will be down for a few days and then they'll get a lot more customers, all those guys who weren't sure before."

"Idiots."

"She'll be hiring more girls. She'll need more too."

"We're going to have to take it easy for a while," Sharon said. "All those cops all over the place last night." She went into the kitchen and got out the beans and the grinder.

Bobbi followed and stopped in the doorway. She said, "How's Zahra?"

Sharon waited while the grinder made its noise and then poured the coffee into the filter, saying, "She's okay. It's weird, you know, a guy she never wanted to see again in her life, but now he's dead and she's full of how good he was."

"He was her husband."

Sharon said, yeah, that was true. She rinsed out the pot and poured water into the coffeemaker. "But it's not like she met him before they got married."

Bobbi said, "Yeah, well, it's not like that always makes a better match."

Sharon looked at her daughter and said, "How'd you ever get so cynical?" then walked past her into the living room. She lit a cigarette and looked at the TV, saying she just knew it would be the wife who ended up on the leash. "Judges."

"Who's cynical?"

Bobbi took the smokes from her mother and lit one. Then

she said, "What's that?" and pointed to a green canvas bag by the door.

"It was Ku's. He was waving it at Zahra, yelling. Then he threw it at her, just before he jumped."

"Holy shit, what's in it?"

"I don't know."

Bobbi walked close and looked at it. "Don't you want to find out?"

"No. And neither do you."

"Well, what are you going to do with it?"

"Throw it out. I only have it here because Zahra caught it and when he jumped I got them out of there and then she wouldn't take it into her apartment. I couldn't just leave it in the hall."

Bobbi poked it with her toe and said, "But you can't throw it out, they'll be going through the garbage."

"You think?"

"Sure, it's what they do, right?"

Sharon thought about it. Shit, she wasn't sure. "Well, they can't get back to us."

"No, but there's probably something that'll link it to Zahra."

"Okay," Sharon said, making up her mind. "Just keep it here, put it in the closet."

Bobbi said, okay, for now, and put it back in the closet by the front door. Then she said, "What are we going to do now?"

"What do you mean? It's over. There must have been fifty cops here last night, but they're all gone now, they didn't find anything. I don't think they're going to bother looking too hard into some illegal immigrant jumping off a roof."

"Well," Bobbi said, "how come there's a cop across the street dressed up like a homeless guy?"

"What?" Sharon walked to the window and looked out. "Shit, are you sure?"

"I saw him when I was coming in. He's one of Becca's regulars, she's got him on her nanny-cam, giving her his tribute."

"His what?"

"Paying her, that's what it's called now. She's got all her clients on camera and they don't even know. Camera's in a teddy bear on her dresser."

Sharon kept looking at the homeless guy. She said, "You're sure?"

"He likes to tell her his stories. Thinks he's quite the hero."

"Shit." Sharon kept watching. "They might have seen something."

"They were on the roof, they might have seen the vents."

"Yeah."

They both looked out the window. He was just lying there on the sidewalk, under a filthy blanket.

The coffeemaker made a loud gurgling sound and Sharon said, you want to get that. "Black for me."

Bobbi went into the kitchen. "Is it the Starbucks?"

"Yeah, the Breakfast Blend."

"Do you have any cream?"

"No."

Bobbi brought the mugs back into the living room and said, "Mom, you can't stare at him all day."

"What the fuck else can I do?"

Bobbi looked at the grey plastic box strapped to her mother's ankle and said, "You have one more week with that thing."

"Why don't they just bust the rooms?"

"I guess they want to see who's coming and going."

Sharon said, "Yeah, well, nobody is now."

"Come on, we can still work."

"If they're going through the garbage, or watching it, they'll see the stalks. Zahra and Katie were starting to harvest in 2404. Shit, they probably have those things, they can see bodies moving inside buildings because of the heat."

"What heat?"

"Body heat. Come on, it was on *CSI*. They've got those things, like radar guns, they can point at a building and see how much electricity is being used, how many lights are on."

"I don't think it works like that."

Sharon, still looking out the window, said, "You remember, that guy was in his ex-wife's house with the gun, threatening to kill her?"

Bobbi said, "Which one?"

"Not the last one, the guy before that. Remember, on the news, they showed how the cops could tell what room he was in, what room she was in. It was all dark and they looked like glowing red blobs?"

Bobbi said, "Was that real? I thought that was on TV?"

"It was real. We can't go anywhere near those rooms. Shit. They probably have those little cameras, they put them in the vents, they can see every room."

"Mom? A little paranoid, maybe?"

"Oh yeah? You mean because we're sitting on twelve hundred plants we can't get to, and we've got a hundred customers, wholesale customers we're going to lose, and the cops are watching us, and I'm on fucking house arrest? Is that why?"

"Okay, chill, relax, take it easy."

Sharon sat back down on the couch and picked up her coffee cup. "Okay, right, we'll figure something out."

"We always do."

Bobbi sat down on the couch and said, "Look, this guy borrowed his friend's car and used it to rob a gas station. It got impounded and now the other guy wants to be paid for it."

Sharon sipped her coffee. It was good, but the coffeemaker never made it really hot enough. She said, "Idiots."

Then she wondered if she was any smarter.

CHAPTER **5**

SHARON WAS SITTING ON A BENCH a block away from her apartment, looking over the expressway and Lake Ontario, thinking how you could get anything out of a guy for a decent hand job. They want more, of course, but they settle.

Guy she was waiting for, he might take some work.

Not like the guy who hooked up her EM, looked like one of those actors you see all the time but never know his name—the main guy's overweight friend, needs a shave, and a haircut, and a pair of jeans that fit. Came to Sharon's place with his equipment, her joking about his little black bag, and he got right to work hooking up the transmitter to the phone line. He held up the ankle bracelet, the ugly grey thing, and asked her which leg.

She said, wait a minute, I don't think I can get these jeans over it, and looked at the guy, standing there looking at her like so many guys she'd lap-danced for. She said, "How far away from that thing can I get?"

"About a hundred yards. Should get you to the store in the

lobby and the laundry room. Any further than that sends the signal."

"But you can set it to any distance?"

"It's preset."

"Yeah," she said, "but you've hooked up hundreds of them, you can change that," and she started to unbutton her jeans.

He wanted a fuck, of course, but he settled. She even had to work to make him last a little longer, so he wouldn't feel ripped off. Just like back in the clubs, timing being everything.

Now her timing couldn't be worse. She'd have to get on her knees for these guys. Shit.

A car slowed down and she looked away, hoping he was just some guy looking for a cheap afternooner. It was some kind of convertible she didn't recognize.

No license plate in the front. Could be stolen, could be from Quebec, the last place for no right-hand turn on red and no front plates.

The car stopped right in front of her and she said, "I don't fucking believe it."

"Need a ride, honey?"

The driver looking at her, casual, relaxed. Short black hair, clean shaven, nice features, he was wearing a teal golf shirt, and very expensive sunglasses. Now she could see the car was an Audi, an A4.

Sharon said, "Richard Tremblay, in Toronto. Is it the end of the world?"

He opened the car door and said, "Step into my office, Shar."

She did. She opened the door and sat down in the comfortable leather seat.

He turned off the ignition. "You look great, Sharon."

She said thanks, so do you, and meant it, thinking he must be forty-five, filled out since he was a skinny kid but no fat on him. At all.

"What are you doing here?"

"I was at the club when you called. Nugs was going to come over himself, but I said I'd handle it."

She said, "You'd like to," slipping into old times right away. He smiled and she heard a song in her head she used to dance to, April Wine, "Say Hello," the first line something about no more living in the past. "Thanks for coming."

"Hey, you know, Sharon, for you, anything."

She thought, yeah, that's what guys always say, all the bikers, after they left her holding three pounds of Quebec Gold and seventeen grand in cash at Hanrahan's peeler bar in Hamilton when the cops turned on the lights. Really, they'd been saying it for years, since Pierre exploded in their Grand Cherokee while Sharon went back into the house to get her smokes, but they mostly thought she'd just gotten lucky then.

Or that she was working for somebody.

Now Richard said, "Nice view."

"Well, you know, it's close to home."

"Can we go somewhere, get a drink?"

She said, no, this was as far as she could get from her place. "Working from home, I'm lucky I can go this far."

Richard said, "Yeah. Lucky."

She held up a bottle of water and said, "I'm drinking this," and Richard laughed and picked up a bottle from the cup holder between them. Same size, different brand.

"Look at us," he said. "Drinking water. How'd we end up here?"

"We're here, though, that's good."

"We're survivors," he said. "You and me."

Sharon drank her water. "Must be twenty-five years."

"No, come on, I saw you a couple of years ago at Sylvie's funeral."

"Since we met. Where was it, Les Amazones?"

Richard smiled and drank his water. "Out on St. Jacques. Had that parking lot, you could look down, see the train tracks, the expressway, the canal."

"I'm always looking at expressways. It's the worst part of this." She looked at the EM on her ankle. "I miss driving. God I love to drive."

"Yeah?"

"Nice car." She touched the dash. "Yeah, that's really what I'd like to do, hop in the car and just drive. All the way to Vancouver, look at the ocean. Maybe down the coast to L.A."

"Be nice," he said. "Just take off like that."

"Like we always said we would but never did."

Richard said, yeah. "We were always working. That was the first club we opened in Montreal. In '80, '81, something like that."

"There was a restaurant upstairs, Picasso, everybody thought the place must have been owned by Italians."

"They were downtown, had Chez Parée and Super Sexe. It was all new then, eh? The old days." Close up she saw a little grey in his hair, figured he left that much to be distinguished. It kinda worked. He could be a banker or work for one of those high-tech companies. Except he never looked like he worried about anything.

Richard said, "I remember, you did that routine, you rolled up your blanket, it looked like a big dick."

"A guy showed me that with a napkin. If I was pissed off I'd bite the blanket."

Richard laughed, put a hand on his crotch. "It hurt when you did that." His slight French accent coming out.

"If you guys had turned on some heat, we wouldn't have needed the blankets. That stage was cold."

"Had to do something to make you look interested." He cupped his hands like he was holding tits and said, "Get your high beams on."

She shook her head. Nostalgia. Twenty-five years ago. Say Hello. Walked out of Harrison Trimble High School in Moncton, New Brunswick, and got on the bus to Montreal. Seventeen years old, but no one checked, and she could dance. She could move her body. The strip clubs were just opening up in Montreal, the first ones in Canada. Burlesque had been dead for years, there were some go-go clubs and disco places through the seventies, decent places to move coke, but then table dancing arrived. The girls all took a turn on stage, then walked around the club with a little table about a foot high. A guy wanted a dance you put it down right there in front of him, wherever he was sitting in the club, and danced. Folded your money and put it under a leg of the table.

Seemed innocent compared to private VIP rooms, contact dances, and whatever the hell they were doing now. Sharon didn't even want to know.

Richard said, "I remember you got that tat on your shoulder blade, the horse with the wings."

"Pegasus. That was my own drawing."

"Nice."

They each drank their bottled water.

Then Richard said, "So, how much?"

"Shit, Richard, get right to business, why don't you? I thought we were old friends here," trying to stall, think of a way to make it sound not as desperate as she really was.

"Do we have friends, Sharon? Or is it always business?"

"You can do business with your friends." She looked up at him and tilted her head, her stylish red hair falling to her shoulders, her eyes looking big.

He leaned in close to her, taking the bait, it looked like, but he said, "Don't bullshit me, Shar, I've seen your face when you come."

She laughed. "Yeah," she said. "That's true."

Richard was smiling then too. Relaxing, enjoying himself.

"Okay, yeah, I need to buy a little."

"Really? I thought you were totally independent."

"I might have rushed that a little." Shit, she hated having to ask these guys for favours. And Richard, look at him, the big guy from Montreal come to town to take charge. She knew she could try to get him thinking about the old days, back when he was nothing but a hangaround, back when Les Amazones first opened, throwing out drunks, dealing a little hash and coke, most of the girls on the Jenny Crank diet, he got them that and did some B&Es and she heard about truck hijackings. Back when he was thrilled the best-looking stripper in the place would fuck him.

But she could never really figure this guy. He didn't even get too pissed off when she moved in with Pierre, already a full-patch member.

Now he said, "You? You rushed into something? I don't believe it."

"Fuck you." But in a playful way.

Richard was one of those guys, you'd never pick him as most

likely to succeed but he was always just there. Whenever something was going on, he seemed to be around it. He was a kid when Mario "Mon Oncle" Bouchard took over the Saints, real bikers then running a few strip clubs, some hookers, dealing drugs, and stealing cars mostly out in the sticks on the south shore of Montreal, and turned them into a multinational. Richard just hung around, the tide raising all boats.

"I just had a little interruption in my supply."

"How much you need?"

The question she'd been asking herself. The little interruption would probably be permanent; she'd never get those rooms running again. She had no cash to get any more started.

She couldn't believe she was on her ass again. On her knees.

"The thing is, you'll have to front me."

"I will?"

"Look, I know, you guys have been great, you've had some trouble, and you still let me have my deal."

"We had trouble?"

She looked at him and she wasn't sure if he was her old friend. He was all business. She said, "You know, I saw, Claude and Denis got killed out at the airport, Nugs got picked up." It had been all over the papers, the biker war come to Ontario, two guys from Quebec in town for a couple of days got shot, "execution-style" as they love to say, in the parking garage at the airport, and a big task-force operation picked up the head of the Toronto chapter at the docks loading a couple dozen almost new SUVs and luxury cars on a ship headed for Latvia.

"I mean, I guess that's why you're here, right? Straighten things out?"

Richard said, don't worry about it. "Doesn't change anything."

Sharon thought, right, and even if it did, Ricky, you'd end up okay, wouldn't you? You'd come out on top somehow. What she said was: "Yeah, well, whatever. Thing is, I'm just getting back on my feet."

"Seems like you're always just getting back on your feet."

She thought, fuck you, but she didn't say it, not even in a playful way. Problem was, he was right, she was always getting back on her feet. But that was because she was always the one getting knocked on her ass. She never wanted to be one of them, she always just wanted to be on her own. Maybe not always. She stared at her water bottle and thought maybe she never really got over Pierre, how she liked the idea that he was going to be big-time and she was going to go with him.

Ever since then, though, since Bobbi was little, Sharon always wanted to run her own show, even if it was small.

"Well," she said, looking at Richard, "I never take anyone down with me." She closed her eyes, thinking if he took it as a threat he might just throw her out of the car, drive away, and that would be it for her.

He said, "I remember you dancing to that song, 'Girls Just Want to Have Fun.' You could really make it look fun."

She was thinking it was fun. Sometimes. "I was never much for 'When Doves Cry.'"

"I used to watch you. And sometimes, you were so pissed off, you couldn't hide it, man, everybody knew. We used to laugh about it."

She looked up at him. "Yeah?"

"Wondered, how could you get naked in front of all those guys when you were on the rag." He shook his head. "But you weren't always, you were just so emotional."

She said, "Like a woman?" and he spread his hands and had

that look on his face like, you said it, not me. She said, "You saying I'm still too emotional?"

"You take it personal, Shar. You gotta learn it's just business."

"So, you'll front me?"

Richard smiled. "Like that, see. Business. Sharon, we can always do business."

"All right. That's good, I really need this."

"But," he said. "Business has costs."

Right, she thought, and she knew he wasn't talking about money.

FIRST THING, Nugs asked Richard about his meet with Sharon. "How much does she need?"

They were sitting in a minivan on Highway 9, north of Toronto, parked on the shoulder just outside a little town called Kleinburg. The two hangarounds, prospects really, had just gotten out, hockey bags over their shoulders, and walked into the woods. Sharon was right, of course, there was a lot more business to straighten out than Richard was hoping for when he came in from Montreal. The whole patch-over in Ontario was a pain in the ass, but, like Mon Oncle said, would be worth it.

"Her deal," Richard said. "She gets the strip clubs, the massage parlours, and the escorts?"

"She pays her cut," Nugs said. "And she just gets the chicks, and just weed."

"You sure?"

"You know, like I said, we could shut her down right now, let the cops do it."

"Yeah?"

"Since she threw that guy off the roof they're all over it."

Richard said, yeah, he knew. "But Homicide."

"Homicide don't give a shit," Nugs said. "Some raghead jumps off the roof. Our cops have it now."

Richard looked at Nugs and saw some confidence. "If you say so." Richard thinking, Nugs could still go either way. Have to sit on this, see how it develops. He said, "How much does she move?"

"Not sure, it's her own supply."

Richard thought, shit, you guys aren't on top of any of this. Every one of those escorts could be moving to her customers, some of them probably wholesaling it, and Sharon with another supplier. In our territory.

She was right too, when she said Richard would be okay. From the beginning, when he was a teenager in Châteauguay on the south shore of Montreal, Richard could sit in a room and take everything in. Course, he could never sit in a classroom and take anything in. Shit, feeling trapped in there, fucking Macdonald-Cartier Catholic High. At least he went to an English high school, his English mother insisting after French elementary, his French father long gone.

Stealing cars, B&Es, dealing dope by sixteen. In and out of Weredale and Shawbridge youth detention centres. Everyone telling his mother that her boy would end up in jail or dead by the time he was twenty-one.

Rush played Macdonald-Cartier once, must have been '72 or '73, Richard in grade seven or eight. It was before their really big hits, before *Farewell to Kings*, even before *2112*. The only song anybody knew was "Fly by Night," but Richard watched the way the girls swarmed Geddy Lee and that guitar player with the long blond hair. Like the song said, fly by night, away from here, change your life.

A few years later, Rush headlining at the Montreal Forum, Max Webster opening for them, "A Million Vacations" is what I need all right. Richard's life changed, he showed up in a limo with his girlfriend, Cheryl Zubis. Stepping out on Ste-Catherine Street, he was on his way to being a full-patch member of the LaPrairie Saints of Hell. No way he would have ever imagined Mon Oncle turning them into the multinational corporation they were now, armies of lawyers, property owners, businessmen.

All by wanting it more than anyone else.

Richard said to Nugs, "So when you go down and all this proceeds-of-crime bullshit gets you, and they take your boat, you want us to blow it up before some pansy-ass biz boy gets it at auction?"

"That's not even fucking funny."

"You love that boat."

Nugs didn't say anything and Richard looked into the dark woods. The biggest thing he had to clean up in Toronto was Nugs. Find out if the guy was really able to run the place. That's why they were here, two top guys actually out doing a job. It was all about looks. Richard had been reading some books, parts of books anyway, and magazine articles, and watching a lot of TV shows about business. One of the shows, *Venture,* had a whole bunch of episodes about top guys, CEOs, presidents and shit, going back to the floor, they called it, doing all the jobs in the company from the shittiest on up. He wasn't sure about it, but Richard liked the idea of showing the young punks he was always willing to get shit done himself, if he had to. And see if Nugs was willing to.

So far, he was.

Came along, no hesitation, no bullshit about being too high ranked. Richard always thought it was possible that Nugs was just pissed off his boys sold out to the Saints too fast, didn't put up a big enough fight, and he sulked about it. He got soft, sitting on his big boat, his rich girlfriend, his don't-give-a-shit attitude. When he got picked up down at the docks, watching the cars getting loaded for Russia, it could have gone either way. He could have just caved, turned informant, given them all up, and died in his cell.

But he didn't.

Richard still wasn't sure, but it looked like the old Nugs was back. Cops made him offers, cops worked him over, dumped him in the Don with some very pissed-off niggers, and let him rot.

He gave them nothing.

Mon Oncle said for that he deserved another chance. Richard wasn't sure but he wasn't going to say anything. There was just too much money to be made in Toronto. Still, they had a lot of work to do. The Italians were operating on their own, Danny Trahn and his Vietnamese buddies were getting uppity, and there were some straggler bikers who hadn't patched over, needed to be brought in line.

Nugs said, "Here they come."

The two hangarounds walking out of the woods, laughing, and falling down.

Richard said, shit, and Nugs said, "I had another day I would have brought Big Boy in from the Falls."

Roy Berger, running the Niagara Falls chapter. Richard didn't say anything, but he agreed. Big Boy could put a bomb together, give Al Qaeda a hard-on.

"Get in the fucking car and shut up."

Richard turned around in the passenger seat and said, "So what are you waiting for?"

"Now?"

"Yeah, now."

The guy actually looked at Nugs and waited.

"You heard the man."

The two prospects were plenty serious by then. One of them, the older one, over thirty and overweight with long hair and a beard, took out a cellphone and punched some numbers.

Nothing happened.

He looked around and said, "Shit."

Nugs said, "You sure you hooked it up?"

"Yes, fuck."

Richard said, try it again, and the guy dialled again, and nothing happened again.

Nugs said, "You checked the battery on the phone?"

"Yes, fuck, it's brand new."

Richard looked into the woods and said, "Go back, start a fire beside it, when it hits the bomb, it'll blow."

"I'll fucking blow too."

Richard said, yeah, maybe. "What are you gonna do?"

The other guy said, "Shit. Give it here." He was probably twenty-five, had short hair, like an army buzz cut, a tight black T and black jeans, looked like he worked out every day.

They heard a loud bang and a fireball rose up into the sky about a mile away.

The buzz-cut said, "You dialled the wrong fucking number."

Richard knew if he looked at Nugs he'd laugh out loud. But it wasn't funny.

The longhair said, "Show those fuckers, you can impound our shit, but you can't have it."

And Richard thought, our shit? But he didn't say anything. In the rear-view he could see the buzz-cut shaking his head. He thought that he'd have to keep his eye on this one, might have potential.

They drove back into town making small talk and Richard thinking maybe it wasn't Nugs, maybe the guy was all right, but when they took over all these guys in Ontario, shit, they got some dumb-ass wannabes. Losers and users. Truth told, they wouldn't have taken half of them if they'd had a choice, but they had to get in before those assholes from Texas had the whole fucking continent. They knew they'd have to clean up after, they just didn't know how much. Claude and Denis killed at the airport—some fucking Russian from New York, it looked like, all for a lousy peeler bar—they should have taken care of all this. Oh well, things were sloppy, but they'd get it together. Richard would get it together.

He said, "Henri back at the Club International?" and Nugs said, yeah, till his trial, why, you want to check it out, and Richard said, yeah, let's have a look.

NUGS SAID, "Not much tits, but check out the door knockers. You get a hold of that." He hooked a finger on each hand and pretended to pull back towards himself, like he would the chain that joined the nipple rings. "The nips are like three inches long, I swear."

Richard said she should get her tits done though—a couple of grand, maybe five, would make all the difference.

"Lot of these chicks, they like the tats and the piercings, not the surgery."

Richard said he was just saying. "It would make a difference."

The club was almost empty. The longhaired prospect thought he was going to get comped in the VIP room but Richard told him he had to pay the chicks. He went anyway and the buzz-cut knew enough to sit by himself at the bar.

"Not much business."

"We're still coming back. From the explosion."

Richard nodded, not too sure about that. He'd have to look at the books.

Nugs said, "Business is way up at the massage parlours though."

"Yeah?"

"We opened two more last month. One right on Bay Street, in an office building."

"Oh, yeah, right, the spa. Business is good?"

"Very good. All the upscale locations. Shit, we got one with guys in it serving chicks."

"No shit."

Nugs laughed. "A couple of broads in it too. City's got a huge dyke market."

"What about fags?"

Nugs nodded. "Oh, yeah, good business. Moving some of that into the burbs too."

Richard said, good.

"It's not just Church and Wellesley anymore."

Richard said, what, and Nugs said that was the gay neighbourhood. Richard thought, yeah, young guys, lots of money, no kids, no family responsibilities. He remembered running dope in Montreal's Gay Village back in the eighties—one of the first places the Saints took over completely. Richard was always suspicious about some of the other bikers, especially some of the new ones, the ones who liked the leather too much and hanging around with each other.

Shit, half the reason he got into it was the chicks.

Chicks like Sharon. Well, he knew there weren't too many like Sharon MacDonald. Too smart for her own good, too quick with her mouth.

He said to Nugs, "How's our supply of weed?"

Nugs said it was good, they could always use more. "We got a lot of growers up north. We're getting a lot from Danny Trahn, Vietnamese guy."

"He's got grow ops?"

"Houses all over the place. Hundreds of 'em."

"He sell to Angelo?"

"I don't think so." Nugs looked at Richard and said, "Maybe."

Richard said, okay. They all knew they had work to do, why bust his balls over everything, they needed each other. Richard said, "Angelo growing a lot?"

"Shit, it's like an obsession with him. You heard about the brewery op?"

Richard nodded. Angelo's guys had turned a closed-down brewery north of Toronto into a giant marijuana-growing operation, had fifteen guys working in it.

Nugs said, "They had a wholesale coffee business next door, roasting the beans to cover the smell. Fuckers made money off their coffee too."

"But they didn't sell the weed here?"

Nugs said, maybe, maybe not. "But they moved a lot of it south, through Detroit. You know, Angelo's brother-in-law has the garbage contract. Toronto ships its garbage to Michigan, a hundred and seventy-five trucks a day down the 401. That's how the brewery got nailed, somebody didn't get paid, somebody thought they deserved more, some fucking shit, a truck gets pulled over at the border crossing."

"In Detroit?"

"No, up by Sarnia, little shitty-ass crossing. Cops trace it back to the brewery operation."

"Fucking Angelo, what, was he shipping it by the ton to the States?"

"Got the city of Toronto to pick up the fucking freight."

Richard thought, yeah, of course, he billed for that truck too. "What's he doing now?"

"He's got a hospital, closed down, up by where we were tonight. Four storeys. Couple other places. He's looking out by Lake Erie, there's talk of closing the Stelco plant."

"Isn't there always talk of closing the plant?"

Nugs said, yeah, but a lot of other businesses were closing, warehouses, factories.

"He's got the right idea," Richard said. "Big operations."

"It works because he can ship it south. We get about twenty-five hundred a pound here, but in Detroit or Chicago it's closer to five grand American and the further south you go the more it sells for."

"You'd think closer to Mexico it would get cheaper."

"Billion-dollar war on drugs, man. Fucking Americans spent all that money on the southern border. Worked out for us."

"We should have a big operation."

"The garbage trucks are what make it work for him."

"Maybe find out some other way to move the garbage, something we could get in on."

Nugs liked the idea. Big operation could be good. He said, "We have a lot of farmers up north but they keep getting busted."

Richard said, well, yeah, you grow fifty acres out in the open, pissed-off farmers all around you, what do you expect. "How many crops do we get in?"

"Three out of four," Nugs said. "About. The cops keep buying more planes and helicopters, and these regional forces, hicks are still gung-ho. Cops we've got onside can warn us, most of the time, but we lose the crops."

"You can't just pay off the hick cops?"

"Working on it. Could take a while. Even still, they'll have to show some results, bust some."

Richard guessed so. "And the farmers can't keep their mouths shut."

"Or hide their money. These guys go from broke, banks taking away their houses, to suddenly throwing money around like nigger pimps."

Richard watched a couple of dancers sitting at a table, drinking shots and laughing. He'd always liked to watch strippers when they weren't working, when they were just kicking back.

Nugs was saying, "Can't blame them, really. They never actually had a cash crop in their lives."

Richard said, yeah, that's true. Then he said, "The chick with door knockers, she got anything else special?"

Nugs said she loved it up the ass, she'll sit right down on your lap, take it all the way deep, look on her face, man, she can't be faking that. "She starts pushing her own button, squeeze you like a fucking vise."

Richard said, okay, he'd be back, and stood up. He waved

and she came walking over, carrying a white towel and a purple Crown Royal bag. Up close she was older than he thought, maybe even thirty, but that was okay. Almost no tits under her tiny flannel shirt tied at the waist but a nice-looking ass under her cut-offs.

She said, "Hi, I'm Frankie," and held out her hand. "Are you a friend of Nugs?" Richard said, yeah, he and Nugs went way back and she said, "Well, any friend of Nugs is a friend of mine." She took him by the hand and led him into the VIP rooms in the back.

WHEN RICHARD GOT BACK to the table Henri was sitting with Nugs.

Nugs said, "So? Is that the tightest fucking ass you ever slid it up?"

Richard said she was all right. "She talks a lot."

"She's got a lot to say."

Richard said, "Yeah, well, she told me there was a guy here offering up large amounts of weed."

Nugs looked at Henri like it was the first he'd heard of it.

Henri, big guy in a suit looking like a bouncer even though he ran the place since his Russian partner got blown up in the change room a few months back, nodded and looked at Richard. "It's taken care of."

Richard said, "You mean he won't be back here?"

"That's right."

Richard took a moment. What he wanted to do was pick up his glass of mineral water and smash it into the big fuck's face. But that was years ago. Now he said, "But he'll still be somewhere, offering it to someone?" Right away he could see Henri saw the problem, pissed at himself for not realizing it before. Richard figured at least that was something. He said, "You think he really has something to offer?"

Henri thought about it—another good sign, Richard thought—he didn't try to bullshit his way out of it. "He might. It was homegrown, but pretty good."

"You think he could be growing a big supply?"

Henri still looked at Nugs before he said anything, but then he said, "Could be. I mean, probably not, but could be."

"Okay," Richard said, thinking, baby steps, man, bring these guys along with baby steps. "Why don't we find the guy and ask him?"

"He could be a cop."

How fucking small do the baby steps have to be? Richard said, "You think they just send a guy in offering up endless supply? What do you think, they call it Operation Stupid?"

"You remember those fucking Mounties in New Brunswick," Nugs said, "undercover assholes. They opened up a fucking store, sold cigarettes, and magazines, and dealt shit. Had that place for fucking months. Bernie walked right into it, telling them it was his territory, they had to deal with him, telling them he could supply weed, and coke, and whatever they could move. You remember how many guys went down then?"

Yeah, Richard remembered. He nodded, thinking, never overestimate the cops, Operation Stupid might not be that stupid. "Still, find out. Use some hangarounds."

But then Richard had an idea. He said, "No wait, I know someone. I'll take care of this."

CHAPTER **6**

RICHARD CALLED AND TOLD SHARON he'd front her the four pounds. "Should get you through."

She told him, yeah, it would, and hey, thanks, and he said, "It's not for free," and she thought, no, of course not.

"Your daughter, Bobbi—"

And she jumped right in, saying, "No way, she's not doing anything," and he jumped right back saying, relax, Shar, shit.

"My daughter's about the same age. Take it easy."

This whole thing was really getting to her. She knew it, and she chewed on her nails, and told herself to just calm down, relax. "Okay, what?"

"You're really starting to lose it."

"I have some shit to deal with."

"Don't we all? So we deal with it."

Great, now she was getting lectured to by a biker in Eddie Bauer khakis, driving an Audi convertible. It wasn't enough she was under house arrest, cops all over her building, had lost her only supply, had customers calling all day. She waited.

He said, "Your daughter, she met a guy a couple of times trying to sell a large supply?"

"Yeah, she mentioned something. A farmer maybe."

"Right. So, I'd like to know who he is and where he's getting it."

Sharon thought, yeah, some poor punk-ass kid tired of watching his old man go broke growing tomatoes out in Leamington, just enough margin in tobacco to barely survive another year, plants himself a little crop, and now Richard and his boys have to come down hard on him.

"Why don't you just pick him up?"

Richard said, "You want me to front this for you or not?"

"Yeah, okay."

"Look, Shar, I'm trying to do you a favour here, you don't have to take it."

"No, no, I'll do it. Who he is and where he gets it."

"Sounds easy when you say it. Let me know," and before he could hang up, she had to say, what about my supply?

"Oh yeah, I guess you can't very well come get it. I'll send it over."

"Okay."

"Aren't you going to thank me?"

Mostly she was pissed off at herself for getting into this situation. She said, "Thanks, Ricky, I'll let you know."

He laughed and hung up.

She lit another cigarette and sat on the couch with the phone in her lap. Now she was going to have to call Bobbi, get her to call Becca or one of the massage girls the farm kid approached, get a number on him, and get him over. He'd have to spill, he was so naive, walking into Toronto telling everyone who'd listen what a big supplier he could be.

Guy that dumb, she was almost surprised the cops hadn't picked him up.

Then there was a knock on her door and it was the cops.

In the hallway, Bergeron saying, "You wanna bet this one speaks any English at all?" and the door opened. They were both surprised, seeing a good-looking white woman, late thirties, maybe early forties, nice red hair, good skin, smooth, no makeup, freckles on her neck, and the tops of her tits sticking out of the low-cut T.

Armstrong said, "Hi. I wonder if we could come in, have a chat?"

"I don't know, I was just going out."

Armstrong said, oh yeah, and looked at the grey box strapped to her ankle.

"To the laundry room."

"We really just wanted to know if you know this guy?"

She looked at the picture of the dead guy taken in the morgue, the blood all washed off his face, the scalp and cheekbones more or less put back in place, and said, no, she'd never seen him before.

Bergeron said, "You sure? You've never seen him in the building, maybe in the laundry room," and Sharon said, "He look like he does his own laundry?"

The two cops nodded and Armstrong said, "Is that racial profiling?"

Sharon hadn't moved from the doorway, and now she put a hand on her hip and stared right at Armstrong. "I've never seen that guy before in my life. I gotta go," and she walked past them towards the stairwell door, down the hall past the elevator.

Bergeron and Armstrong watched her go, neither one looking in her apartment as the door closed.

Armstrong said, "What is with her?"

"You want to find out, don't you?"

They walked to the next door and Armstrong said, "Yeah, I do."

Bergeron said no good could come of it, and Armstrong said he wasn't looking for good.

SUNITHA WAS SITTING on a chair in the waiting room of the massage parlour, feet up on the coffee table, smoking a cigarette. It looked so long in her tiny hands, so white against her dark brown skin.

Bobbi said, "Sorry I'm late."

"You mean the ten minutes now, or the two days?"

"Ha ha."

Bobbi handed her a plastic coffee travel mug from Country Style and said, "Can I ask you a question?"

Sunitha stood up, all the way to her four and a half feet, and shook her head from side to side, her curly black hair in a shag to her shoulders, said, "Sure." She was wearing a black miniskirt and a yellow T-shirt, cut off just below her big, completely paid-for tits. Across the front of the T brown letters said, "Good Things Come in Small Pakis."

Bobbi followed her down the hall, past the massage booths, a couple of closed doors, girls in there with clients, to the very back. One of the booths, size of a small bedroom, was the lounge, where the girls changed and took breaks.

"Little bonus?" Sunitha held up the baggie and Bobbi said, yeah, for waiting. Sunitha got her backpack down from her shelf and took out her purse. Change of clothes, tie back her hair, put on the backpack and she was a university student. Except for all the bullshit she couldn't stand. She said, "How's Zahra?"

Bobbi said she was okay. "My mom's looking after her. And Katie's still there."

Sunitha sat on the couch and rolled a joint. "She must be freaked out."

"I don't know, I mean she left the guy, she was scared of him. She thought he was going to kill her, and then he goes and jumps."

Sunitha lit the joint. She closed her eyes and leaned her head back against the back of the couch. "He was her husband, still."

"Yeah, I guess." Bobbi noticed the "still" at the end of her sentence, Sunitha starting to talk like the Jamaicans. "Anyway, she'll be okay. She might come back here."

"It's pretty slow."

"Yeah."

Sunitha inhaled deeply, then held out the joint for Bobbi, who took a hit to be polite, and handed it back.

Bobbi said, "So, did a guy come in here and offer to sell to you?"

"Guys make me offers all the time."

"Ha ha. Young guy, good-looking, clean-cut. Said he had a lot to sell."

Sunitha still had her eyes closed, her head back. She nodded slowly. "Eddie. Guy's name is Eddie, he says. I tell him, 'Today it's Mike, like all the others.' He says, 'Shouldn't it be John,' but playful, still." She opened her eyes and looked at Bobbi. "Said he had a huge supply, wanted to know who we buy from."

"Jesus, this guy's a moron."

Sunitha shrugged.

"Could he be a cop?"

"Took the full-nude reverse. He's got kind of rough hands, like a construction worker."

"Did he leave a number?"

"Guy's a salesman." She poked around in her backpack and came up with a clear plastic baggie with a phone number written on it in black marker.

Bobbi said, "He's something, anyway."

"WE SHOULD HAVE GONE TO FRAN'S."

"We always go to Fran's."

Fran's, the twenty-four-hour diner half a block from Metro Toronto Police Headquarters on College Street, had been there as long as anyone could remember. Change of shift, end of a long overtime, before a hockey game—it was always packed. Then the Leafs moved to the Air Canada Centre closer to their Bay Street corporate sponsors and the police board cut back on overtime. It was always about the money in this town.

So, the detectives were having lunch in a noodle place on Yonge. Yonge still as sleazy as it ever was, no matter how much talk there was of cleaning it up, still lined with dollar stores and discount XXX places, the Brass Rail strip club still the classiest place on the street. Price said he was getting tired of so many noodle places. "Why is every restaurant in this town Asian?"

McKeon said, have you noticed the population of this city lately, and Bergeron said, "I don't know, this is good, vegetables are fresh, chicken's spicy."

Armstrong drank some tea. "It's not heavy, you know, you don't get too filled up."

Price said, "I remember the old guys when I started, those detectives, man, three-hour lunches, eating steaks, drinking Scotch."

Bergeron said, yeah, and never getting a bill. "Those were the days."

"Here we are, born too late again."

McKeon said, yeah right, Andre. "You, me, and Armstrong over there, the three of us had a real shot at making detective thirty years ago."

Bergeron said, "Not a lot of guys with French names, either."

Price held up his tea and said, "The modern world. Someday we'll be complaining we don't speak enough Mandarin."

Bergeron said, "So, how's that drive-by going? What is it?"

Price rolled his eyes and ate some more Shanghai noodles. For all his complaining, he was pretty good with the chopsticks.

"It's the sloppiest hit I've ever seen," McKeon said. She was finished with her salad and was picking at her spring rolls, no main course at all. Said she was still trying to lose her pregnancy weight.

Bergeron said, "I thought they shot from outside."

"They did. Missed the target completely, hit some guy coming home from a soccer game with his kids."

Armstrong said, "Who was the target?"

"Looks like Eddie Nollo, he owns the place, he was there. Used to be with Angelo Colucci. Apparently there's a new guy in town, actually came in from Italy, he's recruiting, moving into Colucci 's territory."

"And Colucci couldn't find a real shooter, somebody to just walk in and hit him?"

Price said, "Doesn't look like it."

"Shit. Bikers didn't take it?"

Price said it didn't look like it.

"So," Armstrong said, "why didn't they just get some bangers, Malvern Crew or Galloway Boys?"

McKeon shrugged, dipped half a spring roll in the little plastic dish of sauce, and said, "So far they're too busy shooting each other. We had another one last night."

Armstrong said, "Yeah. Levine got it, right?"

"No, it's Dhaliwal and Mastriano. They're doing so much gang work they're practically on the task force."

"And that's who you're giving this to, right?"

"Shit, no way," McKeon said. "Poor bastards, they've got every TV station and newspaper breathing down their necks, they got no budget, not nearly enough manpower and they're supposed to be going after street-level bangers."

"Still," Armstrong said, "doesn't sound like you'll get too far, you could dump it on them."

"You're nice."

"I'm just saying, get it off your plate."

"Like you'd give it up. You're still working a suicide."

Bergeron said today was the last day. "We get the coroner's report, forensics and we're done." He looked sideways at Armstrong, who didn't say anything.

Price picked up the last of his noodles with his chopsticks and pointed them at Armstrong, saying, "Someone wants to talk to you."

"Who?"

Still chewing, Price said, "You remember Loewen?"

"Poor bastard went from you to Burroughs, who could forget? What now? He beat up a Native dealer, needs some sensitivity training?"

Price wiped his mouth with a tiny paper napkin and said he

had no idea. "He'd like to meet with you but he doesn't want anyone to know."

Bergeron said, "What is it now, *Get Smart*? We have to sit under the cone of silence?"

"Give him a break, he's working narco, it makes people weird."

"Yeah," Armstrong said, "or weirdos work it."

They agreed it could go either way.

THERE ARE RULES, Sharon, rules. She could hear her grade-ten homeroom teacher, Mr. Mardinger. Rules, young lady, rules.

And she broke them all.

Now, it turns out, there are just as many rules for dealing dope in the big city, and she had just as hard a time with them.

She lit another cigarette and paced in front of the window. The cop dressed as the homeless guy was still there. She thought about going out to tell him he should eat that half a gyro in the garbage can, make himself look real.

Always have two suppliers.

Rule number one. Supplies are always getting cut, temporary stoppages, missed weeks. But you have to supply customers or they go somewhere else. They have two suppliers too.

If Bobbi was right, this mystery man coming over could be a great supplier. New, nobody knew him, he had a great sample, and he sure was calm on the phone.

Only deal with people you know, people who come recommended. Well, that was shot to shit, but what could she do? Like that Supertramp concert at the Moncton Coliseum, 1975, the Crisis? What Crisis? tour. Might have been Crime of the Century. Sharon, getting in that car with three guys she'd never met before.

Sometimes rules have good reasons.

A cab stopped in front and a guy got out. Must be him, Sharon figured. She watched him glance at the cop, up and down the street, and then at the building. If he knew the guy under the blankets on the sidewalk was a cop, he sure hid it well. The guy who got out of the cab, said his name was Ray on the phone, walked up to the building casual, not hiding a thing, not nervous, not worried. Sharon just knew he wasn't going to see one of the girls in 1019 for a teenage blow job. She could tell by his walk—not a cop swagger, but confident, easygoing—that he was coming to see her.

She would have liked to know where he was coming from.

Bobbi said he wasn't the guy going around telling everyone he had a huge supply; that was a kid. This Ray guy must be his partner, or his boss, or something. Shit, Sharon wished she didn't have to do this.

The doorbell buzzed.

She stubbed out her smoke and looked at herself in the mirror. A black shrug tied under her nice tits, a white T-shirt, jeans. She could be casual too.

The EM on her ankle was covered by the bell-bottom, genuine vintage, hand-done embroidery.

She opened the door.

"Hi, you must be Ray, come on in."

Why was she so goddamned nervous, talking so fast? She was the one in control, she was the buyer; he was some mope trying to unload more weed than he had any right to have.

"You want a cup of coffee? A beer?"

"Coffee'd be good, if it's made."

"Fresh pot."

She went into the kitchenette and he said, "That's what we're here for," and she started to relax. Guy this corny, must be for real.

"Cream and sugar?"

"Black."

She came into the living room with two mugs and handed him one.

He was looking at her CDs, mostly eighties dance stuff, also some Pink Floyd, David Bowie. She said she downloaded everything now, it was all on the hard drive. "What do you want to hear?"

"Got any Allman Brothers? Grand Funk? Maybe Buddy Guy, Chicago blues?"

"I've got some early Rolling Stones, when they were ripping off Chicago blues. Some Led Zeppelin."

Ray liked that and she liked him. Bobbi was right, he was no farmer, or rich guy playing dope rebel. Or cop, she was pretty sure.

"How about this?" Her iPod was hooked up to her stereo and she rolled her thumb around the menu.

Ray said, "Shit, John Lee Hooker, where'd you get into that?"

" 'Cause of the duet with Bonnie Raitt."

Ray said, yeah, "In the Mood," that made sense, but the way he said it didn't make her feel bad, like he thought he was way cooler and she was playing catch-up, it made her feel like it made sense she'd get to John Lee Hooker through Bonnie Raitt.

She looked closer at this guy now. Like Bobbi said, he was a few years older than Sharon, in good shape, looked like he was used to being in charge. Your type, Mom.

Sharon sat down on the couch, crossed her legs, and watched him sit back in the easy chair, looking at her.

He opened the little black bag, like one of those doctor bags in the old movies, and dropped a big Ziploc bag on the coffee table. "One pound."

Just like that, Sharon thought, getting right to it. She put her mug down beside it and opened the bag. She looked up at him, saw him watching so closely as she dug through to the bottom. That was a rule she always followed, make sure what's at the bottom of the load is the same as what's at the top.

He said, "How much longer you doing the Martha Stewart?"

"What?"

"House arrest. I guess you didn't have three or four houses to choose from."

"No," she said, "just this one." Leaning back on the couch she said, "Five days."

"What then?"

The way he was looking at her, made her think he was wondering what he'd be doing in five days. She said, "Work, work, work."

"This what you do all the time?"

"One of the things I do."

"I guess you need something, you can work from home."

She said yeah and looked at him again. He was sitting there looking around her apartment not worried about a thing. How come he didn't think this was a setup? She could be anyone.

She said, "How much more can you get?"

"How much do you need?" He drank his coffee and kept looking at her.

"Can you get four pounds a week?"

"Sure."

Now he was starting to piss her off. She said, "I'll give you eighteen hundred for this."

"Eighteen hundred? I was looking at more like twenty-four."

That was better, now he was starting to look worried.

Sharon said, "This isn't bad, but come on, it's still wet, this pound is pretty damned loose. What, did you stick a straw in the bag and suck?" She kept her lips pursed when she said it and reached for her smokes.

Ray nodded.

Sharon got out a cigarette, held it and her lighter in the same hand, and kept looking at him.

He said, "Two grand each, if you buy four."

She offered him the smokes but he shook his head and took out his own. Players. Sharon thought, shit, what is this guy, a sailor?

She put her cigarette in her mouth and lit it quick, blowing smoke at the ceiling. She tapped her lighter on the coffee table. She was thinking this guy was a real amateur when it came to the dope, but he seemed pretty well put together otherwise. Most guys, she could figure them out right away, push the right buttons and get what she wanted, but this guy was harder to figure. She said, "You really think this is worth two grand?"

"I think it is to you, right now."

Before she could say anything he held up his hand and said, "Look, we don't need to act all tough and full of shit, we're both too old for that."

"How old do you think I am?"

He said, "Old enough to know better, but young enough to do it anyway."

They looked at each other, Sharon thinking, where the hell did you come from?

He said, "Look, you got stuff you need to do and so do I. I can sell you four pounds, just like that, what did you call it, loose, for seventy-five hundred bucks."

Sharon didn't know if it was because she liked this guy or because he was pissing her off so much. She said, "You're going to get yourself killed," and right away wished she could take it back.

Now it was Bonnie Raitt on the stereo, going through the playlist. Next up would be "Redneck Woman."

And Ray just said, "Maybe."

She said, "You come into town, no one knows you, offering to move large shipments, you're either going to get ripped off, or killed, or both."

"What do you think I should do?"

"I don't know, shit, but not this. Don't leave yourself so open."

He was nodding, she couldn't believe it, like he was taking fucking notes. She said, "You offered someone two hundred pounds a month."

"Yeah."

"You expected to get twenty-four hundred a pound?"

"I heard I could get four grand."

"Yeah, if you can sell it in the States."

"I can deliver anywhere."

"You could deliver two hundred pounds a month to Detroit, or Chicago, or New York?"

"Maybe not New York City, but Buffalo. Chicago, Minnesota, Cleveland."

Sharon took a long drag on her smoke, inhaling deeply, and

letting it out slowly. She could see why Richard wanted someone else on point on this one: this guy seemed too stupid to be a cop and way too stupid to be for real.

For a minute she thought maybe it was some new reality hidden-camera show, *America's Stupidest Home Dealers*. Or maybe someone was setting her up, but why? She was a sitting duck, someone wanted to take her out it was too easy. She always figured that was her best defense, no secrets.

Well, not many.

She smoked some more and drank her coffee. Ray was just staring at her.

But man, he's talking four hundred grand a month. American.

What rule was it? If it looks too good to be true, it probably is.

She said, "You're right, we're too old for the bullshit. I'll take four pounds and I guess it better be today, while you're still breathing."

She liked the way he stood up and started for the door. Business over, he wasn't going to stick around and try for something else.

But he just left the pound on the coffee table.

Sharon said, "You want your money?"

Ray stopped at the door and said, "Why, you going somewhere?" He looked at his watch and said, "I'll bring the rest in a couple of hours," and walked out of the apartment.

Sharon sat on the couch staring at the closed door.

Then she realized she hadn't gotten anything out of him for Richard.

———

ARMSTRONG DROVE the Crown Vic all the way through town on Dundas.

Bergeron said, "Why didn't you take the DVP, go across on the 401?" and Armstrong said he liked to drive on city streets, get the feel. He was tapping the wheel in time with the song on the radio, some kind of powwow drum thing.

Bergeron said, "What's that?"

"That's my people."

"What?" Bergeron'd forgotten Armstrong was an Indian. A First Nations, Aboriginal, whatever. "Oh, right."

Armstrong didn't seem upset at all, though. He said, "Aboriginal Voices Radio; 106.5, downtown T.O."

"You like this stuff?"

"I like Robbie Robertson better, and some of the blues stuff. One thing, this station's all over the map."

Bergeron looked at him, Armstrong, in his thousand-dollar charcoal grey suit, his perfect haircut, Ray-Bans, his shiny leather shoes. The guy was so downtown, so hip. Bergeron said, "You ever been on a reserve?"

"Visit my gramma when I was a kid. Spent whole summers on the reserve."

"But you didn't grow up on one?"

Armstrong turned north onto Jane, just after they'd passed through the Junction, another old neighbourhood going condo and getting gentrified.

"I grew up among the country's largest Aboriginal population."

"Where's that, Six Nations out in Brantford?"

"Regent Park, right downtown. Well. You know, you gotta be an immigrant to get to the top of the waiting list there. The urban reserve's a little further east."

Bergeron thought it was weird, to hear Armstrong talk about immigrants like that. The way an Indian-hating redneck would. Bergeron said, "You live there with your parents?"

"My mom. My dad died when I was two."

Bergeron looked at Armstrong closely, but he didn't seem to mind talking about it. He was driving slower now, creeping up Jane, no gentrification here, the street was lined with storefronts that had been brand new in the fifties, probably filled with Woolworth's and hardware stores, now it was all jerk chicken and payday loan places cashing welfare cheques. Whole place used to be filled with British immigrants, came over to work in the McDonnell Douglas factory making airplanes, but now it's all South Asian and black, looks just like an American city on the news, Detroit or Chicago.

Bergeron said, "What happened?"

Armstrong stopped at a light at Lawrence. He glanced at Bergeron, then back to the road. "What? To my dad? He got himself blown up in the Golan Heights. Nineteen seventy-four."

"Golan Heights, what was he doing there?"

"Peacekeeping. He was in the army."

"I didn't know anyone was killed."

"There've been 119 peacekeepers killed since 1950."

"Really?" Bergeron didn't think he was making it up, he'd just never heard that before. It seemed like a lot, like a bigger deal would be made of it.

"All over. Anywhere there's been peacekeeping. It was our bright idea, remember?"

"Yeah, I knew that."

"There's a cemetery in the Golan with a cross for my dad."

"Shit."

Bergeron thought of something and said, "Does that include those guys in Afghanistan? The friendly fire guys the Americans killed?"

"That is not peacekeeping," Armstrong said.

"Oh yeah, right, that's that war we're not in on."

"Right."

"So your father was in the armed forces."

"Hell," Armstrong said, "it's a family tradition. My great-great-great-great-something-granddaddy ran with Champlain. My family was in the War of 1812. You think that Laura Secord shit with the cow was true?"

Bergeron didn't say anything. He was embarrassed he knew all about Laura Secord leading her cow through the night to warn the British that the Americans were advancing, but he couldn't name a single First Nations, Aboriginal—hell, he didn't even know what to call them—fighter who was there.

"There might've been a lady and she might even've had a cow, but the Indians, they knew where every single guy was on both sides."

Bergeron was glad Armstrong had said Indian. Then he said, "Joseph Brant," and Armstrong looked at him, and Bergeron said, "That's all I've got."

Armstrong laughed. "The Chief. My family were in the trenches, we've always worked for a living, but we've been military since way back. Usually, go in for a few years, see the world, get a pension. That's what my grandfather did, Second World War. You know they had Navajo as radio operators, a code the Germans could never break."

Bergeron said yeah, he remembered that movie with Nicolas Cage a few years back.

Armstrong nodded. "That's right, Nicolas Cage, from the Italian Ojibwa. I think they're down by Niagara Falls."

"He was the white guy," Bergeron said, "looking out for the Indian guy."

Armstrong nodded. He was smiling though. "Couldn't make a movie about Indians with Indians, could you? Here we go." He turned into the parking lot of the Metro Police labs, 5050 Jane, practically underneath the 401 highway. There was a big new Leon's furniture store behind the lab, and an old small warehouse that was now something called the Disciples Baptist Church, which Bergeron figured must be all black, right up against the ten-foot chain-link fence.

"So, it doesn't bother you? Guys like Burroughs, right away he thinks your father was a drunk down on Queen Street?"

"Can't be pissed off every minute of the day."

"I guess not."

Armstrong turned off the ignition and got out of the car, saying, "Like Maureen said, we were all something thirty years ago."

"Yeah, I guess." He looked across the hood at Armstrong and said, "Still, it explains why you look so fucked up."

Armstrong put on his Ray-Bans and his most stoic Indian look, and said, "You funny, white man," and then, walking to the front door of the police lab, "Lock the doors, this is a high crime area, we need that radio."

CHAPTER **7**

THERE WERE THREE HARLEYS PARKED in front of the clubhouse on Eastern Avenue, big ones, loud chrome. J.T. and Chuck were sitting on the wooden picnic table when Richard pulled up in his Audi and parked in front of the driveway.

"This place stinks."

Chuck said, "Harleys, man, they leak oil."

"We don't leak," Richard said. "We mark our territory."

J.T. liked that, liked the way Richard said it, this guy so easy-going and in charge. He watched him look around the cement front yard of the old clubhouse, look up at the fully trade-marked flaming skull logo covering up that old hanging dice of the club that got patched over.

Richard said, "Still, man, get this place cleaned up."

"Like how?" Chuck said, not wanting to lift a finger.

Richard looked at him and then looked at J.T. and said, "Clean it up, get a proper sign and do something about those posts." Looking at the four-foot-high concrete posts lining the sidewalk.

J.T. nodded, said okay, no idea what to do about them but not about to ask.

Richard said, "Flowers and shit, you know, landscaping," and then walked inside.

Chuck said, "Asshole."

J.T. said, what?

"What's he doing here? Comes into town all by himself, driving his own car, doesn't even have a driver."

J.T. didn't say anything, but he was thinking, so what, I like to drive, makes me nuts sitting in the back, some asshole stuck in traffic. Gotta feel the wheel in my hands.

Chuck was saying, "You know who drives Mon Oncle?"

"What?"

"You know who his driver is? It's a cop. Guy used to be on the task force, now he's a fucking driver for us, takes Mon Oncle wherever he wants to go, carries his fucking coat."

And J.T. thought, yeah, that would impress these jerks. Chuck and the boys, all the hangarounds ready to do anything, be so tough, can't even tell when they're being used. Or worse, don't even care. Shit, he hadn't seen this kind of bullshit since the army, since those assholes in the Airborne could have run the whole place but shot themselves in the foot over the small shit.

Just like these assholes used to.

Till the pros took over.

It was true, J.T. thought, Mon Oncle took them from a bunch of long-haired thugs dealing dope in strip clubs in the seventies to international millionaires, but he didn't do it alone.

He had guys like Richard with him the whole time

What J.T. wondered was, how much of Mon Oncle was now

show and how much was guys like Richard who actually ran the place. And, yeah, what was he really doing in Toronto?

"You know that woman with the red truck, she has lawn-mowers and rakes and shit in the back?"

Chuck said the one wears the cut-offs, looks like Daisy Duke, but older?

"Yeah. She live around here?"

"Truck's parked around the corner all the time."

J.T. said, yeah, okay, and Chuck said why, you looking for a little action, we could go over to Jackie's, the place'll be empty now.

J.T. said, "No, I've got stuff to do."

LOEWEN SAID, "In the RCMP files they call them OMGs and the TOC, then in brackets, Italian."

Armstrong said, "Outlaw Motorcycle Gangs and Traditional Organized Crime, yeah, I've seen that."

"So, they've been working together for years but things are changing."

Bergeron said, "So we've been hearing."

Price said, "Loewen here has a pretty good contact with the Mounties."

"Yeah? How good?"

Loewen didn't say anything, and Price said, "Very good. Deep," and shook his head.

They were standing beside their cars in the parking lot for the ferry to Rochester. The ferry that didn't run anymore, the parking lot that was empty. But there was only one way in and one way out and they could see it, see that no one followed either car in. The wind was blowing pretty hard,

Indian summer over as fast as it had started and fall coming on hard.

Armstrong thought it was good Price was so amused.

"It's like that Police song, 'Wrapped Around Your Finger,'" Loewen said.

"What?"

"The band, The Police, they have that song," Loewen said. "Something, you know, 'then you'll find, the servant is the master,' something like that." They were all looking at him now—Price, Armstrong, and Bergeron—and he said, "I don't know, it's just, you know, the fucking Mounties, they say it's a big change. Bigger than we thought."

Armstrong said, right, yeah. "I know that song."

"Fuck, it could be a big deal," Loewen said. "For years the bikers were the muscle, did a lot of the dirty work, but the old timers, the mob, they ran everything."

Bergeron said they knew all that.

"Well, the thing about the bikers is, they have brand recognition. They get all the new recruits they want, more than they want."

Armstrong said yeah. He said, "The mob, those guys, you still need to be Italian to be made, right?"

Loewen said he thought so. "Estevao Silva was Portuguese. You remember, the boxer? He was a rising star till someone shot him in the head three times. Don't know how far he could have gone."

"But for the most part," Armstrong said, "the made guys still have to be Italian."

"Oh yeah, for sure. There's all these traditions, it goes way back. They still bring guys over from Italy sometimes. A lot of that shit's true. But for the bikers, it's just business, they don't care where you're from."

Armstrong said that was the thing about Canada. He looked at Price and said, "We're not racists."

Price said, yeah, right.

Loewen said, whatever. "The thing is, they got more hang-arounds, more punks trying to prove themselves to get into the club than they know what to do with. The top guys, the full patches, there aren't more than a dozen in the whole thing, they never do anything themselves, they're untouchable."

Armstrong said, "No one's untouchable."

"They use the cell system."

"Same as terrorists."

"Same as everybody doesn't want to get caught," Loewen said. "So they call them chapters, mob calls them families, whatever. The thing is, there's no official connection. Each chapter operates on its own."

"Even though we know they kick up."

"We allege."

"Yeah, right."

"But you said it's changing."

"Yeah," Loewen said, "looks like it. The bikers are starting to flex, taking over a lot more. They've got more members, more resources." He looked at the other cops. "Inside sources."

Bergeron said, "Is that why we're sneaking around like this, meeting here? Man, I feel like a fucking CI."

Confidential informant. Price said he thought the spot was convenient.

All Bergeron and Armstrong knew was that Price set up the meeting. He seemed to be taking care of Loewen a little. They'd been hooked up while Price's partner, Maureen McKeon, was on maternity leave and then Loewen had been assigned to narco. Guys on the force were getting moved around so much these days, every one of them feeling something coming: new mayor, new civilian police board chair, chief on his way out, new union head, new stories in the papers about corruption all the time. Five thousand cops in the city all lining up to take sides. There'd already been one wildcat strike at 55 Division downtown—change of shift and they'd locked the doors.

Armstrong looked out at the islands a couple hundred feet from shore. There was an amusement park on one, with a little roller coaster and kiddie rides, and on another one there was a nude beach, mostly gay. There were even some houses on one of the islands, people with ninety-nine-year leases the condo developers were always trying to get their hands on. Way over on the far side of the islands was a small airport. Armstrong said, "And these 'inside sources' have something to do with us?"

Loewen said, "Well, sort of. Maybe." He looked at Price, then out at the water, away from the islands towards the big lake, the U.S.A. somewhere on the other side of it, Buffalo, Rochester, New York.

"Tell them," Price said.

Loewen said he just wanted to help out, let them know.

"Let us know what?"

"Your building with the jumper?"

Bergeron said, "The one you guys are watching? The whole top floor is grow rooms?"

Armstrong liked the way Loewen didn't pretend to look surprised or anything.

"Yeah, that one. Well, someone in there's been getting some real attention."

"Who?"

"What kind of attention?"

Loewen looked at Price again and then said, "There's a red-head, got an apartment on the first floor?"

Armstrong said, "We know her."

"She got a visit."

Bergeron said, "Yeah, from who?"

"Guy named Richard Tremblay."

Bergeron said, "Richard Tremblay is kind of like John Smith in French, there are probably a thousand of them in this country."

"Yeah, but only one who's been best friends with Mon Oncle Bouchard in Montreal for twenty-five years."

"Shit. And this Tremblay went to her apartment?"

Loewen said, no, she met him around the corner, sat in his car for a while. "We got a lot of great pictures."

Armstrong said, "But she's under house arrest, she's got an EM on her ankle."

Loewen shrugged. "Don't know about that, but she met with him."

"So tell me," Bergeron said, "why one of the top guys in one of the biggest OMGs, which may be moving on one of the biggest TOCs in the country, would be meeting our girl in a shitty apartment in Parkdale?"

And Price said, "The bigger question might be, why doesn't anyone want you two to know?"

Armstrong said, "What do you mean?"

Price looked at Loewen, who nodded, and said, "Did you get anything at the lab?"

Bergeron said, "Like what?"

"Like, from the dead guy?"

"Come on," Armstrong said, "we don't have time for this shit. What is it?"

Loewen said, "That chick on the first floor, the redhead, name's Sharon MacDonald. The EM's for kicking the shit out of a guy at a massage parlour."

Bergeron said, yeah, so?

"Her handprint was on the back of your dead guy's jacket."

Armstrong said, "Motherfucker."

Bergeron said, "We just got back from the lab. They didn't say a thing."

Loewen nodded, looked away. He was scared and he didn't even know the half of it. He said, "Burroughs was there."

"Fucker."

Loewen said, "I didn't know who to talk to. Price said you guys should know, but, fuck, this could be big."

Bergeron said, "You think?" He was turning in a little circle, disgusted by the whole thing.

Armstrong said, okay, everybody calm down. "It could still just be somebody doesn't want us to screw up their investigation."

Price said, "Sure. Could be."

Armstrong said, "Fuck." He looked at Bergeron and they both knew this was it.

Bergeron said, "Hey, I'm practically out of here, I'm only working this because Nichols feels sorry for me. I got no more promotions to worry about."

Armstrong said he wasn't worried about that at all, and Price said, "How far you think affirmative action's going to take you?"

Anybody else, Armstrong would have hit him. He said, "So Tremblay and Sharon MacDonald, they just old friends?"

"Yeah. Used to live together back in Montreal in the early eighties. She was a stripper and he was just starting out."

Bergeron said, "You're not getting this stuff from our sources."

"No."

"So, this Mountie, giving you all this, you blowing him?"

Loewen said it was a woman, and Armstrong said, oh, okay then.

Bergeron said, "You do whatever you have to do, son, just keep bringing it."

Loewen nodded but he looked scared. He said, "Thing is, Sharon dumped Tremblay for Charles Larose, a much higher ranked guy."

"That's gotta hurt."

"What happened to Larose?"

"Started his car one day and it blew up."

"They do that," Armstrong said, "when you're in a war with another gang."

Loewen looked out at the lake again, and said, yeah, sure. "Sharon was a witness. Apparently she went back into the house for her smokes."

"She's had quite the interesting past."

"She's not all that boring now."

Bergeron said, "What else you got?"

And Loewen said, "What else?"

"Well, shit, where's this going?"

Loewen said he had no idea and he wasn't about to try to find out. "I gave you what I could without anybody noticing."

Bergeron said, yeah, sure, and Armstrong said they'd have to find out themselves.

Loewen said, "You gotta keep me out of this."

Armstrong said sure, "As long as we can."

MITCHELL FUCKING MORRISON was saying, "Once they're in the house they get everything, the plants, the cash, the guns, everything. We have to find a way to keep them out, we have to nullify the search warrant," and Rachel Chin thought she had something.

She just wasn't sure enough to open her mouth in this room.

Oliver said, "We've been over it and over it, there's just nothing."

They were in the boardroom, what Morrison called the boardroom, which doubled as the lunchroom. Three junior associates and the man himself. He was piling authentic Montreal smoked meat, almost all fat, onto rye bread. There were pickles and coleslaw and a bunch of other stuff Rachel didn't recognize. Ryan, the other junior, had spent an hour and half driving up to Bathurst and Steeles, Little Israel, and back to their office on Jarvis to get the man his lunch.

Rachel was the only woman lawyer in the office, the most junior of the juniors, and probably the only Chinese associate the firm had ever had. The firm, Morrison, Woodrow, and Phelps, wasn't what she'd expected at all. Coming out of Osgoode Hall she'd liked the idea of the small, boutique firm that handled, as they said, a wide range of the law, everything from criminal to immigration to financial. It seemed a great way to get experience in a lot of different areas.

When she took the position, she didn't know all the clients were organized crime.

Not that anyone ever called it that. She realized pretty quickly she was there to get some of the up-and-coming Chinese market. She figured at least she'd learn a lot about copyright law and DVD pirating.

Morrison wiped mustard off his chin and said, "Come on, people, we need something today. Let's go, cops fill in these forms, there's got to be something wrong with them. Any translation problems? Rachel?"

"Um, no, I don't think so." She glanced sideways and saw Ryan roll his eyes. She was waiting for him to say, in his Morrison voice, "Don't think, girlie, know," but he didn't say anything. Neither did Morrison.

Rachel wanted to say, "I'm Chinese, you jerks, all these wiretaps are Vietnamese." Besides, she could barely speak Cantonese, growing up in Hamilton.

"And the surveillance?"

"Nothing."

"The undercover report, no holes in that?"

No one would dare look at Morrison.

The boardroom door opened and Stephanie, the receptionist, stuck her head in. She was blonde this week. She said, "Mr. Morrison, Frantisek Wodja is on the phone."

Morrison said, who, and she said, "Nugs."

"I told you, I'm in a meeting and I'm not to be disturbed."

"He's very insistent."

"Yeah, well, he'll wait his turn like everybody else."

"He's called three times, he said you should call him right away."

Morrison turned on the receptionist and Rachel looked away. He said, "I don't think this is too complicated, even for you. I'm busy. I will call him later."

Stephanie looked like she was going to cry as she backed out of the room and closed the door.

Rachel was tapping the paper in front of her, the search warrant for the grow house. She watched Ryan and Oliver, so comfortable with Morrison, or acting that way. She knew they were scared shitless of him too. They just faked it so much better, it was all those years of comfortable entitlement white guys grow up with, going to UCC and hanging out at the cottage with their dads' important friends. She hated the way they treated everything like a game, like there were no consequences.

Of course, for them there weren't.

Morrison said, "Okay, you geniuses, you best of the best, come up with something."

Oliver looked around, said, "Well, a lot of the guns were in the garage and the warrant says . . ." and Morrison shook his head and said, "Once they're in the fucking house, it's all house. Come on, people."

Now Rachel was really afraid to say anything. But she thought she had something, so she cleared her throat and Morrison stared right at her and said, "You got something?"

"Um, maybe."

"Well?"

She tried to focus on the paper in front of her, knowing they were all staring at her. She said, "Um, okay, so we're looking for something that's open to interpretation, something that can be taken two ways."

She kept staring at the warrant, knowing Morrison's beady eyes were boring into her. She could feel Ryan and Oliver waiting for her to say something stupid so they could jump all over her, get Morrison on her and away from them.

"Okay, so, um, in the directions it says that a reasonable time must be allowed for the residents to respond."

Ryan said, "That's standard, on every warrant," and Oliver said, "That's not specific to this warrant."

Morrison said, "Hey, girlie," and when she finally looked up, he was smiling. He said, "Have some cheesecake. There's no fortune in it, but I got one for you—you got something."

Ryan and Oliver couldn't believe it, saying, "What the hell," and "There's nothing there," and that they couldn't use it, but Morrison cut a piece of the cheesecake, getting a lot of the cherries, and slid it down the table to Rachel.

"Reasonable. That's what we want."

Ryan said, "Well, how long did they wait?"

Morrison said, "They didn't wait at all, they just banged open the door with their fucking battering ram. Scared the shit out of little Duong and Hanh Phuc, poor kids."

Rachel thought, yeah, right, we're all really worried about illegal immigrant kids living in grow houses.

Ryan and Oliver were busy flipping through all the papers they had in front of them, Ryan saying, "I don't think there's any precedent," and Oliver saying, "Nowhere does it say how long they waited before they broke the door," and Morrison said, "Exactly."

He took a big bite of the cheesecake himself. "It doesn't say. That's what we've been looking for." He stood up and said, "Come with me, Ms. Chin, we've got some work to do," and walked out.

Rachel packed up her paperwork quick, and followed him out.

She stopped at the door, puckered, kissed the tips of her fingers and pressed them to her stuck-out butt.

RICHARD SAID, "I'm going to Costa Rica in two weeks. We ready?"

Danny Mac said, "We have twelve girls going down next week, the place is almost finished, it looks great, the website's running fine, we're half booked the first week, but we'll be full after that."

There were six of them, all guys in their late forties or early fifties looking mostly business-casual, sitting around the wood-panelled main room of the clubhouse. Nugs was letting his beard grow and his hair was getting past his collar, but he'd clean up before his court appearance if Mitchell Fucking Morrison couldn't get rid of the charges before then.

"And we have enough girls to rotate through?"

"Hey," Danny said, "you advertise full-service, you better supply full-service."

They were calling it the Gladiator Club, the perfect vacation, the real fantasy island. Places were opening up all over the Caribbean: Viking Resorts, Blackbeard's, White Gold. Guy rents a room, gets a girl too, anything he wants. Nice girl too, Russian, Romanian, Hungarian, almost always blonde, and then after his trip the guy flies home with no strings. When they first mentioned the idea, Nugs thought it was some kind of swingers club like Hedonism in Jamaica, or one of those mail-order bride things, but no, they said, it's like a high-class brothel. They were booking three-day getaways and had to start offering group rates for bachelor parties and graduations. It was amazing; even after paying the girls and paying off the locals, it was still cheaper than running a golf course.

"All right," Richard said, "looks good. Now what about this goddamned legalization bill?"

Alex, the most business-looking of them all, said, "It's under control."

"A fucking police chief, two city counsellors, and an MP are talking about legalizing marijuana, bringing a private member's bill to Parliament. That's 'under control'?"

Nugs thought maybe Richard was finally getting pissed about something, but it could just as easily have been something he read in one of those management books he always had around, like the shit about complimenting people. This could be some shit like that, some kind of technique, as if they really were businessmen.

"Overlea cleared the press shit with us, it's just smoke," Alex said. "His buddy Anderson is coming out next week with a new study, smoking dope destroys youth, we're all doomed, blah, blah, blah."

Richard said, "You be damned sure. The last thing we need is for this shit to be legal."

They all agreed, but Richard said, "The only guys we don't want to compete with are Imperial fucking Tobacco."

And Nugs thought he might be serious about that one, guy who wants to be a businessman so bad he's started to think they're something special.

Alex said, we know, man, don't worry and Richard said, yeah, okay, but what about long term?

"Sure, tobacco's slipping here, but worldwide markets are going up."

"So they don't want to get their hands on dope? Come on, they want it bad."

Alex said, no, yes, no. "I know what you mean. But hell, talk about thinking long-term, these guys have been around for hundreds of years, they can be patient."

Richard said, yeah, that was true. "Still, man, stay on your politicians, keep those fuckers in line. They start talking about selling this shit in liquor stores, it'll be tough."

Nugs thought, yeah, but we'll find something. Can't legalize everything. And he was pretty sure it was all a calculated scam with Richard, couldn't have the meeting go too smooth. He tried to remember the first time he met Richard Tremblay and couldn't. Must have been in Montreal, probably in the early eighties when they were both long-haired bikers who actually rode bikes, but the guy didn't stand out at all. He just always seemed to be there after a while, every time they went to see Mon Oncle Bouchard, Richard was there.

And now he was here, saying, "How are we with the Russians?"

Danny Mac said, "They had some disruptions but they're back on track."

Nugs said, yeah, "When fucking Boris shot Anzor and then got himself blown up." He looked at Richard to see if there'd be some reaction. After all, it was Boris's uncle who killed Claude and Denis at the airport, and that was part of this mess Richard was in town to clean up. But the guy never let anything show, nothing ever seemed to bother him.

He moved on. "Shit, O.J., you're moving a lot of guns."

O.J. Dunbar, the only black guy in the room, pretty much no matter how many bikers were around he was the only black guy, said, for sure, my boys need them.

Richard said the press was full of gun violence. "Is it getting too public?"

Nugs knew a lot of people thought O.J. got his name because he looked like a football player, but the truth was the name only happened to stick a few years ago when O.J. started slitting people's throats instead of beating them to death. Nugs said, "They're just fighting for territory."

"That's good, get rid of the weak," Richard said.

O.J. said, yeah, it's all good.

Richard said, if the boys are that ambitious, selling that much dope, maybe we could raise the price a little.

O.J. said, "Just for my guys, or across the board?"

Nugs liked the way Richard dropped that bomb so casual, tossed it off like it was something he just thought of.

Richard was looking around the room, waiting. He took a bite of his steak, then said, "Across the board."

Danny Mac said, "Nugs, man, how come we don't have proper plates? You can't cut a steak on fucking Styrofoam."

Nugs said the hangaround was new. Kid went a few blocks over to a steak house called the Tulip and got six takeout meals. Steak, mashed potatoes, and mushrooms sautéed in pounds of butter. Nothing green ever touched a plate from the Tulip, the place was old-time, went way back to when there was a racetrack across the street and the gangsters wore suits and ties.

"Yeah, well, show him where the fucking plates are."

O.J. said, "You think we can raise the wholesale price across the city?"

Richard said, "Why not the province?" and drank some of his expensive imported water.

"A lot of guys would have to be brought in line." O.J. looked at Danny Mac, who said that the Russians didn't move much weed but he'd talk to them.

"When we did this in Quebec," Nugs said, "it started a war." He watched for Richard's reaction.

"It wasn't really 'we' then, was it?"

Smacked down, Nugs thought, letting him know there'd been a real change at the top. He was only pushing to see what there was to Richard, now that he was talking about taking over the entire drug business in the fourth-largest metropolitan centre in North America. Since they'd won that war in Quebec, it looked like they'd just keep rolling. Now that it was "we."

But Nugs said, "If we raise the wholesale price, most of the dealers won't be able to pass it along, it'll eat into their profits."

Richard said, "Yeah, so?"

O.J. said, "They'll need bigger territories, to make up the difference."

Richard said, yeah, that's right.

"Some guys will have to be taken out."

Richard said, "Cream rises to the top. There enough manpower?"

"Hey, man," O.J. said, "there's always more coming on, best franchise operation in the world, nothing comes close. There were some fat, lazy-ass chumps making easy money. They just happened to be here when it started to flow, didn't earn a goddamned thing. Now they'll have to fight for it."

"Story of this whole goddamned province," Richard said, swallowing down his steak, "this goddamned country. Luck and timing, just happened to have all the natural resources right next to the U.S. of A., biggest fucking market in the world, didn't have to break a sweat."

Right, Nugs thought, more of that management shit Richard's been reading, next thing he'll want to have a fucking lunch-and-learn.

O.J. said, "There's still some other supply coming in once in a while though, we'll have to take care of that."

Richard said, yeah, they would, and looked around.

"We'll have to talk to Danny Trahn," Nugs said. Then he looked right at Richard and said, "And Colucci."

"I can talk to Colucci," Richard said. "We go way back."

That was the first Nugs ever heard of that, but fine with him if Richard wanted to drive all the way up to fucking Woodbridge and put up with all that mafia poser bullshit. He said, "I'll talk to Danny."

"Okay, good." Richard nodded.

Nugs said, "Maybe we should soften him up first."

"Yeah?"

"Maybe get our boys in blue to bust a whole lot of his grow houses."

Richard looked like he was thinking about it, then said, "Maybe. How reliable are your cops?"

"Reliable."

"Okay, let's think about it."

O.J. said to the guy next to him, guy looked like a golf pro, "What about the stragglers?"

The golf pro, Spaz, said, "Assholes. Bosco and his fuck-ups." He looked at Richard. "Guys refused the patch-over? Up in London and some in Windsor, Lone Gunmen."

"They bringing anything into Toronto?"

"Probably."

Nugs looked at Danny Mac, wishing he hadn't said that. He was really starting to get Richard's point now, about not controlling the situation.

But all Richard said was, okay. "And they're still talking to Texas, trying to make a deal with them."

Danny Mac said he thought that was all worked out at higher

levels. "We get Canada and they get Texas and Arizona. We gave up two good clubs in Austin and Houston."

Nugs watched Richard, all this talking about what "we" did back before there was any "we," but now he didn't seem to mind.

"They'll be taken care of. How many are there?"

O.J. said there couldn't be more than a couple dozen, counting hangarounds and prospects. "Who the fuck prospects for the Losers?"

"Still, they've got to go."

They all agreed.

And that was that. The six of them, in five minutes, decided to shake up the entire power structure of a billion-dollar industry.

Ozzie said he had to get going, if there wasn't anything else, and Richard said, "You got some business?"

"No." Ozzie said, "I'm picking up my wife, we're going out to dinner."

Nugs watched Richard, thinking maybe this was it, a guy sits through the whole meeting, this meeting, not saying a word and now he's got to leave for no real reason, this could be where Richard gets tough. But Richard just looked around the room and said, "Anything else?"

Nobody had anything.

"Okay, that's it."

Nugs watched them all leave and looked at Richard thinking, how long has he been planning this? Nugs wondered if he had cleared it with Mon Oncle, or if he was just going to start a war all on his own. Nugs said, "Colucci's still pissed."

"Yeah?"

"Yeah, that botched hit, it's all over the news."

Richard said, "Yeah."

"Well, you know, you told us to not to take it."

Richard nodded. Nugs would swear he saw him smile, but if it was there at all it was gone fast.

Richard said, yeah, so what. "If he can't find someone to do a proper job, it's his own damned fault."

And Nugs thought, yeah, fucking right. Maybe that was the opening Richard was looking for, testing his competition, seeing how strong they really were. There might really be something to all this management crap.

"You know, Nugs," Richard said, "twenty-five years ago we were the muscle, the fucking foot soldiers getting killed in the trenches. Now it's our turn to run things."

Nugs liked the sound of that. "So we have to let everyone know. Get everyone in line."

"Show we're not just talking."

Nugs said, yeah. "Take somebody out. You have someone in mind?"

And Richard said, yeah. "I do."

ARMSTRONG GOT INTO the car and said, "Okay, where were we?"

Bergeron drove the Crown Vic west, away from the College Street headquarters, past Queen's Park and the U of T campus.

"Sharon MacDonald was born in Moncton, New Brunswick, in 1966. She looks good for forty."

Bergeron said, forty's not old, and Armstrong said he knew that.

"She'd even look good for thirty. She was arrested once for possession with intent. That was in Hamilton at Hanrahan's."

"She still a peeler?"

"Doesn't say. You know these files don't give much. She got a year's probation, but she broke that when she assaulted that guy at the Taj Mahal Massage on the Queensway."

"Taj Mahal, that Arab, Indian? I can't tell them apart."

Armstrong said, "From what I understand, if they're Pakistani it could go either way. I mean, whose side are they on?"

"They gotta be on someone's side?"

"Hey, what the man said, you're either with us or you're against us."

"So, who's Sharon MacDonald with?"

"We'll find out."

Bergeron turned south on Spadina, heading through China-town to the Gardiner.

Armstrong said, "There's practically nothing in this file. Shit."

"That the CPIC?"

"Yeah. Names and dates, criminal records. There's nothing here for known associates, no intelligence at all."

"What about ACIIS?"

"Yeah, I pulled it." Armstrong took out another sheet of paper. Automatic Criminal Intelligence Information System. Of course, if she was doing anything in Quebec that wouldn't be in here, it'd be in their own system, G-11.

Bergeron drove up the ramp to the Gardiner, the traffic heavy even in the middle of the afternoon.

"And anything she's done in drugs will be task force," Armstrong said. "And in the RCMP database that we can't access."

Bergeron said, "So, do we do any police work, or just play computer games?"

"It would just be a lot easier if we could get at the information."

"And people think we live in a police state."

"Would make our jobs a lot easier if we did."

Bergeron laughed. "You get rid of the lawyers. What's in the ACIIS?"

"Not much. Like Loewen said, she must go back with the bikers because she was at a few funerals."

The traffic eased up and they picked up speed, passing Sharon's apartment building to their right. To their left was the lake, the yacht club, and the Boulevard tennis club under its year-round dome. Two worlds separated by six lanes of non-stop traffic.

Further along, the lakefront turned into a skinny park, the expressway no longer raised. On the other side what used to be factories and warehouses were either going condo or being knocked down. And billboards. Big electronic ads with giant screens showing TV commercials and flashing lights everywhere.

Bergeron took the Queensway exit. "So, Sharon MacDonald, known to associate with bikers, is running grow rooms, and selling to strippers and hookers?"

"Could be," Armstrong said. "But why is she pushing some guy off the roof?"

They turned onto the Queensway, a divided road lined with strip malls, full of fast-food joints and dollar stores, some new big-box stores, and car dealerships. A big old house had been converted into the House of Essex Gentleman's Club and in the row of stores on the next block there was the Taj Mahal Massage Parlour.

Bergeron parked right in front.

Armstrong said, "It's hard to tell about this neighbourhood."

There was an Indian food restaurant in the same strip of storefronts, but there was also a Polish restaurant and a place selling Chinese CDs and DVDs. Movies still playing in downtown theatres were on display in DVD boxes.

"Man, how come the only parts of this town that have any real integration are where there's crime?"

"It's all business," Armstrong said, pulling open the massage parlour door. "Everybody comes to Toronto to make money."

Inside they saw a short, good-looking East Indian girl with big hair and big fake tits walking down the hall towards them.

She said, "L.E.'s here," and turned around, but they caught up to her and Armstrong said they weren't Vice.

"We might be law enforcement but we don't care what you do here."

"Sure you do," the East Indian girl said, looking at him now and flirting. "You just might not arrest me for it."

And Armstrong said, yeah, that was true.

IN THE BACK of the cab, Ray was going over Eddie's numbers again: two and a half months from planting to harvest, fifty plants to make a pound, and it sells for twenty-four hundred bucks in Toronto.

Or it would, if Ray had any fucking idea what he was doing.

Looking out the window, he liked Parkdale a lot less at night. Queen Street down here was trying hard to go upscale but keep its rough edges. It made Ray laugh, as if any of these art gallery owners had any idea what rough really meant.

Eddie said the cops always take the amount of a bust and work it out to the final payout possible to give it the highest value—like saying how much beef was in a cow by totalling the amount you could get for every Big Mac that comes out of it. Ray'd thought they had four hundred plants, that was four hundred pounds, like the cops said. Eddie said, yeah, and they never lose evidence either. No, it's all press, all looks. Maybe, maybe if you had the perfect growing conditions, the perfect amount of sunlight and water and nutrients, maybe then you could get a pound out of thirty plants.

But they didn't have anywhere near perfect growing conditions.

The cab turned off Queen and right away anything upscale was gone. By the time they got to King it was cheap bars, rooming houses, and hookers. And seven- or eight-storey apartment buildings that were low-rent the day they were built.

But what Ray thought was really out of place here was this Sharon.

She had to be close to forty, almost his own age, and she was living in this low-rent UN, hardly anyone around speaking any English, but she wasn't white trash. Good-looking woman, nice red hair, those freckles on her neck and the tops of her tits, her really nice tits, and her ass in those tight jeans. At some point in her life she worked it and now it just came natural. And she knew what she was doing when it came to the dope. That EM on her ankle, though, Ray figured maybe she got into something she couldn't handle.

But she seemed like she could handle just about anything. Or anyone.

Ray was sure she was going to try to handle him. Hell, Eddie'd laughed about it, saying the only person in town who'd even taken a nibble at the bait was already driving a hard bargain—and she was obviously trapped and strapped.

Then Eddie'd said, "Maybe you just want to get laid," and Ray didn't say anything, but he thought it wouldn't be the worst way to spend the night.

The cab pulled up in front of the building, the tallest one in Parkdale. The other side of the street was dark, a big fence around the grounds of the rehab centre, a couple of hookers in their miniskirts, and halters, and fake-fur coats now that it was getting cold at night, and the healthiest looking homeless guy Ray'd ever seen. Probably a cop.

Ray paid the cabbie and carried his little black doctor bag to the door.

SHARON WOULD HAVE LIKED a new outfit, some retro thing, embroidered jeans, maybe a shawl and boots. She really would have liked nice leather boots with four-inch heels.

She settled for painting the damned thing on her ankle with bright red nail polish and put on her red Jimmy Choos, open toed with the extra-tall heels, a red leather mini, and a low-cut white silk top. If you can't hide it, you might as well embrace it.

She paced around the apartment like a teenager going on a first date.

Not that she'd ever been a teenager who waited around to go out on dates, but she'd seen the Molly Ringwald movies.

A cab pulled up in front, and Ray got out, walked up to the lobby. Sharon watched him all the way, thinking the guy was sure relaxed.

She had the apartment door open when he came down the hall. She said, "Hey, Ray," and he said, hey.

She turned and walked into the apartment, knowing he was checking her out, looking at her ass and her legs, all the way down to that thing on her ankle, but they'd gone over that and he didn't seem to care.

"You want something to drink?"

He said, sure, whatever you've got and she asked him would beer be okay, and he said, yeah.

Bruce Springsteen was playing; Bobbi had downloaded it for her. Sharon came out of the kitchen with a couple of bottles and handed one to Ray.

He said, "That thing on your ankle, can you get it wet?"

She said, you mean like the bathtub, yeah, it's waterproof, and he said, okay then, and she said okay, and they stepped close, and started kissing.

Sharon wanted to put her beer down, she didn't know what to do with it but Ray had no trouble, he had his arms around her, one hand on her back holding her tight, and it felt really good. He kissed good too, not ramming his face into hers, not moving all over, not getting on to the next thing, he was enjoying it, she could tell.

He enjoyed it all the way and so did she. Couple of awkward moments, her thong getting caught on the EM, but Ray just said, you want to leave it hanging there, it's sexy, and she said, I do not, and sat up pulling the thong off, and dropping it on the floor, and then got right back to it, no break in the mood.

Bruce sang about seeing a hooker in Reno, two hundred straight up, two-fifty in the ass, but it didn't give Ray any ideas. He liked it old-fashioned and that was fine with Sharon. And he really liked it when she got on top, pushing her hands on his chest, grabbing him. Even the EM digging into his thigh was okay.

When they were both finished, Sharon said, "You know, not every dealer's going to want this kind of service."

"No?"

"Well, Randy will, but his legs aren't as nice as mine."

Ray was touching her softly and he said, "What about his tits?" and Sharon said they looked really good but they were fake.

"Not like mine," she said.

"No," Ray said. "Yours are nice."

"Damned right. You want another beer?"

Ray said, sure, and Sharon hopped out of bed, full of energy and naked, except for the EM on her ankle.

She came back and handed Ray a beer, put hers on the bedside table, and walked back to the living room saying, "You want a smoke?" and Ray said, yeah, but get mine, in the bag.

Sharon opened the little black doctor bag and got out his smokes, Players, and saw the four pounds of dope, each one in a big Ziploc bag like his sample, all of them loose and damp.

Shit, she thought, who the hell is this guy?

And remembered she was supposed to find out. She was thinking about small talk, how did it work. Neither one of them being too up on it, she figured she'd ask him where he was from, when there was a knock at the door.

Sharon took a step towards it and said, "Just a sec, Zahra, I gotta get some clothes on," and a guy said, "Hey, don't worry about it."

Another guy said, "It's the police."

Sharon closed the little black bag and said, "Well, I'm still going to get dressed."

CHAPTER 8

BOBBI SAID SHE WAS THINKING, when her mother's house arrest was over she was going to take her to a spa, get her the full package.

Sunitha said, "Don't do it. I used to work at a spa."

Bobbi drank her martini and said, "Oh yeah?"

"Yeah, right downtown, The Bitches of Bloor."

"What?"

"What we called it. For busy women executives. Manicure, pedicure, waxing. I hated it. Fucking yoga and massages."

Bobbi looked around the bar, 7:30, no one there yet. She liked the Drake. A hundred years ago or something it was a decent hotel in the west end of Toronto, then somehow Parkdale went from big family houses, practically mansions, to rooming houses and the Drake became a fleabag. Then, Bobbi heard something, a few years ago an Internet millionaire bought it, turned it into trendy-central. The whole area was going upscale, art galleries, little stores that sold almost-antiques and kitschy stuff people said was ironic.

"So, no spa?"

"You think they hork one up into your burger at Mickey Dees? You don't want to know what's in that face mud. Where I worked was awful, they were just never satisfied, the Bitch Brigade. All these women, I don't know how they got their money, but shit, they sure figure they deserve it."

"Yeah," Bobbi said, "I've never heard anybody say they don't work hard for their money."

"Well, they work a lot, these chicks, a lot of hours, I don't know how hard but they sure treat the help like shit." She took a sip of her drink, something in a highball glass.

"Worse than the guys?"

"Hell yeah." She played with her pack of smokes, tapping it on the bar. "I mean, the women, they think they're being nice, you know, pretending like we're pals, but they're so shitty at it, God." She rolled her eyes. "It's like they took some course on how to treat the staff, make sure you give one compliment in each session, be polite when telling them what you want. The one I got most often was how good my English is. Shit."

Bobbi said, "It's all about what they want."

"Yeah, and that's to feel important, like a fucking big shot. Talk about your inflated sense of entitlement. How's that for my good English?" Then she did a really good Punjabi accent, "You hands get rough, you work too much." She laughed. "They always buy the bullshit. I'll tell you, all those things they say they get at the spa, relaxation, recharging, focus, whatever the bullshit is they say these days? Well, a quick rub-down and blow job and that's actually what the guys get out of it."

"And they're nicer?"

"Once in a while you get a drunk, but most of the time? Shit, yeah. The guys actually like you, it's not bull, they don't look down on you all the time like you're the fucking help. The guys know why they're there, they have a good time, they leave."

"Relaxed, recharged, focused."

Sunitha waved to the bartender for another round. "Ready to take on the world."

"Here I come."

"They come all right." She leaned in close to Bobbi. "Those prissy chicks, if they'd admit what they really want and come once in a while, they might not be so fucking bitchy."

Bobbi said, "Well, yeah, but they live for denial."

"Even more than we do."

"So maybe I should get my mom the full treatment at a massage parlour."

"Don't laugh, we're getting more chicks in all the time."

Bobbi said maybe before the next round they should have a smoke. "I can't believe we can't smoke in here."

Sunitha said, okay, sure, but just one thing, and Bobbi said, yeah?

"Yeah. Some cops came into work today."

"You got busted?"

"No."

The bartender put their drinks down and asked them if everything was okay.

"A martini and a cosmopolitan? Yeah, you got it right." He left and Sunitha rolled her eyes. Then she said, "No, they weren't Vice. Or narco. They were Homicide."

"Wow, everybody thinks they can get a free reverse glide."

Sunitha said, it's reverse slide, and no, that's not what they wanted.

"Don't they usually?"

"Depends how many there are. I thought these guys would for sure, just the two of them. If it's more you never know, witnesses and all. It's almost funny these days, the cops don't trust each other at all."

"Their own worst enemies."

"More than you think."

Bobbi said, so what did they want, these two Homicide guys, and Sunitha said, "They wanted to know about Ku."

"What?"

"At first they asked about your mom, about the assault. One of them, guy has shoulders as wide as a truck, I can't tell if he's black or what, he asked a lot of questions. Walked around the place like he owned it."

"Assholes."

"I didn't tell them anything, I swear."

"I know."

"Then, just when they were leaving, the other one, older guy, had really nice eyes, he took out a picture."

"Shit, Sunitha, you got such a daddy complex."

"I do not. But it took me by surprise, you know. I was so glad they were leaving, I just wanted them out of there, and then he shows me this picture. God, it must have been taken at the morgue, looked like somebody put his face back together but missed a few pieces. Gross. And I just said, 'That's him,' and they said, 'Who?'"

"You told them?"

"I didn't mean to."

"Bastards."

"I just wanted them to get out. I had practically the whole ounce in my purse and Sami and Zahra were both doing guys."

"Where was Farhad?"

"I wish I knew. Anyway." She took a drink of her cosmopolitan and tapped the pack of smokes some more. "Anyway, they already seemed to know who he was so I told them. I thought, what's the big deal, your mom's already doing the time for it, she gets that thing off next week, right? If Ku didn't want anybody to know he should have paid for the mirror himself." She took a cigarette out of the pack and tapped it on the bar. "Besides, he's dead now, what difference could it make?"

"Yeah, it's okay," Bobbi said. "Don't worry about it. It's cool." She'd have to tell her mother right away. She didn't know if it meant anything, this connection between Sharon and Ku, and then him jumping off her building. They probably just wanted to know who he was, so they could send a bill for the funeral to someone.

"You sure?"

"Yeah. I'm sure."

Sunitha put her hand on Bobbi's arm and squeezed. "Thanks. Shit, I was so worried. I mean, after what he did and everything."

The bartender came over and said they couldn't smoke in the bar.

Sunitha said they wouldn't dare. "Rules are rules."

The security guys were out front already, setting up the ropes and putting on their headsets. In Toronto, Bobbi thought, a place is only cool if it looks the part.

DRIVING AWAY in her Mini, the first thing Bobbi did was get on her phone to her mother, tell her the cops went to the massage parlour, and Sunitha told them about Ku, and the assault stuff, and Sharon said, "I know, they're here now."

Bobbi said, "Omigod, no way," and got off the phone quick.

Sharon hung up and watched the two cops talking to Ray. Or really, watched Ray talk to the two cops.

Ray was saying it has its moments but it gets dull, "Like any job," and the older cop, the white one was saying, yeah, but people dream their whole lives they can retire and live on a boat.

"They don't usually dream about hauling sixty-five tons of iron-ore pellets though."

"No, but you could still probably sell tours, like those hockey fantasy camps."

Ray said, "You mean get people to pay to work the boats themselves?"

"Sure."

"I never thought about that, it might work. There are plenty of guys out there like to watch us go through the canals."

Sharon was sitting back watching the men talk. She'd put on a T-shirt that barely covered her ass and Ray was wearing jeans and his shirt, unbuttoned. The guys didn't seem to be trying to impress each other or stake out territory, they just seemed to be talking.

She kept staring at the black bag on the coffee table between them filled with four pounds of dope.

The white cop, Gord Bergeron, said, "What do you do in the winter?"

"Since I started running my own ships I do maintenance. Try to get contracts."

"The tough part."

"You know it." He drank some more beer. The cops had turned down Sharon's offer. They'd looked at each other before they did and she knew they hadn't been working together that long. The men were still standing. Ray said, "I guess it's like anything else, we're getting cut to the bone but the service can't slip. Used to be, a thousand footer had twenty-five guys working it. You get a decent crew, it's a great summer. Now you push a barge around the lakes. Got a six-man crew, everybody working their asses off, pissed off all the time."

The other cop, the dark-skinned one, said, "We know what that's like. But they want the same service."

"Always."

Bergeron said, "What do you mean, you push a barge?"

Ray said there were all kinds of regulations on the Great Lakes about what size of crew you needed for what size boat. "Then some genius came up with the idea that if the freight was just on a barge, you could push it around with a tug, which doesn't have to follow the Coast Guard crewing standards. When we get to ports or locks we get helped through."

Bergeron said, "Always looking for a way to screw some guy out of work."

Ray said, "There was a big strike in '96, didn't work. What're you gonna do?" He sat on the couch.

Then Armstrong said to Sharon, "So, that comes off next week?" Taking her by surprise.

She said, "Yeah, the twentieth. Friday."

"You'll be glad about that."

She said it really wouldn't change much. "I've got nowhere to go."

Bergeron said, "No more massage parlours?"

Sharon said to Ray, "Maybe you want to get us something to eat? There's a Portuguese place on Roncesvalles makes great barbecued chicken, you can get takeout."

He took out his cellphone and said, "Do they deliver?"

Armstrong said, "It's okay, we're just talking."

And then nobody said anything for a while.

Sharon couldn't stand the silence, the way it hung there begging to be filled, but she fought the urge to say something. She looked at Ray and saw him sitting there waiting. She knew he was an amateur about selling the weed, but now she couldn't tell if his stories about being on Great Lakes freighters were bullshit or not. He seemed to know what he was talking about, but he also seemed really calm with the cops.

Experienced.

Then Armstrong said, "So why did you smash up the massage parlour?" and Sharon said, "Because I asked for Shiatsu and they gave me Swedish."

"The complaint we usually get," Armstrong said, "is that they paid for a blow job and only got a hand job."

And Ray said, "But that's not really a criminal complaint, they should take that up with the Better Business Bureau."

"That's what we tell them," Armstrong said.

Sharon wasn't about to tell these cops anything.

Bergeron said, "All we really want to know is, this guy who went off the roof, Kumar Nekounam, why'd you push him? He deserve it?"

Sharon said she had no idea what they were talking about.

"You know, we'd like to just write 'suicide' in the report and file it."

"So why don't you?"

"We have to follow the evidence."

Sharon said, "Oh yeah," but she wanted to say, what evidence, what have you got?

"But, you know, if he deserved it, if it was self-defense or something, then we could work with that."

"I didn't even know the guy."

Armstrong said, "First you slammed his head into a mirror at the Taj Mahal Massage Parlour, then you pushed him off the roof of a twenty-five-storey building, and you didn't even know the guy?"

Sharon said, "Look, if I pushed a guy off the roof and you had evidence, you'd just arrest me. There's nothing in it for you sniffing around like this."

She watched the cops look at each other. They didn't say anything, they just looked. She didn't like being used like this. If they were trying to find out if their new partnership was going to work they'd have to try it out on someone else.

"Well, okay then," Bergeron said. "Thanks for your time." He nodded at Ray, and the two cops left.

When they walked out the door, going right past Ku's canvas bag just inside the open closet door, Sharon let out a huge sigh, and looked at Ray.

He said, "You got the number for that chicken place?" and she said, "Who the fuck are you?"

He laughed and said, "I told you, I'm a sailor."

"No," she said, "you told them. The cops. And I don't believe you."

"It's true, I've been on the lakes since I was sixteen years old."

Her hands were shaking as she opened up his little black bag and took out the weed. "And this is just a sideline for you?"

"Something new I'm trying out."

"Well, you don't panic, I'll give you that."

"Neither do you."

She opened one of the Ziploc bags. "So that's how you can deliver to the States?"

"Maybe."

Sharon laughed, felt better again, relaxed. She said, "Okay, if this is gonna work, Ray, don't bullshit me. You can be all Mr. Calm, Cool, and Collected with the cops, but with me you've got to be honest."

"All right."

She looked at him and didn't know if she believed him or not. She wanted to, it had been so long since she'd talked to a man she could believe. She'd just never expected it to be a civilian. When she was a dancer going out with bikers that's what they called regular people, civilians. Or squares. Every once in a while one of the girls would quit, marry a square, head out to the burbs.

Sharon couldn't think of one who stayed away. The money, the attention, the excitement. Just something to do to keep the boredom away. One girl, Diana, spent two years living in a four-thousand-square-foot house in Richmond Hill; she came back downtown, she said, after she pulled into her garage, watched the automatic door close, and couldn't think of a reason to turn the engine off her Honda CR-V.

So, this guy, Ray—sitting back on her couch, four pounds of weed on the coffee table, able to handle two Homicide cops telling him Sharon had pushed a guy off the roof—was he a square? Some amateur getting in over his head, be dead in a week?

He said, "If we order something to eat now, it'll be at least a half hour till it gets here. We can go back in the bedroom."

Sharon picked up her own cell, hit one of the numbers in the memory, and said, "We better stay out here, sometimes I don't hear the buzzer," and straddled his lap, her T-shirt riding all the way up over her ass.

He stroked her thigh while she ordered the chicken and ribs, and she thought, whatever, I'm going to be in here for another week anyway.

CHAPTER 9

SITTING IN THE CAR, Armstrong said, "So, why'd she push him?"

"Drugs, guns, bombs. What do you think the guy was into?"

Armstrong put the car in gear and pulled away from the curb. "I guess the simplest is that he came to the grow rooms. Maybe he's her boss."

"She kicked the shit out of him at the massage parlour, they all said that. The guy ran away, man. If he was the boss, she wouldn't have gotten arrested, she'd have gotten messed up."

"It does seem like the guy was more scared of her."

"So why'd he go to where she was? She wasn't coming after him."

They drove in silence for a while on Queen, the neighbourhood really caught in the middle. A building on the corner had been turned into a shiny new Starbucks. Someone had spray-painted on the side of it, "Drake you ho, this is all your fault," referring to the Drake hotel, a fleabag some millionaire had bought, another rich guy's toy starting to gentrify the whole neighbourhood. The comma in the graffiti led Bergeron to think it was some pampered college kid, all sad because his grotto, the temporary home he could leave at any time, was getting fixed up.

Then Bergeron said what they were both thinking. "Who's protecting her?"

"It can't just be they don't want us to fuck up their narco investigation."

"It's not like this would be the first time."

Armstrong said, "Shit. We going to tell Nichols now?"

Bergeron's phone rang and he answered it. He said yeah a couple times, and hung up. "We got another call, out behind one of those welfare motels on Kingston Road."

Armstrong said okay and pulled a U, heading for the Gardiner. Good to be busy for a while, not have to deal with this shit.

LEVINE SAID, "You know why you guys got this one, don't you?" and Bergeron walked right into it saying, "Why?"

"Because you're the experts on what's homicide and what's suicide. So, what do you think?"

O'Brien, following Levine under the yellow tape, rolled her eyes and shook her head, her long hair loose tonight.

Bergeron said, "Teddy, it's just a torso."

Cruickshank was taking pictures, the scene was taped off and lights had been set up. It was almost midnight.

Levine said, "Yeah, but maybe she wasn't sure slitting her wrists would do it, had to cut her arms and legs right off."

O'Brien said, "And her head."

Bergeron wasn't pissed about Levine at all, he was looking closely at the body, the torso, interested. "And where are they, her arms and legs? And her head?"

Armstrong stood back watching. He knew they'd catch a lot

of shit on this one too. He looked around the scene. Way back in the fifties, Kingston Road was Highway 2 headed out of Toronto towards Oshawa, Belleville, Kingston, and then Montreal. A stretch on what used to be the outskirts of Toronto was lined with two-storey motels, a lot of which managed to stick around after the 401 opened up north of the city, and the whole area went suburbs in the seventies. Mostly the old motels rented rooms to social service agencies as family shelters, places for homeless families, refugees, and people waiting to be deported.

Fast-food places, drugs, and prostitution were pretty much the only businesses along the strip, the real service economy.

Levine said, "You want us to canvass?"

Armstrong said, no, that's fine.

"You sure? We'd be happy to help." Levine with his puppy-dog look, Armstrong couldn't tell if he meant it or not.

O'Brien said, "Can you get anything from the body?"

Cruickshank stopped taking pictures long enough to say, "Won't really know anything till we get the meat off the bone."

"You see," Levine said. "Could be suicide."

Armstrong thought about telling him there'd been a new development on the jumper, but he kept his mouth shut. Too many forensics guys, too many lab guys, too many uniforms. Armstrong was never any good at office politics, but he knew when to keep his mouth shut.

Bergeron said, "Couple of kids found it." He looked at the row of townhouses that backed onto the motel parking lot. There was a beat-up wooden fence as high as the second-storey but the townhouses were three storeys high. "Putting up Hallowe'en decorations."

O'Brien said this'd be plenty scary for them.

Bergeron said, "Why would someone go to all the trouble of cutting off the arms and legs and then just dump the torso in plain sight?"

O'Brien said, "She's carrying a lot of weight, probably over two hundred pounds. Maybe she was just too heavy."

"So we're looking for an angry, lazy asshole. That narrows it down."

Not joking around anymore, now they were on the same team, after the same thing, Levine said, "You're going to get all kinds of shit about this, all the amateur psychologists and profilers."

O'Brien said, "Papers'll be full of it, like he's daring us to catch him, he hates women, hates his mom, all the usual bull-shit." She looked over the scene, all the uniformed cops, the technicians, all looking serious or bored, but no joking around, all part of the same "us."

"Yeah," Levine said. "They'll say he must be a doctor or a butcher."

"Even though it's easy to cut off arms and legs," Bergeron said. "You don't need any special tools at all."

"No," Armstrong said, "but you gotta do something with the blood. There'll be a lot of blood at the scene."

O'Brien said, "Wherever that is."

Cruickshank walked back to his minivan and Armstrong followed him to where it was parked, under the bright red neon sign by the motel office.

Cruickshank said, "What do you want, Armstrong?" without turning around.

"We were at the lab earlier, didn't see you."

Now Cruickshank turned around and said, "You checking up on me, Armstrong?"

"Seemed kind of tense up there."

"Why I spend as little time there as I can."

"What's going on?"

Cruickshank was packing up his camera. He said, "What's it to you?"

"Just wondering."

"Yeah?" He turned around and fiddled with some equipment in the van. "You trying to pick sides?"

"Sides of what?"

Cruickshank craned his neck, looked at Armstrong close, and then shook his head. "Let's see, outgoing chief or new guy—or new chick—whatever PC asshole gets the job. . . . Who you voting for in the' union election, the asshole or the worse asshole? Or, 'cause it's the lab, civilians or cops?"

"What the fuck?"

"Okay, okay, even you would probably side with cops. You haven't noticed the tension on this force? Anybody tell you about the walkout at 55?"

Armstrong stared at the crime scene where everyone else was still poking around at the torso. The reporters hadn't even shown up yet. He said, "I heard."

"There's going to be disciplinary action. There's going to be some shit hitting the fan. Even a big-time detective like you can see it coming."

Armstrong realized the power dynamics on the force were a lot worse than he thought. Truth was, he kept out of this office politics shit as much as he could. Till it started getting in the way of investigations. "But what about the lab?"

Cruickshank said, "You really are out of it, Armstrong. You got your civilian technicians and their bosses are cops."

"I thought it was all nerds and geeks."

"Yeah, right. The cops are still pissed off because we don't have a new contract. Anyone tell you that?"

"I heard something."

"And the civvies are pissed because they think when we get a new contract we'll all get more money."

"So they're just pissed off about money?"

Cruickshank shook his head, like he couldn't believe this guy. "This is Toronto, it's always about the money."

Armstrong thought about it, said, "Or the status. We're big on status too. Maybe the cops are pissed the nerds are starting to get credit for their work."

Cruickshank said, "Okay, why do you fucking care, Armstrong? You want a higher priority on your horror show there? She'll get processed when it's her turn. You find us a head, or some arms or legs, that'll sure help."

Armstrong said he'd see what he could do and walked back to the scene.

The first question Armstrong heard shouted from one of the tabloid guys was if the cuts were made with precision, like an expert, and he wondered: what kind of expert is there for decapitating people?

J.T. WAS ACTUALLY GLAD Richard asked him to get the place fixed up. Not that he was interested in "flowers and shit," as Richard had said, but he was interested in the woman who was walking around the front yard now, shaking her head.

"I wouldn't know where to start," she said.

The place did look shitty. Rundown and dirty. Concrete posts across the front, dirt where there should've been grass, a concrete front on what had once been an old house. A nice, big, old house.

Now she stopped in front of J.T., sitting on the wooden picnic table by the door, and she said, "You really think flowers?"

He thought, yeah, maybe not. Richard had just said to make the place look better, not so much like an armed bunker—which was what it was.

Up close she looked a little older than he'd thought, probably as close to thirty as he was himself, and that made him even more interested. He said, "Some kind of plants anyway. You think we could grow grass here?" and she said, I bet you can grow grass anywhere you want, and he laughed.

"Seriously, with those pillars in front, anything you put back here will be lost. There's not much point."

"Well, we can't get rid of the pillars." He looked at her and she was looking back at him, nodding. Good, he didn't need to explain. "But maybe we could dress them up a little, paint them or something."

"I guess you could cover them up."

J.T. stood up and took a couple of steps towards her. "Like how?"

"I don't know, with planters maybe."

"Planters?"

"Yeah. Wooden boxes with flower pots in them. You just put new flowers in them, and change them once in a while."

"You mean like poppies for Remembrance Day and poinsettias for Christmas?"

She looked at him and said, "Where'd you learn that?"

"Everybody knows that." He didn't smile at her, but he was playing. He liked the way she was kind of making fun of him in a knowing way, but like she liked him.

He liked her.

She said she'd do some drawings, give him choices to pick from. Have them by the end of the week.

He said, "What's your name?"

"Tina."

"Tina, I'm Justin. Well, J.T. Look, why don't you just do what you think would be best? Make the place look nice. How much will it cost?"

She took her time looking around the front of the building and doing the numbers in her head. "Five grand?"

"You sure? I wouldn't want you to go over budget."

"Then make it eight."

"All right. Can you start right away?"

"Sure. But you'll have to pay me up front."

J.T. was already walking back to the front of the house and he stopped and looked back. "You don't think I'm good for it?"

"It's not you."

The front door opened and Chuck came out with a Corona in his hand. He said, "You want one?" and J.T. told him, yeah, and asked Tina if she wanted one, and she said, okay, and Chuck went back inside.

J.T. said, "So if it's not me, what is it?"

"I did something dumb."

"Oh yeah?"

They looked at each other. J.T. figured he'd wait. The more he looked at this Tina the more he liked her. He'd seen her around, driving that red Ford pickup with something landscape designs written on the door, wearing those cut-off jean shorts and the halter top, baseball hat. That's why he thought she was younger, working for someone, but now he realized she worked for herself, and he liked that.

"You'd think I'd learn by now."

Chuck came out with the beers and handed them to J.T. saying, "I've got to take this call," and went back inside, cellphone pressed to his ear.

J.T. sat on the tabletop of the picnic table and handed one of the cold bottles to Tina. "What happened?"

She sat down on the bench seat. "Oh, you know, the usual, some guy needed a job done right away, didn't even argue a price, just took my quote."

"And then didn't pay you."

She drank from the bottle and nodded. "You know, I've been in this business almost ten years."

J.T. figured it was closer to five, and he bet she barely covered her costs month to month.

"He needed it done right away and I figured he could be good for more work."

"How often's the guy going to do his yard?"

She looked at him like how dumb do you think I am. "He's a builder. He buys old houses and fixes them up. At least that's what he says, I'm starting to think this is his first one."

"Around here?"

"The Beaches." She motioned with her chin down Eastern Avenue towards the upscale neighbourhood—the continuously upscaling neighbourhood. There were a few companies specializing in renovating the old houses, but people were always trying to get in on the action. It looked like there was no high end for the house prices, some had even gone over a million.

"So, you know where he is?"

She said sure, for all the good it does. "It's not like I had a written agreement, or could afford a lawyer if I did. When I went after him, all he said was maybe we could talk about it over drinks."

J.T. said, oh yeah?

She took another drink of the Corona, and said, "As if I was gonna fuck him to get my own money back," and that was it for J.T. He really liked this woman.

"So, now he's working on another house?"

She said, "Yeah, but he hasn't sold the first one. He needed the landscaping done right away for the open house. He thought it would sell right away but it didn't."

"So now he's short on cash."

"So he says. He probably is. It's just to put me in my place, you know?"

J.T. said, yeah, he knew. Then he said, "Hang on a second," and went inside.

Tina barely had a sip of the Corona and J.T. was back handing her an envelope. "Okay, eight grand. Can you start right away?"

"Sure."

"Hey, boys, vote early, vote often."

Bergeron said, "You know it, man," and watched Burroughs pick up his ballot and go behind the little cardboard barricade set up on the desk in the lunchroom. There were three voting stations and what seemed like six guys watching: union reps, management, and a guy no one knew, probably a lawyer, some kind of observer.

Andy Sawchuck was with Burroughs, and a woman Bergeron didn't recognize. The three of them stood behind the cardboard dividers. Burroughs said, "I hope everyone sees the need for change around here," and one of the union guys said, "Detective."

Burroughs waved his hands saying, okay, okay. "You're right, no campaigning on site. I'm sure we don't need to by now."

The station house was full, almost two shifts' worth, plus a bunch of detectives. Armstrong and Bergeron waited their turns, then picked up their ballots. They hadn't really talked about this election at all. Not much to say, when the choices were extreme and more extreme, but what were they going to do? Bergeron had joked about Wayne Cotter calling himself the moderate, the voice of reason, saying, "Maybe at a Klan rally," which let Armstrong know what he thought about the other guy, Walters.

Armstrong had said they did need strong leadership; it felt like everybody in the city was on their case.

It was the first time he and Bergeron had stumbled. They agreed they needed strong leaders, but just like every other election, was this the best they could get?

"You want the job?"

"I see your point."

They voted and walked out into the parking lot.

Burroughs was leaning against a car, having a smoke, surrounded by his guys: Sawchuck; Price's kid, Loewen; the woman Bergeron didn't recognize; and a few other guys.

Armstrong and Bergeron were passing Burroughs, who said,

"How's the hunt for the notorious torso killer?" He laughed and so did most of his guys.

Bergeron said it was going fine, moving along. "You know how it is."

Burroughs shrugged, if-you-say-so.

Then the woman—shit, Bergeron realized, it was Barb Roxon, five years on sex assault and now she must be narco—said, "Hey, Gord."

"Hi, Barb."

"I hope you famous detectives voted for change."

Armstrong said, "Yeah. There's a few changes we'd like to see around here."

Burroughs was off the car, saying, "What's that mean? Eh?"

Armstrong stepped up, saying, "What do you think it means?"

They were face to face.

Barb said, "Come on now, put those dicks away."

They stared at each other for another couple of seconds, then Burroughs smiled big, saying, "Hey, we're all on the same team. We start fighting with each other, these clowns who want to take us down will get what they want."

Bergeron said, "You mean the terrorists will win?"

Burroughs started to get pissed off again, but then caught himself and was all smiles. He said, "Good to see you back at work, Gord, we need all the experience we can get these days."

"Right."

Burroughs motioned for Bergeron to step aside for a more private chat and they turned their backs on the others.

Burroughs said he was truly sorry to hear about Linda. "She was a terrific lady."

"Yeah," Bergeron said, "she was."

"Yeah." Burroughs looked sad for a moment. Then he said, "Look, how come you guys are still hanging out at that place on Close Avenue?"

Bergeron thought for a second, then said, "Oh, the high-rise. It's a crime scene, Andy."

"Come on, you're not going to get anywhere with that."

"We're not?"

"Why don't you just write 'suicide' in the fucking file and be done with it?"

"There something going on there?"

Burroughs took a drag on his smoke and flicked the butt away. "We're trying to find out. Would be a lot easier if you guys weren't in and out like the fucking Pizza-Pizza guy."

Bergeron hadn't thought they were there that often. "Do you think there's anything between the dead guy and the grow rooms?"

"I don't see how anything could connect them."

"No people in common?"

"What the fuck? Some sad-sack camel jockey and a big, professional grow op?"

Bergeron watched Burroughs getting pissed off and trying not to show it and wondered what was really going on. He thought he'd like to find out, but pushing this right now wasn't the way to do it. He said, "Yeah, okay, I see your point."

Burroughs relaxed right away. "All right."

"If we have to go back, we'll keep it short and sweet."

"Appreciate it."

But now Bergeron was way more interested in why Burroughs didn't want them going back.

CHAPTER 10

BACK AT THE OFFICE, Armstrong said, "Maybe you don't want to do that."

"What?" Bergeron was sitting at his new desk in Homicide poking around on the computer.

"It's just, every time you type something in, you can't be sure where it goes, who's reading it."

Bergeron was thinking, shit, you go away a couple of years, the whole place falls apart. He said, "Shake some trees, see what falls out."

Armstrong said, okay, just don't stand so close to the branches.

"Right."

Bergeron typed some more, then stopped when he felt someone else standing behind his desk and said, "Price, if you want another secret meeting you gotta take me to a rub and tug, get me blown first."

Inspector Nichols said, no, it didn't have to be secret. "But I'd like it to be in my office."

They followed him in.

Corner office, sixth floor, College and Bay Streets, it could have been an insurance company, or a bank, or some guys selling the newest accounting software.

Then Nichols said, "You find a head, or any arms or legs for your torso?"

And Bergeron thought, yeah, no matter what they talked about, the boss's office was always the same.

Armstrong said, "Garbage man found a hand out in Mississauga, lab's checking to see if it's a match."

Nichols had sat down behind his desk. He said, "Here's hoping."

"No jewellery on it, but it looks like there was a wedding ring, worn for a long time. Years anyway. No fake nails or anything."

"Do you think the victim may have been a prostitute, or frequented the area where the body was discovered for some other reason?"

Bergeron watched Nichols being official. The guy was only about five years older, but he made detective so young, and then straight on to inspector. Toronto's population had exploded in the seventies and eighties—hell, there were still a hundred thousand people a year moving in—and the police force, like everything else, expanded so fast they were grabbing guys off the street, promoting whoever didn't screw up too bad. Made Bergeron wonder about Nichols, guy like him, high-school education, neither one of them would even get hired today, never mind Homicide detective or inspector. But Nichols seemed so natural with it. Maybe politics was what he did best.

Armstrong said, no, he had no reason to think the victim was a hooker, or a drug addict. "What we recovered of the body looks to be in good shape, no drug use. Coroner says probably over forty, had some kids."

"He going to put that in a report?"

"Have to wait and see."

Nichols nodded and Bergeron thought, come on, Alistair, say it, say something about that asshole taking his sweet time to do anything.

But Nichols didn't. He said, "What are you going to hold back?"

Armstrong said maybe the appendix scar. "There's another surgery scar, don't know what it's for yet, we'll hold that back. At least we'll be able to sort out some of the wacko calls we'll get."

"And what about your jumper? You spending a lot of time on that?"

Armstrong looked at Bergeron, and shuffled a little. Bergeron said, "There've been some developments."

"Oh?"

"Couple of days, we'll know more."

Nichols nodded, like it was the end of the meeting. Bergeron stood up, and Armstrong did too, and then Nichols said, "Oh, by the way," and Bergeron thought, now here's the real meeting, like this guy took a course on handling people.

"That was good work on the Bronwyn Miles thing."

"She's okay?"

"As well as can be expected. Disgusting brute like that takes her from the street, rapes her, tries to kill her. It'll be the rest of her life."

Armstrong said, "Yeah."

"The thing is," Nichols said. "Charles Robarts is heading up the defense."

Bergeron said, "This guy's not going to plead?" and Armstrong said, "Most expensive fucking law firm in the country?"

Nichols said, "No, he's not going to plead. He's going to have the best money can buy surrounding him for the rest of his long and comfortable life."

"Jesus fucking Christ."

Nichols said, "Yes, Gord, I know. So, I've been talking to Bill." The crown prosecutor, William Arthur Knights.

"He's doing this?"

"He was going to do the deal till Robarts got on board. If it looks like it's going to trial, and going to get messy, they'll bring in Angie DeRosa."

Armstrong said, good. "She'll rip him apart."

"Of course, Robarts is trying everything. He's starting with the entry into the house."

"What about it?"

Nichols looked right at Armstrong and said, "He says you broke the door, barged in, the guy refused you entry, you had no reason, the usual."

Armstrong shrugged and said, "Exigent circumstances."

"And what were they?"

"He was trying to drown the ten-year-old he raped."

"How did you know she was in there?"

Bergeron watched Armstrong take a breath, get it under control, and he thought, good, don't say anything till you're ready.

Armstrong said, "I heard her."

"What?"

"Yeah, I heard her calling for help."

Nichols said, no, her lungs were full of water, there's a medical report.

"Okay, I saw her, reflection in the bathroom mirror."

Nichols held up his hand and shook his head. He said, "Okay, I'll talk to Angie, we'll deal with this."

Armstrong said, "Shit. You know, I didn't know, I just figured if she wasn't there we'd leave him alone with his two plants or whatever he didn't want us to see and move on."

"It's okay, we'll work it out."

Armstrong nodded and walked out of the office.

Bergeron started to leave, but Nichols stopped him, saying, "Gord, just a minute."

Then it was just the two of them in the office, and Bergeron said, you want me to close the door, and Nichols smiled a little and said no.

"I just wanted to see how you're doing. You sure hit the ground running."

"I'm doing fine. I'm keeping busy. That's what I'm supposed to do, right?"

Nichols nodded. "Right."

Bergeron left thinking, were we ever friends, me and Nichols? Was he always a politician?

ON THE DRIVE OVER, Chuck was saying he wasn't sure they should be doing this, and J.T. said, "It's what we do."

"Yeah, but what about what happened to Oshawa?"

J.T. was driving his own car, one of the new Dodge Chargers. He liked it, it really had decent power and a good enough look, but the interior was shit. Dashboard looked old-fashioned, and the stereo it came with didn't even play MP3s. He said, "What about it?"

"You know, the big case, everybody's talking about it, Johanson and Pike went down for anti-gang. Bill C-24."

"It's being appealed."

J.T. drove along Queen. It really wasn't that far from their club to the Beaches neighbourhood. He remembered when he was a kid, in town for a couple days with his dad—his dad making some deal—they'd go to Greenwood Racetrack, bet on a few horses, then go across the street to the Tulip and eat a steak. The Tulip was still there, but like everything else in this place it was renovated, trying so hard to go upscale. J.T. couldn't believe these three-storey houses—practically touching each other, built on the horseshit-filled swamp where Greenwood used to be—were selling for a million bucks.

The whole place was going upscale.

Chuck said, "They got convicted just because of who they were, who they associated with, not for anything they did."

"They were doing a shakedown," J.T. said. "The crown lawyers just convinced the jury the threat was 'cause of who they were, it was implied, or some shit." He drove across Woodbine and took the first right, one block down to the lake. Most of the houses had been recently renovated or were for sale. All the old-timers cashing out, making way for yuppie money.

"It's guilt by association, that's what it is, it's against the charter."

"Morrison's appealing."

"Could take years."

J.T. said, so, it's not like they're inside while they appeal, they're out, they're earning.

It really was a nice place. Hard to believe it was so close to downtown, out here it was quiet and clean. Didn't look like the new Toronto at all, the only non-white people were the nannies and guys working on the lawns. J.T. drove up the next street.

"I don't know," Chuck said, "it makes things different."

Shit, J.T. couldn't believe this guy. "Well, we're not just going to fold our fucking tent and go home." He slowed down, pulled up on the sidewalk, and stopped. "This is what we do."

There were five little houses, original beach cottages, the real estate agents would call them, set way back from the street. The middle one had been torn down and a brand-new monster house slapped up, towering above all the others, a FOR SALE sign on the lawn.

J.T. said, "That'll be it."

The landscaping was really good: terraced gardens coming down the little hill towards the sidewalk, flowers, plants, all kinds of stuff in a pretty small space, really. J.T. liked it, he thought this Tina really knew what she was doing.

Well, when it came to landscaping. When it came to money, that was more his department.

Walking up to the house, Chuck said, "You're just going to talk to him, right?" and J.T. said yeah, right, just talk, and he thought, shit, this guy. He noticed the lawns on the other side of the new monster house had all been dug up and trampled down, no move to repair the damage at all.

The door was open.

J.T. and Chuck walked in. The first thing J.T. thought was, who puts a wet bar in a room this small? Right in the middle of the living room. Well, that's what it seemed like, right there by the fireplace, there wasn't any room left for furniture.

No wonder the bar was being taken out. There were pieces of brand-new hardwood, matching the floor, lying around and a pneumatic stapling gun was running.

But the guy, J.T. was sure it was the guy owed Tina money, was talking on his cellphone, telling somebody not to worry, he'd get paid when he got paid. The guy, he was big, six inches taller than J.T. and probably had fifty pounds on him, said, "I got another job, this one we're just going to lipstick, slap on a couple upgrades, and turn it over, nice little profit."

J.T. picked up a piece of the new hardwood, about two feet long. It was prefinished, good stuff but not top of the line.

The big guy noticed him and held up a hand, like, wait a minute. He said a couple of uh-huhs into the phone and then, "I told you, when I can," and hung up saying, asshole. He looked at J.T. and said, "What do you want?"

J.T. hit him in the side of the face with the hardwood. One-handed, but a good swing. The edge of the wood hit the guy right on the jaw. J.T. swung it again, two-handed like a baseball bat, hit the guy right on the side of the head. The big guy fell to his knees, his eyes rolling back in his head, blood dripping out of his ear. J.T. hit him one more time, back of the head, put him down.

Then he picked up the pneumatic hammer, stood on the guy's arm and popped a nail through his hand into the new hardwood floor.

J.T. got down on one knee close to the guy's face, grabbed him by his hair and lifted. He said, "You owed your landscaper six grand. Now you owe me eight."

He let go of his hair and the big guy's head flopped onto the floor.

J.T. said, "Someone'll come by tomorrow," stood up, and walked out.

Chuck ran after him, down the walk to the Charger, saying, "You said you were just going to talk to him."

J.T. got in the car and said, "He pissed me off."

"He didn't say anything to you."

"His whole fucking attitude."

"He's gonna bleed to death."

"There was a fucking crowbar on the floor," J.T. said. He started the car and drove away. "He wants to be a tough guy, now he's a tough guy."

And J.T. thought, yeah, this is more like it.

CHAPTER **11**

NUGS NEVER REALLY LIKED GOLF. He only played enough for vacations and the club tournament. Like last year, after the patch-over, at that course down by Niagara Falls, that was a golf tournament. Closed the whole place for the day, had tents set up all over with chicks in them giving out prizes; blow jobs for pars, anything you want for birdies. Danny Mac's wife, Gayle, who'd never played before in her life, chipped in for a fluke par three, walked into the tent, dropped her shorts, and said, "Hey, a par's a par, do me." The way golf should be played.

Now he was riding in the cart with Richard watching Mitchell Fucking Morrison's fat ass send another ball into the woods, Richard saying, "Says he loves the game. Jumped at the chance to come play here."

Emerald Valley, a course that used to be a nine-hole cow pasture way out of town, which got taken over by Clubplay and turned into thirty-six holes, driving range, and big modern clubhouse. And, as Richard pointed out, a housing development where the real money was.

Nugs said, "Maybe he'd answer the phone if I told him I was taking him golfing."

Richard stopped the cart, got out, and said, "He doesn't take your calls?"

Nugs, still looking down the fairway towards the green, said, "Guy takes fucking days to get back to me."

It was quiet on the course. Nugs looked at Richard lining up his shot, taking a practice swing, guy looked like he played every day, wearing those front-pleat khakis and an actual golf shirt. Richard never took his eye off his ball, saying, "Took my call right away," and Nugs got it. He thought, right, break my fucking balls over this too. But he knew he was right.

Richard slammed the ball. None of that easy swing, don't try to kill it, he practically came out of his shoes he hit it so fucking hard. A rising, straight three iron off the fairway, sailing all the way to green.

Nugs jumped out of the cart, grabbed a club, and said he was going to help Morrison find his ball.

In the woods, Mitchell Fucking Morrison was saying, "I'll just hit another one," and the guy he brought with him, some junior partner looked like he grew up on a fancy golf course, said, sure, that's a good idea.

Nugs said, "It must be around here somewhere."

"No, don't worry about it, I'll just hit another one."

But when he went to walk out of the woods, Nugs was in his way.

"It's okay, really."

Nugs said, "Have another look."

Morrison said, it's just a fucking golf ball, I've got plenty more, come on, but his voice was starting to sound worried.

Nugs said, "Yeah, because I pay you too fucking much."

Morrison let out a sigh, seemed to relax, said, "We can talk about finance structure again, if you want, Nugs," and Nugs swung the club, hit him hard just below the knee.

Morrison yelled, oww, bent over, and grabbed his shin. Nugs cross-checked him with the club, using it like a hockey stick, knocking him over, and said, "I called you three fucking times, I couldn't get past your receptionist."

Morrison was crawling away now, still holding his leg, and looking at Nugs, saying, "I didn't know, I didn't get the message."

Nugs swung the club, hitting Morrison's arms he put up over his head to protect himself. "You take my fucking calls."

"I will, I will, I swear."

"How come my fucking trial's not postponed?"

Morrison said, we're working on it, shit, doing everything we can, and he lowered his arms.

Nugs smacked him in the side of the head with the golf club, said, "Do more."

"We will, shit, we will, we'll do more."

Nugs stood up straight, looking down at the pathetic lawyer. "Good."

Then Morrison said, "But they got a lot of information from your girlfriend."

Nugs pulled the club back to swing and Morrison covered his head with both arms.

Nugs slammed the club into his ribs, said, "Find out where that cunt is."

"It's impossible, the fucking Mounties have her wrapped up. She's their whole goddamned case."

Nugs pulled the club back again, and Morrison curled up into a ball, whimpering. Nugs said, "So find her, I'll take care of her." Then he said, "And take my calls."

Morrison said, "I didn't get the message, I swear, fucking receptionist. That bitch, she's fired. First thing I do."

Nugs swung the club and moved closer, watching the fancy-ass lawyer crawling away in the dirt. "You ever put me on fucking hold, I'll fire you. Got it?"

He didn't wait for Morrison to say anything, he just turned and walked out of the woods thinking, okay, this is good, this feels better. Maybe this Richard asshole from Montreal is a good thing, get our fucking ducks in a row, see what we can do.

Nugs saw the junior partner rushing into the woods asking Morrison what happened, and the fucker saying he tripped on a root. The junior helping him up.

RICHARD WAITED IN THE CART by the edge of the woods and when Nugs came out he thought, yeah, now he looks like a guy ready to take on the world. Richard said, "That went pretty well."

Nugs put the club in the bag, got in the cart, and said, "Yeah? I don't know, maybe I should have used the wedge."

Richard said maybe. "Might not give you the distance." Started driving towards the green.

Nugs said, "Asshole. He's still going on about fucking Amber. She's their whole case." Nugs's girlfriend Amber, hung around for a couple of years, the whole time on the RCMP payroll, now she was in witness protection getting ready to testify against him.

Richard said, "What would you do if you found her?"

Still looking ahead towards the green, where Richard's ball was, Nugs said, "What the fuck you think I'd do?"

That was the question. Richard hadn't spoken more than ten minutes to Nugs before this trip. Heard all the rumours about how he was soft, no ambition, couldn't run a big organization, but now he wasn't so sure. The guy seemed to be stepping up fine.

Richard said, "There might be something we can do."

"You still testing me?"

"Maybe not."

Richard thinking, give him Amber, see what he does, then he could go see Angelo Colucci, tell him how things were going to be.

SHARON WAS TRYING TO THINK if there was anyone she knew in Cleveland. Not likely. Be nice to see the Rock and Roll Hall of Fame though. Chicago? Buffalo? Shit, nobody was in Buffalo. She knew a couple of guys from Detroit, black guys worked their way up through Young Boys Inc., might be able to talk to them.

Then she thought, am I really thinking about double-crossing Richard and the Saints?

Half a million bucks a month in weed, get a piece of that, pretty good reason.

Yeah, like they'd let that go.

She paced the apartment. Three days left on the house arrest. Couldn't get to her own supply. The five pounds she got from Richard and the four from Ray would get her through but wouldn't get her ahead. Next month she'd be begging again. If she had any customers left. This Ray guy would probably be dead, the way he was walking around waving a flag.

Unless he had someone knew how to do this.

She laughed. Yeah, right, someone like you, Sharon? You want to jump into this fire?

Like back in Montreal when she first started dealing, dancing at Les Amazones out on St. Jacques. Bobbi just a baby, named for that Springsteen song "Bobby Jean," you hung with me when all the others turned away, that was the idea. Bobbi and Sharon were going to stick together. And they did. Bobbi growing up with no secrets, seeing everything. She was like a little adult when she was nine. Sharon couldn't take the hours dancing so she started dealing. Pierre dead by then, Richard and Mon Oncle moved uptown, upscale, and they let her have her deal, let her take it to Toronto. She had plans to be legit by the time Bobbi got to high school, open a store or something, but nothing sold like this. And the time just slipped by, Sharon always putting things off, living for the moment.

She went to her iPod and scrolled through to find that Springsteen album, that was so huge in the eighties, must have been '84 or '85. Sharon had no idea who he was, she'd heard "Born to Run" on the radio back in Moncton, but it didn't mean anything to her then. "Born in the U.S.A." though, that was fucking huge. Some of the girls danced to "I'm on Fire," or "Cover Me," or even "I'm Going Down," but Sharon loved "Bobby Jean." Maybe it was because in the song Bobby Jean just left town, just up and walked away, and never said goodbye.

But now, shit, now Sharon didn't want to just walk away. What was she going to do, start dancing again? Start a mother-daughter adult website with Bobbi like that chick Roxanne, used to be in real estate, tried to talk them into last year?

There was a knock at the door and Sharon was surprised

because the front-door buzzer never went. She walked over and said, "Who's there?" and some guy with a heavy accent said, "Hello, Sharon?" Like it was a question, like he might not have the right door.

Sharon said, "Sorry, you've got the wrong address."

The guy, his accent was some kind of Middle Eastern, she was pretty sure, said, "I am sorry, Miss Sharon, I am a friend of Ku, I'm looking for him."

Shit. "A friend of Ku, or a friend of Zahra?" Then she thought, shit, why'd I say that, should have kept up with the wrong door. She looked through the peephole and saw a pretty pathetic looking guy, actually had his hat in his hand.

He said, "I am sorry." Sharon watched him through the peephole, him looking up and down the hall like he was embarrassed. He said, "I am friend of Zahra also. No one has seen her too. We are very worried."

He didn't look like he was going away and Sharon was pretty sure that cop was still out front so she opened the door.

As soon as she did she knew it was a mistake. The guy was way bigger than he looked through the peephole, broad shoulders and a huge chest and with the door open he wasn't pathetic at all, he was all business. Sharon tried to close the door fast but he got his big shoulder in the way and pushed her back inside, saying, "We can do this easy or hard."

In the living room he said, "I want Ku's bag."

Sharon said she didn't know what he was talking about and he slapped her across the face, called her a filthy whore, and said, "Give me the fucking bag."

Sharon said, okay, okay, let's do this the easy way, and he said it was too late for that.

She said, "Come on, you sure?" And gave him that look. She'd been giving that look to men since she was fourteen years old and he did what they always did, he got full of himself believing she was weak and in love with his manliness.

He said, "Yeah, sure, you make me happy, maybe I don't kill you."

She kept right on giving him that look, saying, "Sounds like a deal to me."

Right away he started undoing his pants. Sharon said, "Hey, let's take a shower."

"A shower? Oh, you know some tricks?"

He walked to the bathroom and she stopped in the kitchen on her way.

She said, yeah. "I know some tricks."

CHAPTER **12**

ARMSTRONG SAID, "YOU KNOW, I can understand the whole being trapped in the wrong body thing. You're born a guy but you're really a woman."

"Your spirit is a woman," Bergeron said, and Armstrong asked if that was a crack about Native religion.

"Yeah, now I'm making racist remarks." Bergeron put the car in gear and pulled away.

"I just don't understand why you'd get all the plastic surgery, get the breast implants, do all the electrolysis, hair removal, all that and leave the dick? I mean, isn't that the most male part?"

Bergeron pulled onto Church, heading north, and said, "Takes all kinds."

"I guess."

"Looks like our torso's really her sister, though."

"Do we say 'her' when there's a dick?"

"You didn't actually see the dick," Bergeron said. "Did you?"

Armstrong folded the tabloid newspaper on his lap and said, "It's in the ad—36-24-36 and eight inches FF. What's *FF* mean?"

"No idea. But everything I saw was female, so I'm saying she."

"But you didn't see everything."

"Face, hair, legs. All looked female to me. Looked pretty good."

"Holy shit. When was the last time you got lai . . . oh, sorry."

Bergeron thought about the woman he met in Montreal when he drove Amanda down in September. They met in the hotel bar, the Sheraton on boulevard René Lévesque, she was in from Ottawa on some kind of government work. It was smooth, the way they fell into it, comfortable. The woman, Ghyslaine, had separated from her husband almost a year before. She was two years younger than Bergeron and their small talk went by quick. As he'd said, they were two grown-ups in a hotel. They had a good night together and never mentioned seeing each other again.

He said to Armstrong, "A while," and Armstrong said, "Well, you better look into it soon, if that's starting to look good to you."

Bergeron said, "I saw a woman at Cinematheque, looked pretty good."

"Oh yeah, you talk about French movies?"

"It was Clint Eastwood movies, the spaghetti westerns. We didn't talk."

"You didn't even talk to her? Man, you gotta do something."

"That's what my daughter says."

The woman at Cinematheque was also around Bergeron's age. When he first started coming back to work, going out for beers after shifts, some of the guys pointed out much younger women, thirties, shit, some of them in their twenties looked like Amanda's friends, said he should go for it. He was in good shape, no fat on him, had all his hair, but he just thought, what would we talk about? The woman watching the Clint Eastwood movies though, she looked really smart, probably called them Sergio Leone movies, a serious look on her face. Made him think if she laughed it had to be something actually funny.

Bergeron turned right onto Bloor and asked if Armstrong wanted to get some lunch. "Souvlaki maybe."

"Yeah, okay, let's go to that little place, the takeout place on Logan."

THEY SAT ON A PICNIC TABLE in front of the takeout place. Logan and Danforth, right in the heart of Greektown, most of the restaurants were souvlaki joints, but now a lot of them were upscale places, names like Myth and Lolita's Lust. There were Greek video stores and a bunch of travel agents specializing in vacations and "trips home."

Armstrong said, "You remember when Greece won that big soccer game?"

"European Championship. Place went nuts."

"It was a good party."

They ate their souvlakis and then Bergeron said, "You want to go talk to the husband this afternoon?"

"We should wait till we get the DNA run."

"Why, you think there's any chance she was wrong?"

The transsexual—the TG girl she called herself—Madeline, knew all about the appendix scar and the other one on the torso, said it was a hysterectomy. Told them about the three broken ribs and how when they found the rest of her what other broken bones they'd find.

Armstrong said, no, he was sure. "I just want to make sure we get him."

Bergeron said, "We'll get him."

He thought of the look on Madeline's face, a female face, that's for sure. Ten o'clock in the morning, all made up waiting for her first client. Telling them not many TG girls were escorts, it just looked that way in the back pages of the free tabloid. "Where they call them Shemales. We don't like that." Explaining they did it in their ads so the customers could find them, guys with issues who'd seen too many porno movies.

She'd called the tip line, said the victim was her sister, offered DNA to prove it. Asked if they could come by, said police stations made her nervous. Armstrong said that was fine, they didn't care what she did, they just wanted to catch this guy who killed her sister, and Bergeron believed him.

So did she, he could tell by the look on her face. He had to admit, she had a very pretty face.

She'd said, "It's not like on TV, is it? I don't have to go to the lab or anything, I don't have to go to the morgue?" She'd shivered when she said it, pulling in her small shoulders, squeezing her breasts together.

Armstrong had said no, she wouldn't have to do that. Then he'd said, "One thing's like TV, though, the swab," and handed her the thing that looked like an overgrown Q-tip. She'd made a face and laughed, then put it way in her mouth, and closed her lips around it, joking, all flirty, puckering up, moving it back and forth.

Bergeron and Armstrong had both laughed.

She'd handed it back saying, "Poor Louise."

Bergeron had taken out his notepad and starting writing. Madeline had said they grew up in a small town with two alcoholic parents. "We had an older brother but I have no idea where he is. He was actually the first one to touch us, even before our father." She'd said they had all the usual abuse and self-esteem problems. Then she'd said, "You know, not every prostitute had a shitty childhood and suffers low self-esteem," and Bergeron had said, of course not, before he realized it was a straight line and she'd said, "Just every one I've ever met."

She and her sister Louise had come to Toronto almost twenty years ago, both teenagers. "I didn't know what I was. I was so attracted to guys but I didn't see myself as gay. Louise said she knew what she was: a slut. It was our joke." Alcohol, drugs, the usual. Madeline had said they both hit bottom, sleeping in the ravine beside the Don Valley, getting raped by homeless guys.

"You know, I used to hate my penis. When I was a kid I used to shower in the dark so I wouldn't have to see it. Then, of course, I hated all men."

Armstrong had said, "Of course," and Bergeron hadn't been able to tell if he was being understanding or sarcastic.

"But I didn't know about me."

"What do you mean?"

"I just thought I was a fucked-up man. Then I met a transgendered person, a nurse stitching me up. It was like a freaking bolt of lightning, like my whole life I was seeing the world blurry and now it came into focus. I am a woman. Changed everything."

"That's good." Bergeron had figured Armstrong really was sincere and he hadn't known if he should be surprised or not.

Madeline had said, yeah, but poor Louise. "She wasn't so lucky."

"Lucky?"

"Once I realized I was actually a woman, that I have the spirit of a woman, it really was like being born again. All that shit I went through in my life really was someone else. I got to start all over again."

"But not Louise."

"No."

Bergeron had said, "She didn't have any drugs or alcohol in her when she died."

Madeline had said, "No? Well, she was on and off the wagon. She really wanted that whole white-picket-fence, mommy-and-daddy life. At least she thought she did. When we were both on the street, she had a baby and gave it up for adoption. She was straight for the whole pregnancy, but then for a while she was worse than ever. Then she met Ross, that's her husband. The one who did this." She'd been sure and so was Bergeron. "She got pregnant again and they got married, but then Tiffany died. She only lived a few hours after she was born."

"And Louise, she was still married to this guy?"

"And it was never good. He smacked her around, he verbally abused her, all the greatest hits of the shitty husband."

Bergeron had said it did get to start to look the same, they see it so much.

"We talk on the phone once in a while, me and Louise, but it always ends with us fighting, hanging up on each other. Seems like no matter how much you change, you change right back around your family."

"Yeah." Bergeron had told her they'd run the DNA and if it was a match they'd pick up the husband. He'd wondered how come no one had reported her missing.

"I guess because no one's missed her. She didn't really have any friends. When I saw the story in the paper I wondered. I tried calling her and got nothing."

"Well, we really appreciate you calling us," Armstrong had said, standing up.

Then Madeline had tried to lighten the mood, joking about big strong men like them might need a massage sometime, and they'd played along, joking around, and then gotten out quick.

Now Bergeron finished his souvlaki and said he'd like a coffee.

Armstrong said there was a Starbucks a couple blocks up Danforth, they could walk. It was a nice day for October, a little cool, but sunny. A lot of people were out and for a few minutes Bergeron thought, they could just act like everything was fine with the world.

Then they'd go pick up a guy, cut off his wife's arms and legs and head.

SHARON SAID, "You see, it's a big problem."

She was standing in the little hall outside the bathroom and Ray said, "Yeah, big all right."

He didn't make a move to come out so Sharon stepped closer and looked past him to the tub.

Ray said, "So that's a myth, they don't really come when they die."

"Well, I had a pretty tight grip on his balls," Sharon said, "and he didn't really see it coming."

Ray said yeah, he guessed not. The big guy was on his back in the tub, his pants around his ankles, his throat slit and a butcher's knife stuck in his chest. There was blood everywhere, all over the floor and the walls, the ceiling, the sink, the mirror, the whole bathroom covered in it.

"Who is he?"

"I have no idea."

Ray looked at Sharon and said, "I can help you with this, but you have to tell me the truth."

"I swear, I don't know who he is." She gave Ray a look, another look she'd perfected in the clubs, but it didn't get to him at all. She said, "Okay, seriously, I don't know who he is, but he came here for Ku's bag."

Ray said, yeah, who's Ku?

"It's a bit of a story. You remember the cops mentioned that guy went off the roof?"

Ray said, "The guy they think you threw off?"

"Okay." Sharon decided what the fuck. Tell him. "The truth is, I've got a few grow rooms, a few Iranian women farming. One of them, Zahra, her husband, Ku, jumped off the roof."

"Jumped?"

"I swear. She was working in the rub and tug when I met her. Ku—or his friends, I'm not sure—pimped her out. They have all kinds of wives and sister-in-laws working in the trade, massage parlours, escorts. Anyway, a couple of these women, they know their way around the plants. I got them out of the parlours and set them up."

"And you beat up this Ku guy at the massage parlour, broke a big mirror."

"And now this guy comes looking for him."

Ray said, "You really have a problem with anger management," and Sharon said, "What's that supposed to mean?" and then, "I'm just so fucking tired of getting pushed around."

Ray said, yeah, he could understand that.

Sharon said, "So now we have a problem."

And Ray said, "We?"

Sharon said, "If you want."

"Guess I better not piss you off."

She looked up at him, serious, no flirty looks now and he said, okay. When she'd first killed the guy, she didn't know what to do. She'd started to call Bobbi out of pure instinct, but then thought, maybe this guy wouldn't freak out too much, and might be able to help. Now she was glad she'd called Ray.

Ray said, "If we can get him out of here, I can dump the body."

Sharon said, okay, sure, they could do that and walked into the living room.

Ray followed her, saw her sit down on the couch and light a cigarette. She motioned to the pack on the coffee table and he picked it up.

She said, "What if he has other friends, what if other guys come looking for him?"

"What about it?"

She smoked and said, "Like in that movie with Gina Gershon and the other chick, they kill the guy but someone else is coming?"

Ray said, oh yeah, they were lesbians in that one, *Bound*, and Sharon said Gina Gershon was, she wasn't sure about the other chick. "She may just have been using her." Wondering what she was doing herself.

"Yeah, anyway," Ray said, "what I never figured about that

movie was why didn't they just say the guy didn't show? People are always trying to take simple situations and make them complicated." He lit his cigarette and blew smoke at the ceiling.

"You don't think this is complicated?"

"It doesn't have to be."

Without getting up to look, she said, "Is that cop still out front dressed like a homeless guy?"

"What?"

"The night Ku jumped there were cops all over the place, even on the roof, that's how they found the grow rooms. But they didn't bust them, they're just watching the place."

"You invited me over to do a deal, you knew they were watching the place?"

Sharon looked up at Ray, thinking he was bullshitting but not sure and decided, again, just to tell him. Hell, they were in it this far. She hooked the heels of her boots on the coffee table, the EM on her ankle still painted red, and said, "The cops are the least of your problems."

"Why is that?"

"Come on, you roll into town telling everyone who'll listen you can supply hundreds of pounds a month, deliver to the States, no questions? Most people think you're a cop."

"You didn't."

"I was too desperate to care. Anyway, I'm supposed to be finding out about you."

Ray sat down in the armchair and said, "For someone who could use that kind of supply and delivery?"

Sharon laughed. Then she took a deep drag on the cigarette and let the smoke out slowly, saying, "How many guys you think could deal with that much every month?"

"Not many."

"That's right." She looked at him and she still couldn't tell. Shit, this guy, either the dumbest guy she ever met, or maybe the house arrest was getting to her. Not able to get out and circulate, she was losing it. "Okay, look, I've been hearing rumours. If you were at all connected to anything you'd be hearing them too, but since your spaceship just landed, I'll tell you. There's gonna be a takeover."

"Of what?"

She shook her head, smoked some more. "Of everything. You ever heard of Les Saints?"

"Motorcycle gang?"

"Yeah, well, it's been a long time since they rode motorcycles. They look like businessmen now." She was thinking of Richard in his khakis and golf shirts, driving his Audi convertible, his Ray-Bans. Mon Oncle in Montreal still looked the part, the leather vest, the big chains, always smiling like he knew something no one else did. "They used to work for the mob, then they got bigger than the mob. Now they're going to run the whole show themselves."

Ray said, yeah, so? "They need supply and delivery."

"You are too stupid to live."

"Look," Ray said. "You just said they're businessmen. What I have is a business arrangement, an offer. If you think you can deliver it to them, if you can set it up, we can maybe make this work."

Sharon thought, wow, she was going to try to talk him into giving her a cut and here he was offering it up. If they didn't kill him outright, Richard and his boys would kill him in business. She said, "I can make a couple of calls."

"All right then. We better get rid of old Mohammed there."
He stood up and Sharon said they could dump him in the grow
rooms.

"Top floor? They probably have cameras in there by now."
He took out his cellphone and said, "No, I know a place."

And Sharon thought she'd never met a guy who was so
stupid and so put together all at the same time.

J.T. FELT LIKE HE WAS starting over again, doing all the dirty
work. The first thing he did when he got out of the Army was
rob one of those cheque-cashing, payday loan places. It was in
North York, the last unit in a strip mall, a place he remembered
used to rent tools. He stood by the back door of the place thinking no one in the old neighbourhood did any work anymore,
they just cashed welfare cheques. When the nice-looking woman
stepped out the back door for a smoke he walked up beside her
and said, hey.

She smiled at him and it took a second for her to see the gun
under his coat, the Tokarev. J.T. came back from Afghanistan
with a dozen guns from all over the world: Russian, American,
German. Hell, some of the British ones had pictures of Queen
Victoria stamped on them from the 1800s. Those Afghans could
get all of them to fire. He said, "Why don't we go inside?" and
when they did a guy said, "If you come back in now your
break's over and I'm going out."

The woman didn't say anything. There were no customers on
the other side of the double-reinforced, extra-thick, bulletproof
Plexiglas. J.T. said, "Why don't you put all the cash in here,"
and tossed the guy a gym bag.

The guy turned around and looked like he was going to shit

himself when he saw the gun, but then he started saying J.T. had no idea who he was dealing with, and you don't just walk in here and rob this place, and shit like that, but he filled the bag with cash and tossed it back.

Before he left, J.T. said to the guy, "Don't blame her, if you'd come out for a smoke, it would have been you."

Over the next week, J.T. hit three more and moved out of the rooming house on Parliament into a short-term apartment rental on the Danforth. Then he looked up his old buddy, Chuck, used to be with the Demon Keepers, but J.T. heard they'd been taken over by Les Saints from Montreal and now they were part of a worldwide operation. Chuck was still an asshole, but he was an in.

So now J.T. was walking into a twenty-five-storey apartment building a block up from Queen and John, by the MuchMusic building, had that half a car bursting out the side about three floors up. Getting his own hands dirty again. Sometimes it felt just like the Army, new guy doing all the shit work, but here the payoff looked a lot better.

He waited just outside the door, walking slow, no one noticing him till he saw someone coming out, young Chinese guy, and he held the door as the guy opened it and went in. There was no one in the little office just off the lobby and J.T. got in the elevator and pushed 25.

The payoff would have been a lot better in the Army if his cousin hadn't gone and got himself killed. J.T. was in Afghanistan, the Canadian peacekeepers, what bullshit that was, driving around the desert with the SEXY unit, "sensitive site exploration," looking for IEDs, improvised explosive devices, and cleaning up body parts. More Army bullshit but very useful for making all kinds of contacts: guns and explosives, sure, but mostly dope. J.T. was impressed, that was for sure. These guys could make bombs out of anything, but their real skill was growing dope. They could grow it anywhere: in sand, on the sides of mountains you couldn't walk up, in fucking caves, it seemed like. And good stuff, the plants were ten feet tall. They could turn over a poppy crop in no time and package it however you wanted.

J.T.'s cousin, James Crouch, wheeler-dealer, running the supply centre in KAF, Kandahar Air Field, which serviced about seven thousand multinational Coalition Forces, could get you anything you wanted too. It was a match made in heaven. They were going to set up a solid network, use the Army to ship everything back to Canada.

Then James got blown up in a suicide attack. That was the official story, but J.T. knew he was dead when they put him in the Jeep, bullet in the back of the head. Wheeling and dealing with all those Romanians, and Swedes, and Nigerians could be an iffy business.

Walking down the apartment hallway to the very end, last door on the left, J.T. thought, now here I am, starting over again. Shit. Oh well, has to be done.

He knocked.

A woman's voice said, "Who is it?"

J.T. said, "Sergeant Sagar sent me, I've got more paperwork."

From behind the door she said, "Shit, it never ends," and the second she opened it knew she'd made a big mistake. Recognized J.T. from Nugs's boat.

J.T. was inside, closing the door, and walking after her down the hall to the living room. There was a galley kitchen on the left, then a dining room that opened to the living room.

The woman, maybe thirty, blonde streaks in her shoulder-length hair, great body, nice tan, wearing jeans low on her hips with a black belt, two rows of silver rivets and a tight sweater, standing in the middle of the room lighting a cigarette said, "You don't have to do this."

J.T. could see past her through the open door to the balcony, the great view. "I don't?"

She took a drag on the smoke, said, "No, you don't. I can just disappear."

He said, "We'll find you again."

She put the cigarette down in an ashtray on a table at the end of the couch. She was starting to get it together, thinking that because he didn't do it right away he might not. "You want a drink? I got some vodka."

J.T. said, yeah, okay, why not. She went into the kitchen and he stepped out onto the balcony, looked at the view. Twenty-five floors didn't sound that high, but looking down it was a lot. He could almost feel the concrete building sway. They were facing south and west, looking out at the Tower, and the Dome, and the big lake with the six-lane highway running along it.

She came out onto the balcony, and handed J.T. a vodka and orange juice, saying it was the only mix she had.

"You're not Amber anymore, right?"

She went back inside, sat down on the couch, picked up her cigarette. He followed her, but left the balcony door open.

She smoked and drank her vodka and orange juice. Her fingernails were long and black. She said her name really was Amber, she hadn't gotten into this thinking it would end like this.

"So now it's Susan?"

"My grandmother's name." Then she said, "Look, I won't testify."

"No, you won't."

"I mean, really, I don't have to, I can just disappear. I mean, you could find me here, this is a fucking RCMP safe house and you just walked right in, you can find me anywhere."

J.T. said, yeah, they could. This Amber, she had been Nugs's girlfriend for over a year. He took her everywhere, showed her everything. J.T. remembered her sunbathing naked on Nugs's boat, treating everyone like the help. The whole time she was meeting with some lady Mountie, giving them everything. Almost everything. She kept herself pretty close to it, this Amber, and doled it out. Now that Nugs's trial was coming up, she was the key witness. Really, the only witness. The mistake she made was thinking that Nugs was really in charge. She'd got to know him pretty well and thought he was soft and really slipping, that he was weak. She didn't know how the takeover was going to change things in Toronto. Change everything.

"If I don't do it, somebody else will."

She stared at him without blinking, said, "Not if they think it's done."

J.T. sat down across from her in the chair. They were close, their knees almost touching, and she leaned forward, looking right at him. She had a plan, this Amber.

"I mean, as long as I don't testify, you don't care, right?"

"Yeah."

"I mean, as long as I'm not here, it doesn't matter where I am."

"Not really. You got somewhere to go?"

"Hell, anywhere. There's lots of places I could disappear. I was a pretty good dancer before I met Nugs. I could go to Vegas, be one of a million. Florida, there's lots going on, I could just disappear."

"Just like that? I don't know. Be a loose end, always hanging out there."

"But it could look like I was really gone." She stood up, took another drag, stubbed out the smoke, and said, "They've got me stashed in Niagara Falls in some shitty retirement condo. Fuck, I hate it. That's why they have to let me come back to town once in a while, do a little shopping, get out."

J.T. said, yeah, he heard.

"So, I've been pissed off, I've been moody, like. I've been depressed."

"Oh yeah?"

"Yeah." She was walking around the living room now, getting into her plan. "So, if I couldn't take it anymore, it wouldn't be a surprise."

"No?"

"You know what I could do, I could write a note and leave it in my car, leave my car in that parking lot by the Falls, you know the one?"

"Across from the lookout, the gift store?"

"Yeah, by the power plant, always full of a million Japanese tourists and buses. I could leave a note in my car there and then just be gone. Lots of people do it in the Falls, they don't find everyone."

"I don't know."

She stopped right in front of him, put her hand on his knee, and said, "We could go down to the Falls together, have a last night on the town, get a room in the new hotel. You could take me across the border and I could get on a bus, go to Miami."

And J.T. thought, a fucking bus, you didn't save a dime? He said, "It might work."

"Sure it would." She was happy now, going into the little kitchen and coming out with a pad of paper and a pen, saying, "Here, like this."

J.T. stood up and watched her write.

She said, "This is all true, you know, I can just say it like it is: I feel so fucking trapped, I'm so scared, I don't know what I'm doing. I don't know how to get out of this fucking mess I made of my life."

"Is that what you'd write though?"

She looked up at him. Thinking about it, not scared at all, she'd already moved on.

Which was really what her problem was, moving on with nowhere to go.

"Yeah, this is what I'd write, all this stuff. It's true."

She held out the note and J.T. looked at it. "Yeah, that seems about right. Seems sincere."

"Fucking right it's sincere." Walking back to the kitchen, saying, "Let me pack up my stuff, make it look like I couldn't take it anymore and ran away from here."

J.T. said, hang on.

She came back out of the kitchen tying her hair back, saying, what?

"I don't know if this is going to work."

"Sure it'll work, it'll work great." She stepped up close to him, smiling, and he said, "You know what else would work though?"

"No, what?"

He grabbed her around the throat with one hand and picked her up by the belt in her jeans with the other. Walked out onto the balcony and tossed her off.

In the kitchen he looked at the suicide note stuck to the fridge with a magnet from a pizza place and thought, yeah, this'll work fine.

He rode down the elevator with a couple of guys who looked like students at the art college around the corner. In front of the building, a crowd had already started to gather, and J.T. walked up Beverley and into Chinatown, thinking, just like the Army, big risks, but if you're flexible and can think on your feet, it can really pay off.

CHAPTER **13**

PRICE AND MCKEON WERE BOTH SITTING at their desks reading files when Bergeron and Armstrong came in, Price saying they just had to hang in there.

McKeon saying, "Forever?"

"This your drive-by?"

Price said, "That's so fucked up."

McKeon said, no, "This is that stripper and her boyfriend. The little girl died."

Armstrong twisted the top off a bottle of water he got from the vending machine and said, "They did it, right?"

Price said, that's right, and McKeon said she didn't know. "Coroner says the little girl was killed, but these people?"

Bergeron sat down at his desk, turned on his computer, and said, "I remember this one, it was last year. Stripper's like, nineteen, boyfriend's thirty, illegal immigrant?"

McKeon said, no, he's in the country legally, from Jamaica. She's from somewhere down east, Pictou, Nova Scotia. "In fact, they never broke any laws in their lives. Their pathetic lives."

"We've been tapping them for almost a year," Price said, picking up the file and dropping it on the desk. Inside it were the transcripts of the wiretaps of their phones and the conversations recorded in their apartments. "They've moved five times, every time to a shittier, more expensive, fleabag, piece-of-shit apartment."

"They're in a motel now, charges by the week," McKeon said. "Tech guys were scared to go there to do the install."

Armstrong said he didn't blame them, that neighbourhood.

They were the only ones in the Homicide office, nearly six o'clock.

Bergeron said, "And they're still together?"

McKeon said, yeah, she knew what he meant. "A year ago their little girl dies. Kid was almost two. Home with the boyfriend."

"He the father?"

Price looked at Armstrong and said, yeah, he's the father. Then Price said, "She was working late at the club. Kid woke up in the night, boyfriend tried to get her back to sleep, couldn't. Says he left her in the crib, crying, finally she stops, he figures she's asleep, then the girlfriend gets home, checks on the baby, and she's dead."

"That's their story?"

"And they're sticking to it." McKeon shook her head. "We pick him up, get the lab report, charge him. But there's not much evidence. Coroner's report says definitely homicide but the crown wants more."

"So," Price said, "we've been following them around."

McKeon said, "We keep waiting for them to turn on each other, you know. The girlfriend wasn't home at the time, we keep waiting for her to say something to him."

Bergeron said, "Maybe she's scared."

Price said they thought so. "But we've got hours and hours of this." He flicked at the thick file on his desk. "They're talking about everything, but they believe each other."

Armstrong said, "What do you believe?"

Price and McKeon looked at each other. They'd been partners a few years, no politics between them. It was a good, professional relationship.

McKeon said, "I don't know." Price shook his head.

"So," Bergeron said, "the only evidence you have to make this a crime came from the lab," and let it hang there, no one saying anything for a minute until McKeon said, "I'm getting tired of this shit."

Price said, "What's going on?" and Bergeron looked at Armstrong, then said, probably nothing.

Armstrong said, "But you can feel it, right? I mean, it's not just us."

No one spoke. What Armstrong was talking about was huge. He was talking about cops with agendas of their own, the lab out of control, not answering to anyone, a lame-duck chief just chomping at the bit to make his move into politics, ready to sell out his own guys if he had to, and their own union so divided they were just waiting for it to explode.

But like most people working for companies with screwed-up management, what could they do? They did their jobs the best they could and stayed out of the way.

McKeon said, "It can't last forever."

Price said, "Till we do something."

Bergeron, the oldest guy in the room, the guy way past any ideas of promotions or career choices, really just there to keep busy, said, "Maybe I should talk to Nichols."

McKeon opened her purse, took out some gum and said, "God, I'd love a cigarette right now."

Bergeron agreed with that, asked her how long it'd been.

"Since I got pregnant. Well, since we started talking about it, but it seemed like it happened right away."

"Coming back to work here, I quit. I stopped when the kids were little, but then after Linda's funeral, that night, I started again." Bergeron looked at Price and Armstrong, both of them in their tailored suits, so cool looking, and said, "You never started?"

Neither one ever had.

Price said, "If you talked to Nichols, what would you say?"

It was getting dark outside and the office was dark too, no desk lamps on and only half the fluorescents, all the new energy-saving crap.

"Just talk, you know. See how management feels."

Nichols being the highest-up guy they could talk to. Once in a while his name got floated for the new chief, though he never admitted wanting the job. Maybe that was the best reason to give it to him. Anybody admitting they wanted to take over this mess needs to be questioned.

McKeon said, "If you want to."

Bergeron said he had to talk to him anyway, they needed to get authorization to put surveillance on the husband, guy who cut off his wife's arms and legs.

"And head," McKeon said. "Don't forget that," chewing on her gum.

"Yeah."

Then Bergeron said, okay. "Maybe we should meet up later?"

They said, yeah, okay, and went back to work.

———

EDDIE DROVE AND RAY SAT in the passenger seat of the car, a PT Cruiser, down the QEW to Hamilton, Ray asking how come this one highway didn't have a four-oh number like all the others.

Eddie said, "I think it's a four hundred series, there's a 410. This one just seems older." Six lanes, eight lanes, sometimes ten, Toronto to Buffalo, heavy traffic all day and night. Cars, RVs, trucks, a constant stream, millions of them every day.

Ray said, yeah, it seemed older, but like they were working on it all the time, adding new interchanges and hooking up more roads. Made him realize that the whole area, the Golden Horseshoe they called it, all around Lake Erie and Lake Ontario was really one big place: Detroit, Chicago, Cleveland, Buffalo, Toronto—might be two countries but it was all one place. He said to Eddie, "I think you were right, we're better off doing this on the Canadian side."

Eddie said, yeah. He cut across four lanes to the right, staying on the highway to Hamilton instead of Niagara Falls and the U.S.A., as it said on the sign. "These guys are more organized, not as many to deal with. And they really want the transport system to the States."

"That'll be a big selling point."

"You think this woman will be able to make the deal?"

"She seems to know all the players. Seems to go way back with them."

"Yeah," Eddie said, "but do they trust her?"

"As much as they can, I think."

"Does she trust us?"

Ray looked into the back of the car, the backseat folded down and the tarp covering up what was crammed into the trunk. "We get rid of this she will."

"Man," Eddie said, "she's got some set of balls on her."

They were passing subdivisions and big-box stores. Ray thought it was too bad, really, the area looked like it was really nice before, when it was trees and rocks, part of the Niagara escarpment. Pretty soon it wouldn't be golden, it'd be an asphalt horseshoe.

Ray said she was really backed into a corner, had no choice, and Eddie said, oh yeah, "We wouldn't know what that's like."

"No." Ray said Sharon was talking to a guy named Richard, came in from Montreal.

"United the biker gangs," Eddie said. "Or took them over, whatever you want to call it. Pretty soon they'll run all these ports, not just the big ones. They've got all the drug business now."

Ray asked if Eddie knew this Richard guy and Eddie said, no. "I told you, I knew a few guys further up, Owen Sound, Thunder Bay. They weren't connected with these guys from Montreal, but the way I get it now is they all joined up, they're all one gang."

"But the guys from Montreal call the shots."

"I think so."

Ray said, okay, that was fine, that would work out okay.

Less than an hour from Sharon's place in Toronto, they crossed over the Burlington Skyway, a bridge that seemed too high to hold itself, the wind moving the car back and forth, big rigs shaking as they passed, and turned onto Kenilworth Street in Hamilton, in the middle of steel mills and factories. They drove down to the harbour, passed through the security gate, and headed to Pier 12.

Eddie pulled up as close as he could to the tug, the *Dream-*

boat Annie, and said, "Here we are." The barge, the old *Chris Kidd* that had been converted, its engines pulled out and the hull lengthened to almost 400 feet and cut into a wedge at the stern, was joined to the tug.

It was dark, almost midnight, and quiet in the harbour. There were a couple of boats docked. The *Algolake* from Algoma Central, one of those with all the cabins aft, was closest to Ray's tug, but all the lights were out. Further on was the *English River*, from Canada Steamships, the *Canadian Provider* still in long-term lay-up in Berth 10, and then a few more Ray didn't recognize in the dark.

Eddie said, "Where we going to put this guy?" and Ray said, don't call it a guy.

"Right. Where we going to put this?"

"Let's put it in the pilothouse, we can keep an eye on it."

They each took an end and carried the bulky tarp up to the tug, Eddie saying, you think he's going somewhere?

In the pilothouse they dumped him by the door and sat down. Eddie stood up again and said he wanted a beer, and Ray said, sure, get me one too.

Looking out at the lights on the Stelco plant, the big coke ovens going twenty-four seven again, the Skyway, the city beyond, Ray said, "We'll go out tomorrow, dump this in the middle of the lake."

"You sure you want to? What's the rush? It'll look pretty weird, unhooking the barge just to go for a ride."

Ray said, you think anyone'd notice, and Eddie said, why take the chance? "We could put him in storage." He motioned to the old pilothouse in the aft of the barge, empty now. Well, almost empty.

Ray said, okay, and they carried the tarp-covered body all the way across the deck. The old pilothouse had been cleaned out of anything salvageable, anything they could get a nickel for. It had been picked clean when Ray bought it five years ago and he never did anything with the space. Until Eddie came along and asked if there was still power, and Ray told him, yeah, the diesel generator still worked, needed it for running lights, and Eddie asked about other kinds of lights.

Ray didn't get it till Eddie explained about growing dope. It was just for his personal use, sometimes they could give some out as bonus to the crew. Ray never smoked himself, but he didn't see the harm. He said he'd never once seen a brawl between stoned crew members, the way drunks would try to kill each other.

Now, when they brought in the dead guy, the pilothouse windows were boarded up and there were tables set up with lights hanging over them. There was a drying machine in the corner, a drum that turned the harvested leaves. Ray didn't really understand and Eddie would always over-explain everything so Ray stopped asking.

They dropped the guy in the corner and Eddie said, "You going back to Toronto now?"

"No, I'm staying here. You?"

"Might as well. We got some beer in the galley."

They walked back along the deck of the barge, Eddie asking about the deal and Ray saying Sharon was setting up the meeting.

"Out of the goodness of her heart."

Ray said she was looking for a finder's fee, he was fine with that, but, "She wants something long-term too."

"Yeah, like what?"

"She put the whole thing together in her head, half a million a month delivered to the States every month. I think she wants a big piece."

"She was running those grow rooms," Eddie said. "She knows what she's doing."

"She does."

"Shit, Ray, you like her."

"In a business sense."

Eddie laughed and said, no, in every sense.

"I'd like to get to know her better."

"This may not be a good time."

They were standing on the deck, between hatches. Four hundred feet long, seventy-five feet wide, a lot of growing space, harvesting, drying. It was a turnkey operation, Ray had said.

"Why not? This is a good deal. For everybody."

Eddie said, yeah, maybe. "But you know what would make it better?"

Ray said, what, and Eddie said, "If we were actually growing some dope on this boat." He tapped his foot, the sound echoing through the empty cargo hold.

"Yeah," Ray said, "that would make it better, but it's still a good plan. These guys know what they're doing."

Ray started walking towards the tug again and Eddie said, "But these aren't the guys who fitted out the brewery, that was the old-time mob."

"I think they all work together now," Ray said. He wasn't too worried about it, that was up to them, they could fit it out just fine. Sharon could get that part worked out. Ray was always less worried about the world when he was on his boat.

Well, on any boat, he realized, don't want to get too sentimental about a hunk of steel.

Eddie said, "I hope they can work together. This isn't something we want to be caught in the middle of."

"That's why we're doing it this way, sell them the idea."

"Okay, but that's not what we're telling them."

No, Ray said, it's not. "Not until it's too late to matter. This is just another major grow op for them, but it's even better because it's the delivery system too." He opened the door to the pilothouse on the tug. "This is really the only way it can work."

Eddie said, okay. They'd been through it before and it always made sense to him, they just didn't have the resources, the connections, the capital.

But shit, the guys who did, did you really want to double-cross them?

SERGEANT JEN SAGAR CRAWLED back up to the pillow and said to Loewen, "Are you laughing?"

He said, "No."

"You better not be." She picked up the glass from the night table and took a drink of water. "After what I do for you."

He said, "Hey, I do plenty for you."

"Oh yeah? In your uniform?" She pulled off the brown leather, knee-high boots. They were all she was wearing.

Loewen said, "I wear a suit to work," and Sagar said, so do I.

"Yeah, but you have the fancy red jacket." Loewen could see it in the closet.

"What's sexy about a Mountie dress uniform?"

Loewen said he wasn't sure. Who knows why somebody

finds something sexy. The idea of the Mountie going down on him though, just seemed that way. Especially after Bergeron said that about where was he getting his information.

He said, "I talked to those Homicide cops."

She said, "I knew you would. But do we have to talk about it now?"

"No."

Loewen didn't move, lying on his back in her bed. She got up and went into the bathroom. He wondered about male-female stuff, all those lines from all those comedians, the difference between men and women. She was a tough cop, all right, a Mountie working the task force in Toronto, he wasn't even sure what she had going on. He'd met her a few months back when he and Price were investigating the murder of a Russian mobster and she had some background. But then the Mounties swooped in and busted up a car theft deal that another Russian had going with the bikers. The whole thing blew up in their faces. But Loewen and Sagar had stayed together.

Now he wondered what she was working.

She came out of the bathroom, brushing her teeth, and said, "Can you get back into Homicide?"

"It's what I'm trying to do every day."

"What about back to Fraud?"

She went back into the bathroom and he was thinking, shit, she has a great ass. Wonder what it looks like in those black pants with the yellow stripe.

"Anything but narco, right?"

She came back out and said, yeah. "That would be good."

"Why don't you just tell me what's going on?"

"If I knew, I would. You think they tell me?"

"Look, I won't say anything."

She stood there at the end of the bed, naked, looking at him. "You already told them about the lab."

"I told Price and the guys working the case. Come on, I've got to have some friends when this thing blows up."

"How do you know it's going to blow up?"

He said, "Doesn't it always?" Then he started to sit up a little. "You're looking into cops, aren't you? You're investigating us, right?"

"I'm not high enough ranked to even know."

"Come on, I can keep you out of it."

She smiled at him and said, yeah, you think so? Then she went to the closet and got her red dress-uniform jacket. Slipping it on over her bare flesh she said, "You're going to do whatever I say."

And Loewen thought, yeah, now why is that so sexy?

Maybe it's just her.

IT'D BEEN ALMOST twenty years since Armstrong was out driving his first night patrols with Old Man Murphy up at Jane and Finch. Somebody's idea of payback for the Indian who got onto the force through some affirmative action program: send him to the worst division in the city and then partner him up with a guy, fifty years old still working a night shift in the jungle.

Now here he was going back.

He could still hear Old Man Murphy saying to him, "Who owns that corner?" Pointing to a couple of black guys. "Who owns that bench?"

It was the late eighties, it hadn't quite exploded, not every punk on the corner carried more weapons than the cops, but the gangs were there. Armstrong knew they had names like Crips and Bloods but he wasn't sure if they were actually associated with the big American gangs in L.A. and New York and Chicago.

"Who owns that alley?"

They were fighting for territory. Guys who'd been around had kids making deliveries on bikes, modelled after Young Boys Inc. of Detroit.

Old Man Murphy had pulled the car into the Jane and Finch shopping centre. There were a dozen high-rise apartments all around, row after row of townhouses, must have been twenty-five thousand people within walking distance and the only shopping centre had no stores Armstrong had ever heard of. Dollar stores, a place that sold "Coffee and Donuts," not even a store name. Half the storefronts were boarded up, covered in graffiti.

Guys, all black guys, standing in front of the tags carrying on their business.

"Who owns this parking lot?" Old Man Murphy getting out of the car, looking at Armstrong.

Armstrong a scared kid, not wanting to say the name of the wrong gang and admit he didn't know anything about this part of his hometown. Even if no one else in Toronto had any idea what was really going on up here.

Old Man Murphy hiked up his gun belt under his huge gut and pointed at Armstrong, saying, "You do. You wear this uniform you own all this. You own this whole fucking city and don't ever let some asshole behind a desk tell you otherwise."

And Old Man Murphy walked through Jane and Finch like he did own the place.

Those kids went by on their bikes, he stuck his nightstick in the front wheel, flipped them right over. Leaned down and said, "Kid, that young offenders act don't mean shit up here in the jungle." Some pimp smiled at him with gold teeth, Old Man Murphy knocked them out.

Somebody probably thought it was funny, Armstrong with racist Old Man Murphy, but it turned out he wasn't racist at all. He hated everybody equally. He hated his bosses just as much as he hated the wimpy politicians and the crooked union guys. What he taught Armstrong was that at the end of the day, people were going to fuck you over. "Someday you're going to go down," he said. "If you don't, you're not doing this job right. And no one's going to stand up for you. Every guy you ever worked with is going fuck you over to protect his own career."

Armstrong said, "Even you," and Old Man Murphy said, "Hell, kid, I'd enjoy it."

They drove that night patrol together for two years and Armstrong learned how to be a cop. He saw Old Man Murphy give kids candy and saw tears in his eyes when he drove a six-year-old girl, hit by a car, to the hospital, telling Armstrong the ambulances were too fucking slow up here. He worked overtime with him on Hallowe'en so the kids could trick-or-treat.

And they watched the gangs get stronger and more organized. They watched the top guys get smarter every time they came out of jail, and insulate themselves with more and more layers of kids.

They watched their city become a big American city just like Detroit, or Chicago, or Philly, or Washington.

Except here no one noticed. Or no one cared. After all, it

wasn't keeping people away from downtown shopping or bringing down real estate values. Toronto built its ghetto way out in the burbs, never thinking it was a growth industry.

The one mistake they made in the fifties, Armstrong's old neighbourhood of Regent Park, a few high-rises and some townhouses a little east of downtown, was being emptied out and razed. Armstrong could hear Old Man Murphy saying the people in this fucking city, so naive they actually think it's being renovated, as if happy people in rent-controlled public housing will live side by side with happy people in expensive condos. Like that's worked anywhere in the world.

Old Man Murphy had his stroke and lasted a few months in a nursing home. Armstrong got promoted and started wearing suits.

And now here he was, back at Jane and Finch.

And it was even worse.

He pulled into the parking lot of the shopping centre, still no chain stores, still half boarded up, guys still doing business. Now he noticed a few Asian faces, could be Vietnamese or even Chinese. Still a lot of BMWs, but now they were SUVs: the X5, and the new Jeep Commander, looked like an armed truck, a couple of Hummers. He parked and walked to a bench where a white guy was sitting by himself.

The guy said, "You come all the way up here so you wouldn't be followed?"

"Who'd follow me here?"

A black guy walked up carrying a couple of coffees in paper cups and said, "Shit, Armstrong, you actually came up here."

"Taylor, I lived here."

"Yeah, back in the day."

Taylor sat on the bench beside the white guy, Smith, and they took the lids off their coffees, looking up at Armstrong.

"We'd get you one," Smith said, "but they don't make lattes."

Armstrong said he was fine. Then he said, "This what G&G do, you sit on a bench drinking coffee all day?"

"Sometimes we get donuts."

"They have Boston cream up here," Armstrong said, "or just plain?"

They were both in their early thirties, these Guns and Gangs task force guys. Armstrong knew Smith from when he was in uniform downtown. He'd changed a lot. Gotten a lot more comfortable in his skin, not the kid running around trying to impress everyone. Well, Armstrong figured, he was still trying to impress people, just in a different way. That's why he was up here talking to him, he thought Smith might have something to say.

Armstrong said, "So. You guys getting ready."

"What for?"

"Could be a war coming."

Taylor said, "Every day's a war up here, man."

Anywhere else Armstrong would have thought the guy was watching too many rap videos, but looking down the storefronts at the kids, twenty-one max, wearing parkas in the fall cool, getting into their Commanders, Armstrong guessed Taylor was probably right. "Lot of movement at the top," Armstrong said.

"Yeah, yeah, new boys in town," Smith said. "These kids were the first to the meetings. Prices going up, territories getting bigger, a lot of dealers getting pushed out."

Armstrong said, "You guys must be working with narco a lot."

He could feel the change in tone. Up till then they were having fun, they were hanging out playing cops and robbers with real guns, and they liked it. Now everybody tensed up.

Taylor said, "Yeah, some. Why?"

"Just wondering."

Smith stood up, got close to Armstrong, and said, "Leave it alone, man."

"Why, 'cause it's just fine?"

"It's either just fine, or it's not. Either way, leave it alone."

"But you guys," Armstrong said, "know what I'm talking about."

Smith said, "We don't know nothing. We're babysitters."

Armstrong said, yeah, okay. "I get it."

Taylor said, "No, you don't."

A kid rode by on his bike, twelve years old riding a thousand-dollar mountain bike, yelled at them, "Hey, you find the mutha-fucking nigga boost my iPod?" Turning fast, laughing, and catching up with his running buddies on the bike path between the buildings.

Armstrong said, "Anybody else talk to you?"

"You think the rat squad's coming up here?"

Armstrong looked at the two cops and said, "I think something's coming. I don't think it can go like this much longer."

"Why," Taylor said, "because it's finally getting downtown? You think that makes the difference."

Armstrong didn't know Taylor at all. Looking at him on the bench now, he couldn't tell if he was even thirty. He'd figured he was some suburb kid out of Brampton, playing it tough on the force, doing what Armstrong had done, using his skin colour to get noticed.

But he was still up here in the jungle.

"You know Burroughs is everywhere."

Smith said, "Shit, man, you're not going to get specific now, are you?"

"I'm just wondering," Armstrong said, "if things got pushed, which way they'd fall."

Taylor and Smith looked at him.

Then Taylor said, "Depends who's doing the pushing," and that was better than Armstrong had hoped for.

These guys, the guys on the street were fed up too. No cop was ever going to rat out another cop, but if things got too bad, if it became too obvious to too many people, they'd have to do something. Or not do something, really. Not offer as much protection as they could, not destroy all the evidence, not get in the way too much. That way it could be contained, a few guys could go down, but it could be kept quiet.

Or it could explode in their faces.

"That's what I'm trying to find out," Armstrong said.

"No one talked to us," Taylor said. "Not yet."

And Armstrong thought by the way Taylor let it hang, if someone did talk to them they might have something to say.

"Okay. Well, I guess you guys are busy. Someone's stealing iPods, you want to find out who that is."

"Broken windows, man," Taylor said, and they all laughed.

Armstrong drove around the neighbourhood a little. Broken windows everywhere. That was New York's plan, Giuliani's plan, treat all crime as serious, don't let anything go. If you leave the broken windows, it escalates.

Well, that and you have major investigations into organized

crime and police corruption, you break the union's stranglehold, and you keep the politicians out of it.

Armstrong was all the way along Sheppard to Bathurst by then, all the signs were for the United Jewish Appeal and Israel Bonds, and he was in a completely different world. By the time he got back downtown, he realized they had a long way to go. Things could stay just like this for a while.

Or they could explode any minute.

"HOMELAND SECURITY?" PRICE SAID. "What do they want with you?"

Armstrong said he'd tell him when he found out. McKeon sat down at the table and said that was the cleanest ladies room she'd ever seen in a place like this.

Bergeron said, "What do you mean, a place like this?"

Almost two in the morning, they were in a small bar in East York called Scotch Corner. There was a time, seemed a long time ago now, that the place would be filled after hours with city cops talking about soccer games back home. All of them from someplace in Scotland or Ireland—Ayr, or Larne, or Glasgow, or Belfast. Somebody with Scottish roots tried to join the force now, it would be a strike against him. Or her.

Levine and O'Brien pulled up chairs around the small table, all of them drinking Blue Light out of bottles. The bartender, Gladys, found something to do in the back.

McKeon said, "Where's Ray and Lou?" Rahim Dhaliwal and Luigi Mastriano.

Levine said they were working a double just got called in. "Two black guys, twenty years old, shot in the head sitting in a brand-new Jeep Commander. We're not speculating on any previous legal histories or involvement with law enforcement." No, everybody at the table doubted they'd have priors and known associates.

O'Brien took out her cigarettes, Belmont Milds, and lit one, blowing smoke over McKeon's head. The two women sat across from each other at the end of the table.

Levine said, "I remember when you could do that, the bar was still open."

Armstrong said, "It's really heating up." He was going to tell them he talked to the G&G guys up in the jungle, but then he thought he'd just tell Bergeron later. It was heating up faster than he'd expected.

"Whatever it is." McKeon drank her beer and said, "Okay, so what did Nichols say?"

They all looked at Bergeron. He drank a little and the place was totally quiet as he put the bottle down on the table. It was suspenseful for a second, and then he said, "What do you think he said? He said to be patient."

"Fuck that."

"Big surprise."

"Patient till he retires."

"This is such bullshit."

Bergeron said, so, what are we talking about here?

Maureen McKeon said, "We can't do nothing." She picked up O'Brien's pack of smokes on the table and turned it over and over. She looked at Bergeron and said, "What impression did you get, Gord?"

Bergeron said, "You mean my totally non-admissible,

didn't go in my official notes, personal feelings about the meeting?"

"Yeah," Levine said. "Your gut, like they say on TV."

Bergeron said, well, if you want to talk about that. "I did get the feeling something was going on." He looked at Price.

Price said, what?

"If we're going to talk about this," Bergeron said, "about doing something, we're going to have to talk."

Price nodded.

Levine said, "You ever see the movie *Eight Men Out?*"

Louise O'Brien said the one about the baseball players who threw the World Series? Shoeless Joe Jackson, those guys. "With John Cusack? Yeah, I saw it."

"It was *fercockta* from the get-go. Some guys thought they were throwing one game, some guys thought the whole series, some guys had no idea what was going on."

McKeon said that sounded familiar and Levine said, "But it shouldn't be a surprise. Look, they were proud guys and they were doing something they were ashamed of. They didn't really want to do it, they thought they had no choice."

"Yeah, so?"

Levine shook his head, used to being interrupted and for people not to wait while he made his point. "So they didn't plan it well, they didn't really talk it through. There weren't exactly minutes taken at the meetings, you know? They said as little as they could, too little, and they moved on."

O'Brien took a drag on her smoke and exhaled, looked at her partner, and said, "And that's why they got caught?"

Levine said, yeah. "My sister would probably say they wanted to get caught."

O'Brien looked around the table and said, Teddy's sister's a psychiatrist.

"Psychologist, but you get my point."

Price said, "There is no way we're going to sit here and talk about going outside the force to the fucking RCMP or OPP to investigate our own guys and take fucking notes about it."

Levine said, "I'm just saying."

They all drank. There it was, on the table.

Bergeron said, "What if Nichols meant it?"

"That the feeling you got?"

Bergeron noticed that Armstrong hadn't said very much of anything, didn't know what that meant, still getting to know his partner. Everybody else looking at him. Bergeron said, "I've known Ali Nichols a long time. Had a few drinks with him in here."

They all waited, giving him time.

"And he's still hard to read. He knows we all feel it, every time we're working something that comes close to IS, or narco, or the task force, we all feel it."

"Feel it's fucked up."

Bergeron said, "I'm saying he wasn't surprised."

"You told him everything we've got?"

Bergeron said, yeah, he told him everything. "He asked me, could we wait?"

McKeon said, "Can we?" Looking around the table at almost the entire Homicide squad, the most senior detectives on the force.

And they all knew that if they couldn't wait, if they had to go outside the force, it would be more than just a career-limiting move, a CLM as Levine called it. It would be career-defining, it would be with them the rest of their lives. The cops who turned on cops. They'd have to gather evidence and give testimony. They'd have to watch outsiders, smug fucking Mounties, come right into their house. They'd have to spend years on it, it would never go away.

And it could all blow up on them, they could get nothing, no one. It's not like they thought they were wrong, they knew the shit that was going on, but putting everything on the line for it? Shit.

Bergeron said, "Look," and everyone did, they all looked at him. He said, "I guess I'm the senior guy here. I'm the only one not worried about promotions or pensions."

"Fuck that, that's not what this is about."

"Okay, okay. But if you want my impression," and he looked at Price again and this time Price got it, this time he understood, "I do think we should wait. Something might be going on."

Price said, "Something with somebody was in our squad for a while?"

"It's just a feeling I got."

"Your gut," Levine said, but by then they were all thinking about the kid, Loewen, filled in for McKeon during her mat leave, now working narco with Burroughs. Sleeping with that Mountie, Sagar, on the task force.

McKeon said, "If he's as lousy at keeping his work a secret as he is who he's banging, we'll be back here in a week."

Bergeron said it might be over by then.

"Holy shit."

"So we wait."

"We wait."

The tension went right out of the room. Decision made. They weren't traitors, not yet.

Price said, "So why does Homeland Security want to talk to you?"

Chairs were scraping on the floor, people standing up, beers finished off.

Armstrong said, "We got an ID on our jumper, Kumar Nekounam. Ran him through every database and he's clean, but we get a call from Homeland Security, want to talk to us."

"You going to Washington?"

Bergeron said they were going to the U.S. Consulate tomorrow. "But now that we know who he was, we want to find out a little more about him."

Price said he guessed so.

"Big international incident."

"Yeah, right."

They all sat down and had another round, some of the tension coming back.

THAT FIRST TIME HE MET Angelo Colucci, at the old Voyageur Restaurant on the 401, just outside Kingston before all the stops were fast food, Richard was such a kid. Twenty-five. Colucci was probably just over thirty, but he seemed so much older, sitting there drinking that shitty coffee and eating pie, wearing a dark blue suit and Ray-Bans.

Richard was so excited, doing a real mob hit, thrilled to be invited to the party.

Now he was driving his Audi convertible out of Toronto, heading north up to Woodbridge. Wearing his own Ray-Bans and four-hundred-dollar khakis. About to shake up the party.

Back then, Richard, with his long hair and his beard, rode his Harley out of Montreal for the meet. He had no idea who these guys were, really, just how Mon Oncle told him this was going to be a big break for them, really get them noticed. Mon Oncle, he studied it, knew all the players, and Richard saw early on how it could only help in the future.

There was a real struggle going on then. Like every other business in Canada, crime was run out of American branch offices. One of the New York families, one of the five, ran Montreal through the Costas. Toronto was run out of Buffalo. Back in those days, Mon Oncle said it was so small that Toronto was really run out of Hamilton, since the day Johnny Pops beat the shit out of that Jewish bookie in the Towne Tavern and let everybody know they'd have to deal with him.

It went on like that for years, through the sixties and seventies until Toronto really started to take off and there was big money. Construction boom, office towers and subdivisions going in, people moving in every day. Half of Montreal moved to Toronto after the PQ got elected in '76 and passed Bill 101, making French the official language in Quebec.

And the Costas moved in too. At the time, Richard didn't really know what was happening, but now he saw how it worked. Angelo Colucci was Pietro Poletti's driver, right-hand man, second in command. But he was ambitious and saw that they didn't have to drive out to fucking Hamilton every time they wanted to do something. He saw that Toronto was just going to keep getting bigger and they were going to move on from running unions and extorting donut shops. The Montreal guys, hooked up through New York, had already run the whole French Connection, supplying pretty much all of North America with its heroin. That's who Angelo wanted to deal with, so he did. Went to Montreal and offered them a big piece of Toronto.

He just had to get rid of Poletti, and that was where Mon

Oncle and the bikers came in. It was probably the Montreal guys, Little Vito Costa or someone, who suggested using bikers. They'd already been working together in Quebec, Les Saints taking over a lot of the street-level drug dealing and strong-arm work. They were good muscle.

Richard took the twenty-five grand from Angelo that day in the parking lot of the Voyageur, went back inside and had a hot chicken sandwich, putting some time between them. Then he hopped on his bike and rode to Toronto. Waited in the airport parking lot. Richard had a lot of ideas about how to do it, but Mon Oncle, he was always a little smarter, a little more forward thinking, he said, do it right away, direct, show these guys we can do fucking anything.

Pietro Poletti drove himself to the airport, parked, got his bag out of the trunk, and Richard shot him in the back of the head. Stuffed the body in the trunk, hopped on his bike, and took off down the 401. He was back in Kingston visiting his brother in Millhaven maximum a few hours later.

There was a lot of talk at the time about how Colucci wasn't with him at the airport, but it was Johnny Pops himself who had Angelo in a meeting, going over some shit about the Carpenters Union.

It was pretty quick after that Angelo Colucci and the Costas took over Toronto. To avoid a war they left Johnny Pops in Hamilton, but Richard seemed to remember something about someone shooting the old man last summer. Guy was walking on Elizabeth Street in his bathrobe, somebody put two in his head.

Richard pulled into the parking lot of the golf course and wished he had his clubs. He was pissed Colucci picked this place to meet but didn't invite him to play a round. It was really looking like Colucci's problem wasn't just not being able to find someone to do a simple hit.

Colucci was there on the practice green, a dozen balls at his feet, and Richard thought, look at him all bent over and stiff. And like always with these guys, Colucci made him wait, standing there with his thumb in his ass till he'd hit every ball on the green, not one going in, finally he looked over and said, "You must be Richard."

Richard thinking, asshole, pretending he doesn't know me, doesn't remember me. He smiled and held out his hand, said, "Good to meet you."

Colucci handed his putter to a clean-cut kid and took his time taking off his golf glove and walking over, Richard standing there like a dick with his hand out. Then they shook and Colucci said, "You want a beer?"

Richard said, yeah sure. Might as well let the guy think he's in charge for five more minutes.

On the patio overlooking the eighteenth green, Angelo said, "Looks like we're getting Indian summer," and Richard said, yeah, thinking it never gets as cold in Toronto as it does in Montreal.

"You enjoying your trip?"

Richard said, "Yeah, I'm starting to find my way around Toronto."

"That's good. How long you here for?"

A waitress came over to their table and asked them if everything was okay. Looked like she should still be in high school, but Richard knew he was getting really bad at figuring out ages. He said, yeah, everything was fine. A Caesar salad and a light beer. He'd watched Angelo eat a roasted eggplant sandwich, on some kind of sourdough bread, thinking he'd rather have that Voyageur restaurant hot chicken.

She picked up the empty glass from in front of Richard and said, "You want another round?" Angelo was drinking red wine, for shit's sake.

Richard said, yeah sure. "I've got time," and saw Angelo want to leave but instead order another glass.

When she was gone Richard said, "You know, we're pros, let's not fuck around. I'm raising the wholesale price to four grand a pound."

Angelo laughed. "You are? Just like that?" He waved to a couple of guys who had just come out onto the patio. When they saw Richard they didn't come any further.

"Yeah," Richard said. "Just like that."

The waitress put down a glass of wine in front of Angelo, then she put down her little tray and picked up the chilled glass, pouring half the beer into it. Angelo waited till she left and then said, "You have any fucking idea what you're doing?"

"Some."

"Mon Oncle know you're doing this?"

"Come on, Angelo, look at us, couple of guys in Toronto, the centre of the universe, we don't need to ask permission."

Angelo shook his head, but he was still smiling. "You're fucking insane, you think you can ride in here on your little scooters, start giving orders."

Arrogant bastard, just like he was back in the day, handing over the twenty-five grand, telling Richard how to do it. Richard didn't say anything, just okay, sure, but he was going to do it Mon Oncle's way and he was glad he did. Learned from one of the best.

He said, "Things have changed, Angelo. You saw what happened, some guys got on board, some didn't." Meaning the biker gangs in Quebec fought them for territory and Mon Oncle and his Saints killed almost two hundred of them, a bloody war that lasted ten years. Then the gangs in the rest of the country, including the biggest ones in Toronto, patched over, got on board.

So, now Richard was laying it on the line. Angelo just stared at him.

A couple of women, probably in their early fifties but really well put together, both of them wearing short golf skirts and tight sweaters, came up to the table and said hello to Angelo. He said hello, smiling, casual, and then one of the women, the one with the most blonde streaks in her hair, looked at Richard and said, "Who's your friend?"

"This is Richard Tremblay. From Montreal."

The woman doing all the talking said, "Well, hello, Richard. How are you enjoying Toronto?"

He looked at Angelo and said, "So far so good."

"Will you be staying long?"

Richard kept looking at Angelo for another second and then back at the almost blonde and said, "I might be, it's starting to grow on me."

She gave him a flirty look and said there were all kinds of things to do in Toronto. "Maybe we'll see you around?"

"Maybe."

Then she and her friend went inside to the bar and Richard was pretty sure he heard the friend start to give the flirty one shit right away.

He looked at Angelo and said, "It's true, you know. This city isn't as bad as everyone says it is."

"It does all right. The thing is," Angelo said, "it was never meant to be number one, you know? It wasn't headed in that direction, but then Montreal took its ball and went home." After the PQ got elected in '76, and 150 head offices moved to Toronto. The separatists passed the official French language law, Bill 101, and people left Montreal like refugees, saying it was 101 or the 401.

Angelo drank his wine and looked at Richard. "Everybody thinks they want to be number one, but when you get there, it's not so easy."

"Nothing worth having's ever easy."

Then Richard stood up and looked around the golf course and then back to Angelo and he said, "You shouldn't bend over so much when you putt, it's really hard on your back. You still want to be able to get out, play a round when you're retired down to Florida, or Aruba, or wherever you're going."

Then he dropped a fifty on the table—for a Caesar salad and a light beer, shit, and it made him think of when the strippers called a fifty a "brownie," and then he thought about Sharon and this civilian she was working, promising two hundred pounds a month.

Have to get rid of him too. Maybe make a show of it, let everybody see what they could do.

CHAPTER **15**

ARMSTRONG SAID HE WANTED to stop in at Bay Bloor Radio, look at MP3 players.

Bergeron said, you don't have the fanciest iPod there is yet? And Armstrong said he needed something to hook it up to his car stereo. "But I don't want to get a new setup in the car."

Bergeron realized he had no idea what kind of car Armstrong drove away from the job. He wondered if Native guys had the same tricked-out cars as the black guys, then he wondered if that was racist. It was hard to keep up. He said, "I'm going to wait in the bookstore," and walked out into the mall, the Manulife Centre on Bloor Street, downtown Toronto. It was crowded in the middle of the afternoon, people with shopping to do.

They had a possible ID on the jumper, Kumar Nekounam, though the lab admitted there were a few guys with that name in the system. They'd run the name through everything and Bergeron was surprised a few hours later to get a call from the Americans.

From Special Agent Jones of Homeland Security out of Buffalo. She sounded military on the phone, wanted to meet to discuss Mr. Nekounam. Bergeron told her there were apparently a few guys with that name and she'd said, "We are aware, Officer." Bergeron was going to say, call me Gord, but he didn't.

Instead, he and Armstrong decided they'd try to find out as much as they could about the one Kumar Nekounam of Toronto. There was no one at his last known address, no one there knew him, but somebody thought he'd worked at the bookstore in the Manulife Centre, in shipping. Some other "Arab guy" had gotten him the job, the neighbour thought.

So Bergeron walked into the bookstore and saw a lot of scented candles, and calendars, and CDs, and movies. He looked over the staff picks table, thought the staff here probably didn't party together that much, the choice of books being so different, and then he saw her at the magazine racks.

The same woman he'd seen at the Clint Eastwood movies at the Cinematheque. She was younger than he was, probably mid-forties, dark hair to her shoulders, and she wore a kind of suit, the pants snug around her ass, then loose straight down to her high-heeled boots. She stood there, one foot flat on the floor. The other one she absently turned with just the heel on the ground, leafing through a magazine.

Armstrong walked up and said he was ready and Bergeron said, oh yeah, still looking at the woman.

Armstrong said, "You like her? Go for it."

"She's the one I saw at the movies."

"Oh yeah, the spaghetti westerns."

Bergeron was surprised he remembered, but he said, yeah.

"So, man, you should talk to her. That's twice, you may never see her again."

Bergeron said, yeah, that was true.

He walked over having no idea what to say. When he was a couple of steps away from her she looked up and said, *"Fistful of Dollars."*

Bergeron said, "I'm trying to figure out if you call them Clint Eastwood movies or Sergio Leone movies."

"Because you think it'll tell you something about me?"

"That I don't want to just come out and ask."

She said, no, it wouldn't tell him anything. "But you could just come out and ask."

Bergeron looked around and saw Armstrong standing with the manager, waving for him to come on, and he said to the woman, "Look, I have to go. But this won't take long, ten or fifteen minutes, maybe." He motioned to the Starbucks right there in the bookstore and said, "Would you mind waiting, maybe I could buy you a coffee?"

She looked at him for a moment and then said, "Yeah, okay."

"Great."

RUTH GOLDBACH WATCHED the good-looking guy walk across the Indigo to where the Native guy in the expensive suit was waiting, and wondered, what are those guys? They couldn't be salesmen, they were too confident. They walked through the store like they owned the place.

She thought, okay, this might be something in her otherwise dull day.

THE MANAGER HAD THE GUY waiting in the break room by himself and when they walked in Bergeron thought it was just like an interrogation room back at 52 Division. He bet the guy thought so too.

Siya Kahn. Maybe twenty-five years old. Nervous? Hell, he was scared. He wasn't wearing the same blue shirt and black pants as the salesclerks, he was in jeans and a T-shirt. He worked in shipping.

Armstrong asked him if he wanted a cup of coffee, or a Coke or something, and the guy said no. "Well, we really appreciate you meeting with us."

The guy just nodded into his hands.

Bergeron said, "We're trying to figure out what happened to your friend."

The guy said, "Behrouz Mahmoud wasn't my friend."

Bergeron glanced at Armstrong and was glad to see he was just going to go with it too. Bergeron said, "But you knew him pretty well."

Siya shrugged.

"And you weren't too surprised we were coming to see you."

"Guy like that goes missing," Siya said, "you don't expect to find him alive."

Bergeron looked at Armstrong who was doing his best stoic Indian, staring the guy down, giving Bergeron the lead, letting him lead. Good. He said, "No, you don't. Not with a guy like that. How long did you know him?"

"Since I get here. Him and his . . . associates. Talk to all the new arrivals."

"How much did you have to pay him?"

"I'm not illegal," Siya said. "I'm refugee."

"But the board hasn't decided. You still need to have a hearing. Did Mahmoud say he could help you with that?"

The guy finally looked up, pityingly, at Bergeron and said, "He doesn't offer to help, he offers not to hurt."

"So you're glad he's gone."

Back to staring at his hands, shrugging.

This wasn't what they expected at all, whole new case opening up.

"What about Kumar Nekounam?"

"Yeah, maybe Behrouz kill him, I don't know."

Or not.

"So you don't think it was suicide?"

Shrug. "Could have been. He was depressed. Hated it here, his wife left him, had no job."

"And he had some enemies."

"He did everything they asked." Siya looked up at Bergeron, and said, "Ku was an artist, if you saw his work, it should be in galleries, in museums. He couldn't do that back home. He was brilliant, you know."

"I'd like to see his work," Bergeron said, and he meant it.

Siya shrugged. "He wouldn't be the first artist to kill himself."

"No, he also wouldn't be the first guy refused to pay a blackmailer got thrown off a roof."

"No." Back to staring at his hands.

BERGERON AND ARMSTRONG walked out, saying there was a lot more to look at here.

Bergeron said, "We have that meeting with Homeland Security, you want to tell them," and Armstrong said, hell, no. Then Armstrong laughed a little and said, "Your lady's still waiting, that's good. I'm going to go check out CDs."

RUTH WATCHED THEM SPLIT UP, the Native guy going downstairs to the music department and the guy from the Cinematheque coming towards her, and could not figure them out. That swagger, confident, in charge. Nice suit. The Native guy was a little flashy but this guy, he looked like he asked Saul Korman down at Korry's menswear to dress him up nice, but not too nice.

Then she saw the gun under his arm and thought, of course, cops. She'd just never met any real detectives.

He said, "You already got a coffee, hang on, I'll get one. You want anything else?" And she said, no, she was fine.

This could be interesting.

They told each other their names, she watched him register Goldbach, but not say anything, and she told him she called them Clint Eastwood movies. "Even though he's won an Oscar, I still think he's underrated as a director."

"Not too flashy, he doesn't draw attention to the directing, lets the characters tell the story."

Ruth said that was it. Then she said, "You're a cop, right?"

Bergeron said, "Almost thirty years."

"That's a long time. Are you good at it?"

"Pretty good, yeah."

She leaned back in her chair and looked at him over the top of her mug of black coffee. She liked this guy, the way he was straightforward and not trying to impress her. Different from what she was used to, he didn't seem all wrapped up in himself, or insecure and overcompensating. She said, "So, you want to have dinner sometime?"

He didn't look surprised at all. He said, "Yeah, that would be good. What's a good night for you?"

They decided tomorrow. There was a sushi place in Yorkville she liked and he said that'd be fine.

––––––––

THE FIRST TIME Tuan Danh Trahn saw *The Godfather* he was ten years old at his cousin's place in Hamilton. It was really the first two movies, all the scenes put in order as some TV miniseries called *The Godfather Chronicles*, and he loved it. Must have been '78, '79. When he got a VCR it was the first tape he bought, and when he got a DVD player it was the first disc he bought—by then it was the special edition with all three movies. He had different favourite scenes over the years, and now, parking at the airport and walking to departures, it was the scene where Al Pacino goes to the restaurant, goes into the can and gets the gun taped inside the toilet tank, walks back out, and shoots Sollozzo and McCluskey. Starts that whole war.

But they're all businessmen now, no more wars. Right?

Security still tight this long after 9/11, even on these Toronto-to-Montreal flights that leave every hour like taking the bus. The nice blonde lady smiled at Trahn, standing there in his brown leather coat, khakis, and two-hundred-dollar blue shirt. He wore a gold ring and a thin gold necklace. He took off his sunglasses. She told him he'd have to hurry, he only had a half hour to make his flight.

At the security check, the guard, a really tall black woman with long braided hair, asked him if he had any carry-on, and Trahn said, no, I'm just going to a meeting and coming back tonight. Like every other businessman on the plane. He dropped his BlackBerry, keys, and some change in the tray, and walked through the metal detector. The other guard waved him down with the wand and he picked up his stuff. He didn't think all the new security could really stop some suicidal fanatic, but it sure worked for him.

There was Nugs sitting in the lounge.

Trahn bought a coffee from the Tim's and walked over. Said, "Hey," and sat down across from him.

"Danny, man, good to see you."

"Yeah?"

Nugs said, what's that supposed to mean, and Trahn said, you know, the ground is shaking.

Nugs had a bottle of Perrier on the little table and he twirled it slowly. He said, "Adjustments are being made."

"You fuckers."

They were casual, leaning back in the chairs, drinking their drinks. Just a couple guys waiting for their flights.

Nugs said, "Hey, I called you, I made sure you were out in front on this."

"I'm supposed to be happy you're starting to give orders to everyone?"

Nugs drank his water from the bottle.

Trahn was thinking how it was just more bullshit, but maybe the Canadians were finally starting to wake up. Shit, bound to happen someday. He remembered getting off the plane in Canada, just a kid. Called them the boat people, but they left the boats behind in the Gulf of Tonkin. Canada, so generous to take them in. Trahn's father and his two uncles looking like scared refugees in front of the nice white people, got right to business doing exactly what they'd done back home. Pretty soon they had a nice little distribution network up and running. Didn't even have to kill that many people.

Now Trahn and his cousin were real players, importing heroin, sure, but they were also exporting weed. Had grow houses all over the province, starting to move further out too. Trahn had just been in this exact airport the week before, going out to Moncton, New Brunswick, to start buying up houses. He was amazed you could get a decent house there for a hundred grand, fifteen grand down. A quarter what it cost him in Toronto. He could run a dozen of those for eight months, a year, pull four or five crops out of each one, make a couple million bucks.

The immigrant dream come true.

Now he said to Nugs, "These guys come in from Montreal, they're going to raise the price across the board?"

"Just think of it as us raising the price."

"Greedy bastards. We've got a good thing going here, Nugs. It's quiet. You start pulling shit like this, it's going to explode."

Nugs said, so.

"You think you can just do this?"

"You think we can't?"

Trahn didn't say anything. It was clear, get on board or get out of the way. He knew, like everybody else, these guys had so many hangarounds, so many punks wanting to join their club, they could get them to do anything. He'd never been too sure about Nugs, always seemed like every other rich Canadian he'd ever met, just happened to be in the right place at the right time. Americans needed trees for paper, Canada had billions of them. World needed wheat, hey, look. Coal, nickel, oil, fucking uranium, you name it. Next up, water. Assholes always acting like they did so much, they fucking tripped over it. Trahn would like to see how these fat white bastards did in a rice paddy, a fucking bamboo fishing boat in a typhoon. See how rich they got then.

He said, "Your cut going up?"

"No, same percentage."

"What did Colucci say?"

Nugs said, "Danny, you know I'm going to talk to you first, give you the heads-up."

"Right, what did he say?"

"Don't worry about it."

"Change anything at the ports?"

Nugs drank some more water and said the ports were solid, they'd stay the same. "And the cops stay away from your houses."

Fucking veiled threats all over the place. Trahn thinking, it was so easy for these guys to buy off cops. He said, "Yeah. I heard your trial's getting delayed. Some problem with the witness."

Nugs said, yeah, some problem. Then he said, "Look, Danny, we been doing business for years, you and me. We're going to be doing business for a lot more years. It'll work out. It'll be very profitable for us."

"Sure."

"Just have to get everybody on board, on the same page."

"Right." But Trahn knew somebody had to go down to show everybody. Somebody had to be a very public example.

It's what he would have done.

CHAPTER **16**

SHARON SAID, "SO YOU CAN DELIVER two hundred pounds a
month, four hundred grand."

Ray said that sounded about right.

Sharon scratched her ankle, her long red nails leaving white
lines on the skin, and Ray said she shouldn't do that.

"Oh yeah? You ever wear something for a year?"

"I thought it was six months?"

Sharon thinking, imagine that same guy taking it off, expecting another hand job. She said, "So, there's interest."

"I figured there would be." Ray drank some of his beer,
sitting in the bar on Lake Shore West, a neighbourhood that
still had its own personality and felt fifties. Three-storey apartment buildings still called "efficiency units" and mom-and-pop
restaurants. The forty-storey condos were getting closer to the
lakefront though, and almost all of the old motels were gone.
Pretty soon any memories that this was where people stopped
on their way from Niagara Falls or Buffalo would be completely
gone.

Sharon said, "If you can deliver to the States."

"I told you, no problem."

She looked at him, this guy showed up out of nowhere with two hundred pounds a month to deliver anywhere. "Could you deliver something else?"

"Like what?"

Sharon, thinking on her feet, never knowing where this kind of contact could lead, saying, "What do you care? Put it in with the other product."

It was the middle of the afternoon. The bar they were in was empty. They were sitting in a booth, sunlight coming in through tiny windows.

Ray said, "Sure," and Sharon was thinking how this was all too easy.

The bartender, only other guy in the place, was sitting on a stool reading a magazine. Sharon picked up her empty glass and then decided she didn't want to stay here for another gin and tonic. The music playing was that old Foot in Coldwater song, "Make Me Do Anything You Want," always got a lot of play because it was Canadian content.

She said, "Okay, good. When can you do it?" She expected him to give her another one of his annoying answers, really piss her off, saying, whenever you want, something like that, but he didn't.

He said, "I'd like to do two shipments at once."

"Why?"

"Because I can. Four hundred grand doesn't seem like that much. Eight would be better."

She thought, wow, he's not even asking for something to move the other product. She was thinking how even with the damned EM off her ankle she was still trapped. She was seeing

Richard, not some kid from Montreal anymore but an honest-to-God businessman taking over the whole country. She knew they'd get rid of this guy, find out his supplier, and take it over. Take over his delivery system, whatever it was.

She said, "How often you think you can do this?"

"Make a delivery? I can go back and forth to the States once a week. The supply takes longer."

She said she knew about the supply, how long it takes. She said, "You grow it yourself?"

"What difference does it make?"

Sometimes he was the dumbest shit she ever met and then he seemed to know when to shut up. Sharon wished she knew something more about this guy. She pushed her empty glass aside, held his hand on the table, and said, "Hey, Ray, you married?"

"Why, you never slept with a married man?"

"Never say never. I'm just wondering."

"Who you're getting in bed with?"

"We've been to bed," she said. "Now we should get to know each other."

"Yeah, I was married. I was married for fifteen years."

"Any kids?"

"No."

Sharon was nodding, listening to him, looking for a way to get him to open up, and then he just told her. Told her how he was born in Rogers City, Michigan, his father a captain on lakers, those big freighters on the Great Lakes, and how he started working them as soon as he got out of the Army. Worked his way up fast, his family connections doing things for him, he had an older brother who worked on the lakes too, and a sister who worked in the office, but she was in Arizona now, married to some rich guy twenty-five years older than her. His brother was dead, had a heart attack in a hotel room in Las Vegas. Ray said he got divorced about a year after his brother died.

Sharon asked if it was because he went through a midlife crisis, and he said not so much him, his wife.

"I guess I got a little moody, you know, like you do when you turn forty and people close to your age start dropping dead, but Jenny, my wife, she wanted some big changes."

"She live in Michigan?"

"She did then. I thought she'd never move away from her family, she's got a bunch of sisters and they all have kids. Jenny was the perfect aunt. Then, I don't know, she got a little pissed at me, but mostly she started thinking her life was passing her by." He looked at the empty bottle of Bud Light on the table and said, "She's in Florida now, Orlando, cleaning pools and partying."

"You didn't want to go to Florida?" Sharon still held his hand on the table.

"Jenny said I could work at Disney World, drive the ferry, or maybe get a fishing boat, take rich guys out." He shook his head, and Sharon said she knew what he meant, spend all day as the help, sucking up to guys think they're something special.

Ray said, yeah. He said, "The only thing I really knew was the laker business."

And then Sharon saw it. She said, "Oh, right, so now you can deliver to the States. Duh, I feel like an idiot."

Ray smiled. She thought, he really looks good for a guy his age, and then thought, shit, he's only, like, five years older than me and I look great.

He said, "A few years ago I got my own boat. I actually bought a tug and an old barge. The barge used to belong to a cement company here in Toronto and I went to Brazil to get the tug. That was a trip."

Now it was AC/DC playing, they seemed to be on all the time since they stole the show at that huge benefit concert, the one after SARS hit Toronto, when everyone was worried the tourists and Hollywood productions would never come back. Those guys got on stage just as the sun was going down—Bobbi was there with her friends, told her mother, "They fucking rocked, Mom, like you wouldn't believe." By the time the Stones came on a couple hours later, people were too tired to care.

Sharon said, "This isn't exactly where I expected to go when I could finally get out."

"Where do you want to go?"

"What did you say it was like in Brazil?"

Ray smiled again, said it was the Wild West. "Lot of money on the streets for a place so poor."

"Do you want to get another drink?"

Ray said they should get some off sales, he was staying just down the street. Sharon said you couldn't do that in Ontario, and Ray said, empty bar in the middle of the afternoon, cash in my wallet? So they took a few cold beers with them in the cab to the motel.

SHE LIKED TO BE ON TOP and it was a lot better now that the EM wasn't digging into his thigh. Ray hardly moved, looking up at her, her eyes closed, pinching her own nipples. He was thinking, yeah, this woman can make the deal if she thinks she's in it for the long term. She can take care of herself. Then she reached down between her legs and did just that.

When she was finished, she got on her hands and knees and said, why don't we finish like this? Ray said sure, and didn't she reach down and do herself one more time.

Ray sat up in bed after and lit a smoke while she went into the bathroom.

Coming out, naked, a glass of water in her hand, she said, "So you've never done anything like this before?"

He said, "Honey, I work the ports, I've been in more sleazy motel rooms than most hookers."

She sat on the bed, took the cigarette from him, and said, you know what I mean.

"Yeah." He figured he'd have to tell her the truth, and why not, he was telling her everything else. "Till I got divorced I was actually faithful to my wife."

Sharon took a drag on the cigarette, blew smoke at the ceiling. "When I'm with a guy," she said, "I'm only with that guy."

"Well, I never moved anything illegal on my boats before."

"Why not?"

He took the smoke back and took a drag. "By the time I got into a position where I could, where I didn't want to have a boss, I didn't want to deal with those guys. They look like they're used to being in charge."

Sharon said, you got that right. "So why now?"

He looked at her, sitting there on the edge of the bed, a couple of lines on her stomach but she was in her forties, it was hardly anything, and her tits were small but standing up nice. Really nice. She was looking right at him, waiting for an answer.

"I was going to lose the boat. I just couldn't get enough contracts to cover the payments. Hell, I've been living on it for a year, I lost my house, my car, everything." He smoked some more and then stubbed it out in the ashtray on the table beside the bed. "I figured I could get another year or two out of it and then I wouldn't even be able to cover the maintenance. I'd be fifty, what then? Sail relief for the big boys? I didn't think I could do it. So then Eddie was growing a few plants in the old pilothouse on the barge. He said we had all this space we weren't using."

Sharon shook her head and said, "And you're stopping at ports all the time."

"I just thought, you know, if we could sell a little extra, just enough to put us in profit, keep sailing for another year."

Sharon shook her head and then stopped suddenly, and said, "Wait a minute." She turned sideways on the bed and looked right at him and said, "You're growing it on the boat?"

"The barge, yeah. When Eddie read about that old brewery, turned into a giant grow room, he said we had more space than that."

Sharon was staring at him, a smile starting in the corners of her mouth, corners that were usually turned down. "That was Angelo Colucci's boys. They have the garbage-hauling contract, that's how it worked for them, the garbage trucks going to Michigan."

"I go to Michigan all the time."

She slapped his thigh, playful, and said, "You clever bastard." She was really smiling now.

"It was really Eddie. He said they had twenty thousand plants going in that old brewery. A good grow-op house is five hundred. We've got twenty-five thousand."

Sharon said, shit. "How do you harvest? I mean, I had maybe a thousand in the apartments, Zahra and Katie working full-time, and Bobbi and I had to help. It's a big job."

"Money takes care of everything."

"It sure does."

"Eddie said we could just leave the hatches open when the weather was good, and when it's not, we have a generator on the barge. Eddie worked it out with solar panels and now you can even get windmill generators at Home Depot."

Sharon said there was probably even some kind of government grant program for them, and Ray said he didn't know about that.

She said, "And you can move the boat anytime. And deliver anywhere."

Ray stood up, not quite as casual being naked as Sharon was, and got a beer from the sink in the bathroom he'd filled with ice earlier. He walked back into the bedroom and stopped to open the bottle, saying, "You see, it's a good deal."

"It's a very good deal," Sharon said. She started to look serious again.

Ray said, well, it seemed to make sense.

Looking up at him, Sharon said, it seems to excite you, too, and looked from his rising dick to his face.

Ray could feel himself blush. He said, "Something in here does," and she made a kind of "what me" face and he stepped closer, and she took him in her hand.

He was thinking this really could work, this Sharon leading the way.

He'd just have to make sure he didn't really fall for her, let those feelings get in the way when it was time for him to make his move.

The Marine at the front door said they couldn't bring their guns into the consulate and when Armstrong asked where they could check them, the guy said they could put them in a locker in the bus station across the street.

"It's what the last guys did."

Bergeron said, "Well, son, it's not what we're doing." So they waited in a lobby big enough to put another building in, and when Homeland Security Special Agent Jones finally came down the stairs, they went across University Avenue to a Second Cup.

Jones was a black woman, tall and thin, who looked like a movie star or an athletic model. Maybe a Halle Berry with long, thick straight hair past her shoulders. Bergeron wondered if Jones got the job of going out and meeting people in public because of the way she looked. Figured it sure couldn't hurt, give them a better image than the black SUVs pulling people over.

Sitting at the little round table, Jones said the latte was just as good as Starbucks.

Bergeron said, "Yeah, and you get change from a five."

"I've been looking at your money," Jones said, and Bergeron thought, here it comes, she's going to say it's colourful but what's it worth? Looks like pesos, something like that, but she said, "It's a lot easier to see what you've got in your wallet when they're not all the same colour."

Armstrong said that was true.

"Looks like play money though, might make it too easy to spend."

"Maybe if we had more of it," Armstrong said, and Jones smiled. Then she said her partner was out and it was clear she didn't want to talk about where that might be.

She wanted to talk about this Iranian guy, and the other guys he knew.

Armstrong said, what they do, these guys, these Iranians,

they go to businesses, usually places owned by other Iranians or Iraqis, guys from around there, and they set up with their card readers. "A few hours at a time, each place, every debit card gets read, and they clean out the accounts. Then they move on."

"These places, usually restaurants," Jones said.

"Yeah, or gas stations, corner stores. Guys working them too scared to say anything. Sometimes we can trace to where the cards were stolen, not stolen, the victims still have them, but read, the info stolen, and we can tell right away the guy working there or the owner of the place, he's just too scared to talk."

Bergeron couldn't tell if Special Agent Jones was twenty-five or forty-five, but she had a military background, he was sure of that. She drank her latte and said, "Yeah, we get that too. Used to be just in L.A., they called it Irangeles because there were so many Iranians, but now it's all over."

"And not just Middle Eastern guys."

Special Agent Jones nodded at Armstrong, thought for a minute, and said, "Are you Cree?"

"Ojibwa."

"I've got some Blackfoot in me, way back on my mother's side." Bergeron looked at her full, thick black hair, not curly at all, but he knew that might not have anything to do with heritage.

Armstrong said, "You from up north?"

She said, yeah, "Well, from all over, my family's always been military. My mom and dad both."

"What about you? Military?"

"Oh yeah. I was in the first Gulf War."

Bergeron watched these two flirt over Army training and military families. Finally he said, "So why are you interested in

Kumar Nekounam?" and Jones had to pull herself away from looking at Armstrong.

She said, "Because he's in jail in Maryland."

"I guess it's a common name over there."

"And he was shot during a robbery in Michigan. And he's under surveillance in Florida."

Bergeron said, "He's busy."

"His passport is, anyway."

"They all using the same one?"

"These guys pulling the frauds? They're almost organized. Looks like they take the paperwork from legitimate immigrants and doctor it, use it to get more identifications."

"But leave the names. Shit, they're stupid."

"Or they think we are. Or worse yet," Jones said, "we really are. Sometimes they change the spelling, just a letter or two so the computer doesn't pick it up and the human eye misses it."

"The English-speaking human eye."

"So we're trying to follow the money, see if it's just plain old crime for personal gain or if they're using it to finance terrorist activities."

They all drank their coffee and watched some kids, students probably, in their early twenties, come into the place talking in loud voices about the American Consulate across the street, saying it looked like an armed camp, big fence around it, "And those guys with guns."

Jones watched the kids get their coffees and walk out again. She looked at Armstrong and said, "I know, I know, none of the 9/11 guys came in through Canada."

"And we tipped you to the one crossing the border, on his way to do the L.A. airport."

She nodded and said, "You know, I've been here a day and a half, so I shouldn't say anything, but I have to admit, you people don't seem to realize what side you're on in all this."

Armstrong said, "We don't?" and Bergeron said, "Which side?"

"From what I can see, Canadians think the world loves them and hates us."

Bergeron and Armstrong both looked at her and she shook her head.

"I'm just saying, the truth is, to the rest of the world, you are us. Or just as bad. You've got troops on the ground in Afghanistan, and a lot of the corporate money we're protecting around the world is yours. Everywhere there's an oil rig, there's a little Canadian flag on it somewhere."

Bergeron said that was a little political for him.

"Yeah," Armstrong said, "we're just trying to find out if a guy jumped or was pushed off a roof."

Jones said, sorry, said she was just getting a little tired of being the ones putting their face in everything so everyone else could benefit from it.

Bergeron said that was a little out of their department.

She said, yeah, okay. "So did he jump or was he pushed?"

Armstrong said, "It looks like he might have been pushed by another guy. Another Iranian, maybe. Well, he might not have done it himself, he might have arranged for it. When the guy first went off the roof, no one recognized him. No one admitted it anyway. The building super didn't want to look at him, and when we made him, he was relieved it wasn't the guy he thought it was."

"But now," Bergeron said, "we find out another Iranian guy is missing, and we show his picture to the super, and this guy he knows. Very scared of him."

Armstrong took out two pictures and handed them to Jones. She looked at the one of Kumar Nekounam, the one from the morgue with his face mostly put back together, and said, no, she'd never seen him before.

"We haven't found anything about him. He entered the country legally, worked for a while, then dropped off the radar."

"This one though," Jones was saying, looking at the other picture, "this one's familiar."

"He in jail somewhere?"

She looked at Armstrong and said she wasn't sure. "I just know the face. I'll look him up and let you know."

Bergeron watched her keep talking to Armstrong and thought maybe she really would. He was pretty sure she'd be instructed not to share any information with anyone, the Americans being notorious for having five different investigations running at the same time about the same things, bumping into each other and spending more time keeping stuff away from other departments than getting the job done. DEA, FBI, CIA, ATF, state police, local cops, and now they'd added this Homeland Security.

But he saw the way this Jones was talking to Armstrong and he thought maybe she really would let them know. Maybe not. It was hard to tell.

ARMSTRONG SAID, "So what we have is an Iranian guy involved in some kind of international crime, pushed off a building, the whole top floor is grow rooms, by a woman meeting with a major biker from Montreal."

"Yeah," Bergeron said. "But what we really want to know is why do Burroughs and the narco squad want to keep us away?"

And that was it. Protecting someone, but who?

They were walking north on University towards College Street. Bergeron looked across the street and pointed at an old brick building with a cannon in front, and asked what it was.

Armstrong said, "Royal Military Club."

"You sure?"

"Of course I'm sure. I told you, it's the family business. I've got uncles who are members, they stop in for a drink when they come through town. Some of it, it's like a museum. In the basement, by the coat racks, they have weapons, from flintlocks right up to C16 automatics."

Bergeron said he had no idea that's what the place was.

"We'll see," Armstrong said, "if Jones is right and we have to take up sides, get even more involved."

They walked into the parking lot behind the hospital where they'd parked, and Bergeron said, "I hope it's not as hard to pick the right side as this thing. I mean, I can understand if narco is in somebody's pocket and they're just trying to protect them." Then he leaned against the door of the car, looked away from Armstrong, and said, "You hear what the fuck I'm saying?"

Armstrong, also not looking at his partner, said, yeah, I do. "It's almost understandable, you run an operation for years and some homeless immigrant gets himself killed, who cares? You want to lose the whole thing?"

"But that's not what we've got," Bergeron said. "And we know it. This chick, MacDonald, she might have pushed the guy, but who's she working for? Did the biker, what's his name,

Tremblay order it? He in bed with these Iranians? Kumar what's his name, he's not some guy just happened to be there."

Armstrong said, "Maybe we should just keep shaking the tree, see what falls out."

Bergeron unlocked the car and opened the driver's-side door. He looked over the roof at Armstrong and said, "That's a good idea. There's so many bad guys here, we've got to be able to get one of them."

CHAPTER **17**

RICHARD SAID, SO, WHAT'S IT like to be free, and Sharon said she'd let him know when she found out.

He shook his head at her, and smiled, and she thought, screw you, you bastard, but she smiled at him and said, "It feels good, Richard."

"Good. So now you want to be some kind of broker?"

She sipped her drink, just about finished it, and Richard picked up the pitcher of sangria, and refilled her glass. They were in a Mexican restaurant, Margarita's, on Baldwin, a short street that was almost all restaurants. When they'd parked and walked over, the whole area kind of wedged in between the U of T campus, Chinatown, and the art galleries on Dundas, Richard had said the concierge at his hotel called it Baldwin Village, so he was expecting more. He'd said, "They should close this street off like Prince Arthur in Montreal, let the restaurants have huge patios."

Sharon had said, "Not let cars on a street in Toronto? Are you kidding? This city is all about cars."

Richard said, "Yeah, but it's fucking hard to drive here."

Sharon said, "You're still in a hotel?"

"I'm only here on business a few days."

She looked at him and said, yeah, but she had an idea that Richard was going to like Toronto. She picked up another nacho chip and dipped it in the guacamole, some of the best she'd ever had, a whole avocado mashed in a stone dish, and took a bite. She said, "You've been here a while now."

"Yeah," Richard said, looking around the restaurant. "Getting to know the place, the feel of it. It's a big market here."

"An international hub."

"It's easier to deal with Europe from Montreal, but yeah, Toronto's practically American."

Right, Sharon thought, and you like that.

They were sharing a totopos, the hot metal plate covered with nachos, chorizo sausage, olives, sliced jalapenos, and jack cheese melted all over it. And that guacamole.

Richard said, "A good place to do business."

"Yeah." She watched him drink his sangria and thought it was like any other business, they send some VP out to get the branch offices in line. She wondered how long Richard would be happy taking orders from Mon Oncle Bouchard in Montreal.

He said, "So, you don't know where this guy's getting his supply, but you think he really can deliver to the States?"

"I'll tell you, Ricky, he's the smartest dumb guy I've ever met."

Richard leaned back in his chair, finished picking at his food, and looked at Sharon. Shit, calling him Ricky, like old times when she was the experienced woman and he was the kid.

Sharon said, "So, yeah, I really believe he can make the deliveries. That's what he's been doing his whole life."

"What?"

"It's really beautiful. He's got a laker boat."

"Like Canada Steamships?"

She drank some more sangria and said, "Small time. Just him, just one boat. He used to work for one of the big companies, an American one, I think, but got laid off. Apparently lots of those guys are."

"Them and everybody else."

"Some industries are better than others," she said, "when it comes to recession."

Richard smiled and said, yeah.

"Anyway, he's been in the business a long time, and he got himself a boat and a few contracts, salt from Goderich, iron-ore pellets, stuff like that, but it's not really enough to make him any profit, barely enough to keep him going."

Richard said, "Interesting."

"Yeah. So he's running all over the lakes, he figures why not ship something more profitable."

"He could move tons."

Sharon said, "Yeah, I guess," but was thinking, no, Richard, you could move tons. This guy can barely move a few pounds without everybody in town knowing about it. "So, that's his offer."

"But where's he get his supply?"

Sharon took a bite of sausage and shrugged. "Don't know."

Richard nodded, drank, and said, "You telling me, with all your feminine wiles you couldn't find out?"

Sharon thought, feminine wiles, where'd you get that shit?

But she just shrugged and looked him in the eye. Hoping he'd go for it and not press the issue. She could already feel her stomach getting twitchy and it wasn't Montezuma's revenge. Her knee was bouncing up and down under the table.

"Okay, truth is he is his own supply."

Richard leaned forward, like he expected her to whisper. Shit. She said, "His boat's the supply. I mean, what is a laker boat but a giant empty space? It's huge, the cargo hold is four hundred feet long, divided into four sections. He fitted a couple of them out like Angelo's brewery."

And Richard, he just sat there, calm, looking at her, thinking about it. She started to realize how people could have been fooled by Richard, thinking he was dumb, or slow, just sitting there most of the time not saying anything, but she could see him taking it all in, considering. She figured Mon Oncle had taught him well. Those two guys, she wasn't surprised they were taking over the whole country.

Then Richard said, "That is pretty good," and she said, no shit.

Richard said, "It's better than a fucking tunnel," and they both laughed a little, thinking about those guys in B.C., some town on the U.S. border, Abbotsford or some shit, bought land on both sides and dug a tunnel. They got caught, their suspicious behaviour giving them away, cops saying they'd never seen dope dealers break a sweat before.

"Yeah, he's got a history, this guy. His boat's been on the lakes for years, no one even notices it anymore."

"Someone'll notice." Richard didn't look too happy. "I don't know."

Shit, she couldn't tell what he was thinking. Richard was

never one to take too many chances, she knew that. It was why people thought he had no ambition, he never seemed to step up. Of course, it might also explain why he was still here, wearing a twelve-hundred-dollar watch and thousand-dollar shoes.

But for Sharon, it was worth the risk. Nothing to lose.

She said, "Ray said you have a lot of options. He said you could unload at small ports, like Fort Howard or Cedarville, or even big places, like Detroit or Cleveland."

"Use the contracts he's already got?"

"That's right," Sharon said. "Taking salt from Goderich to Fort Howard, it's in Wisconsin. Hell, you could unload to smaller boats in the middle of fucking Lake Michigan, let them bring it in."

Richard thought about that, and Sharon thought, good, he's still interested. He said, "He set this up himself? Some amateur, no history, goes big like this?"

"Yeah." She thought, shit, yeah, maybe not. Maybe those stragglers, those Lone Gunmen up in Sarnia and London who hadn't patched over. Maybe Ray was actually working for them and there was some kind of falling out. She really didn't want to be in the middle of these guys falling out. Shit, now she was seeing why Richard wanted her out front on this.

Richard said, "But it's not a bad idea, it's something we'd like to look into." He drank a little more and said, "But maybe not just as buyers. This supply and delivery system together, it looks interesting."

Sharon thought, shit, you really are taking over. "You want to buy him out completely?"

"I'm thinking," Richard said, "that might be possible."

Sharon said, okay, I'll talk to him, see what he says. "What kind of money are we looking at?"

Richard smiled and said, we? Then he said, "Guy's looking at doing four hundred a month, almost five million a year? Maybe we'll pay him for the whole year, buy his boat, and send him on his way."

Sharon said, "I can talk to him about that."

"I bet you can."

She shook her head, looking around the restaurant, maybe five other people in the place, thinking, look at us now. Seems like yesterday we were sitting in that place, Picasso, upstairs from Les Amazones in Montreal, eating souvlakis and poutine after a long shift of table dancing, looking forward to a big party out at the house out in Candiac. Spending every cent we made the day we made it, not giving a shit about the future. Richard, and Pierre, and Mon Oncle, and the boys, shit, she thought they were so cool then, actually riding big Harleys and not afraid of anybody.

Looking at Richard, she realized he still wasn't afraid. It was just now he could talk about a five-million-dollar deal like it was dime bags in the old days. She was pretty sure Ray would go for it. Or, she was pretty sure she could talk him into it, he was a man after all.

She'd just have to find a way to get her cut.

Or maybe get it all.

THE CRIME SCENE GUY stood up in the garbage bin, bright blue rubber gloves on both hands, plastic suit covering his whole body, puffy plastic hat, and said, "Yeah, it's a foot, part of the leg," and held up a torn-open garbage bag. "All below the knee, no thigh at all."

Bergeron said, okay, thanks.

Cruickshank pushed past him with a camera, telling the guy in the garbage bin to hold still, for Christ's sake.

They were in an alley behind a strip mall in Scarborough, a place that was built in the fifties and was all mom-and-pop restaurants and hardware stores back then, even a fish-and-chips place flying the Union Jack, but now was completely Chinese and South Asian: restaurants, grocery stores, an aquarium store, even a bar that showed nonstop kickboxing from Thailand on its big screen.

Bergeron said, "Jeannie's waiting for us," and he got in the passenger seat as Armstrong got in behind the wheel. It wasn't quite midnight, less than half an hour since they'd got the call from the surveillance team that the husband was driving around dropping off garbage bags. He'd dropped two, both behind restaurants, Chinese and Thai, and gone back home.

Armstrong said, "You having a nice date?"

Bergeron said, yeah, it was okay. "We went to this sushi place in Yorkville."

"You like sushi?"

"It's okay. I'm not really good with the chopsticks so it can be awkward on a date, you know?"

"Yeah."

Bergeron was thinking he didn't need any extra nerves, been so long since he was on a date, but it had been going really well. "I expected it to be really snobby, you know? But the people in there, they were a lot younger than I expected."

"Could be young snobs," Armstrong said and Bergeron said, oh, yeah, I'm sure if we gave them the chance.

"But the place wasn't bad, the atmosphere, the attitude, it was okay."

"She didn't mind you had to leave early?"

They were driving further into Scarborough along Eglinton, away from downtown, the whole area going through a major change. It had been built in the fifties when there were factories and warehouses, when all the little houses were bought by young guys moving over from the U.K. or soldiers bringing back their war brides. Now, they were all dying off or moving out, and the next wave of immigrants was moving in, South Asian, Chinese, Tamil, Sri Lankan, some Jamaican. Along with the small houses, now there were a lot of twenty-storey apartment buildings and condos. The place was transient and it could go either way—people could settle down, make it a neighbourhood again, or it could be a stopping-off point, never get any character back. Too soon to tell.

"Kind of a relief, probably. You know, we're not kids, but neither of us really knows how to date anymore." If he thought about it much, Bergeron would admit he'd never really known how to date in the first place. "This way, we make plans to see each other again and there's none of that awkwardness at the end."

Armstrong turned off Eglinton into another strip mall parking lot. "So, you're going to see her again? She doesn't mind why you had to leave?"

"No, she didn't." And really she didn't. Bergeron didn't think there was much awkwardness at all during dinner. He didn't think Ruth was serious all the time, he just felt she was too smart to be light about everything. He didn't think either one of them felt they had to work too hard at being with each other. When he got the call, he told her he had to go and she seemed okay about it. As his daughter would say, she seemed like an actual grown-up. So he told her he was probably going to be up all night, processing the torso killer.

Ruth said she'd read about it in the paper, didn't know they'd even ID'd the victim. They walked to the parking lot off Avenue Road so she could get her brand-new Dodge Magnum station wagon, some kind of dark silver, the car Bergeron thought looked like a cool hearse with those small windows. And he said, yeah, the victim's transgendered sister gave them DNA, enough to get a warrant on the victim's husband. The guy's been under surveillance a few days, now it looks like he's dropping off the rest of the body. And Ruth had said, there's a whole world out there we don't see, isn't there? and Bergeron said, yeah. He was thinking, he'd usually have said something like, you don't want to see it, or better that you don't see it, something like that, but Ruth was straightforward, clear-eyed about it. No drama. He liked that.

He said he'd call her after it was done and he'd had some sleep, maybe they could go out again, and she'd said that'd be good.

Now he was sitting down at the donut shop across from another woman, this one in her thirties, her hair pulled back in a loose ponytail, wearing jeans and a hockey jacket, looking just like a suburban mom.

She said, "Patty's with him, he went straight home."

Armstrong said, "Okay, we'll go get him." He drank some coffee and then said, "You're looking good, Jeannie."

She said, "Yeah, well, I lost two hundred and thirty pounds," and Bergeron thought there was no way. He'd never seen her before in his life, but she couldn't be more than one-twenty and he didn't think she'd ever been much more than that. She looked at him and said, "I lost five pounds and I got a divorce."

Oh, well, in that case.

Armstrong said, "Good for you."

Jeannie drove the minivan and they followed in the Crown Vic, a few blocks south through some winding roads to a townhouse development. Jeannie stopped at a bus stop and the woman waiting there stood up.

Armstrong parked behind the minivan and the four of them stood on the corner. The woman who'd been waiting for the bus, Constable Patty King, pointed out the unit on the end of the townhouse, said the guy had parked in the driveway and gone in.

Bergeron asked if there was a back door and Jeannie said, yeah, leads to a completely fenced-in backyard. They had a camera set up there, no one came out.

"Okay, let's go get this guy." Armstrong called it in and the backup patrol cars moved in, each end of the street. Armstrong and Bergeron knocked on the door and waited, and waited and knocked again, and finally the guy opened the door, saying, what the fuck do you want, and who the fuck are you, and they grabbed him and cuffed him right away. By then the patrol cars were in front of the townhouse, red lights turning.

Taking him out to the car the guy said, did that dickless bitch turn him in and Armstrong smashed his head into the roof of the car putting him in, thinking sometimes the job has perks.

A couple of uniformed cops took the guy to 52 Division and Armstrong went with them. Bergeron stayed and supervised the crime scene guys, going over the townhouse until the sun came up. The guy had killed her in the kitchen, it looked like, and done a half-assed job cleaning up. Then he'd cut the body into pieces in the garage. There was a brand-new reciprocating saw, the cardboard box still there, the blade covered in blood and snapped off. Bergeron figured the saw broke and the guy was too lazy to finish up right.

He wondered how much of it he'd be able to tell Ruth and thought probably quite a bit. He was looking forward to seeing her again.

THE NEXT MORNING, driving down Bay Street, Richard knew two things: he liked Toronto and he had to get out of his hotel.

The city just smelled of money. New, old, Canadian, American, there was money everywhere. But, as much as he liked hearing the stories about the movie stars who stayed at the Sutton Place for the film festival, he had to get out. The bellhops were great, mostly Latin American kids with stories of how many guys were in Lindsay Lohan's room, how many chicks in Colin Farrell's. Who threw up what in what hallway. It was great, it was Hollywood.

But last night, just as he was trying to get to sleep, Richard hears this banging on the wall, slapping and crying. He knocked on the wall and heard a guy say, go to sleep, asshole. So, Richard, he got up and walked right out into the hall, flicking open that brass thing that flips over for an extra lock to keep the door from closing, and he walked up to the door the banging came from, and he knocked.

A guy opened the door, younger than Richard, maybe thirty, very stylish but too dramatic, saying, "Look pal, this is none of your fucking business, go back to your room."

On the way down the hall in his bare feet and boxers Richard thought he was just going to tell the guy to keep it down, but then, looking at him, the asshole standing there in his Hugo

Boss suit, his tie still pulled tight, and looking past him to the woman, good-looking chick no more than twenty-five, her mouth covered in blood, one black eye, tears and makeup dripping everywhere, he just punched the guy.

Busted his nose, you could hear it all down the hall. Blood all over the place. Richard hit him again a little lower, busting his jaw, then he grabbed him by the tie and dragged him to the stairwell, bashing his head against the door as he opened it and threw the guy as far as he could. There was a landing five or six stairs down and the guy rolled around there, his hands over his face, moaning and crying.

Richard walked back to his room passing the open door, the woman backing in, and he said, "Close the fucking door." Back to his room and he was able to fall asleep right away in the quiet.

So now he was driving down Bay Street right into the financial centre of the city, of the country, and he was looking at condo buildings. He saw a sign for the new Toronto Trump Tower and thought that could be fun, living in one of Donald Trump's buildings, but it didn't look like they'd even started construction.

There were a whole bunch of buildings going up around the ACC, the condo development called Maple Leaf Place, and Richard thinking they might as well call it Loserville. Then he thought how the Leafs made more profit than any sports team and decided they won where it counted. Still, he could never live that close to where the Maple Leafs always lose in the playoffs.

He turned right onto Front Street and drove past the old train station, Union Station, and the Royal York Hotel, now called the Fairmont. Nice old buildings, too bad they weren't going condo. Like everything else downtown seemed to be. If it wasn't a brand-new building going up then old office buildings and warehouses were being turned into condos and lofts. Richard didn't know exactly what a loft was but it sounded too small for him.

Past the SkyDome, now called something else after some corporate sponsor but he couldn't remember which one, Richard saw a whole bunch of new high-rise condos going up. Some already finished. He seemed to think the last time he was in town, for those negotiations with the local bikers, guys practically giving Ontario away, there was a golf course here. Now there was a two-storey building with silver art deco letters across the top spelling out Presentation Centre. He pulled into the parking lot thinking, this town, can't just call it a sales office, and hoped they had something ready to move into facing the lake.

The sexy woman in her twenties, wearing a low-cut top and a miniskirt, said, "I'm really sorry about this wait, it'll only be about twenty minutes," and the older woman said, "Could you do us both at the same time?"

Then she looked at Richard and said, "That didn't sound right."

He said, that's okay, I know what you meant, but he didn't really. She was older than the sales rep, but still probably not forty yet, and she was looking at him playful, letting him know she was interested.

The young woman, "Leah" printed on her card, said, "If you don't mind, it would be a lot quicker?" Like everybody else her age, Richard thought, she says everything like it's a question.

They were standing in the lobby of the Presentation Centre, just an open room with a few leather couches, a giant fish tank built into the wall, and a counter with a receptionist behind it. The receptionist was Chinese, barely spoke English, and the form they gave Richard to fill out asked where he heard of the development and offered choices: *Sing Tao Daily,* some other Chinese name, the *International Herald Tribune,* or referred by friends/business associates.

The other woman, the only customer besides Richard, said, "I don't mind."

So Leah stepped up to the chrome doors and they slid open like something on *Star Trek*.

Leah started right into her sales pitch, telling them the development was entering Phase Two, the north tower was under construction and would be ready in the spring of '08, the south tower in the fall. There was a model of the area laid out on a big table, looked like a kid's train set without the train. SkyDome, Richard saw it said Rogers Centre now, the CN Tower, Spadina, Queen Street, and dozens of buildings. The ones that weren't part of the development were grey boxes, but the Pacific Concord ones were neon blue and red. Leah used a laser pointer to explain as she went through her pitch.

What Richard noticed was how self-contained the whole place was going to be. Thirty acres of prime downtown real estate. Nine condo towers, all over forty storeys, and rows of townhouses four storeys high made a ring around the outside. The amenities buildings with gyms, and pools, and grocery stores, an elementary school, and a huge park were all inside. It was like its own little city.

And that was pretty much the way Leah was pitching the place. Richard listened a little and looked at the pictures on the walls.

And at the other woman, the other customer. She had blonde streaks and was wearing tight, faded Levis, leather boots with spike heels, a leather jacket, and a red silk blouse. Richard figured she could be in some kind of business like fashion or makeup, or she could just be spending her husband's money.

But what Richard started to finally notice was that the whole place was really Chinese. All the other sales reps and the other customers, the people in the pictures on the walls and the stack of brochures on the table. He realized Leah was the only English sales rep the place had.

She said, "Are you looking for a one bedroom or two?"

The blonde said, "All by myself, I only need the one," and looked at Richard.

He said, "Yeah, just one."

Leah continued her sales pitch, telling them about all the services, including a full-service bank, four teller stations, financial planning, full brokerage services, and high-speed, fibre-optic connectivity throughout the premises. Then her phone beeped and she said, "Excuse me, I'll be right back."

The woman said, "My dad used to say, 'I wonder what the poor people are doing?' They're paying 60 percent interest and an arm and a leg to get cheques cashed at those pretend-a-banks because no one will open branches in their neighbourhoods, that's what they're doing."

Richard thought, yeah, but we do pretty good with those cheque-cashing places. Started out as just another way to launder money and now they're making a profit, but he didn't say anything.

She said, "They have one of these developments in Vancouver too," and Richard said, oh yeah.

"Yeah, it looked okay, so now that I'm relocating here, I thought I'd check it out."

Richard said he was relocating, too.

"Wow, what a coincidence. Did you go through a nasty divorce too?"

"No. My wife died."

She looked really worried, started apologizing right away, but Richard said, that's okay. "Really. It was a couple of years ago."

"Well, still, I'm sorry. Not that many happy marriages these days, it's a shame to see one end too soon."

"Yeah."

"Oh wow, sorry. Look, my name's Kristina Northup." She held out her hand and Richard shook it, still looking around the presentation centre, and told her his name was Richard Tremblay.

She said, "Are you from Quebec?"

"Yeah, Montreal."

"I love Montreal."

Richard said, yeah, everyone says that. "I have a place there too, a condo. It's on the Lachine Canal, used to be an old factory, fifteen-foot ceilings, huge windows, you can see Atwater Market, Mount Royal."

Kristina said she'd like to see that.

Richard said, yeah, it's nice.

They looked at each other and then she said, "I was thinking, I don't really know anyone in Toronto, just business contacts, so maybe I shouldn't live somewhere so insular."

Richard said that could have its advantages.

Kristina said, "Do you know a lot of people in town?"

"Like you said, business contacts."

"What business are you in?"

He looked at her and said, "A few different ones."

She said, oh yeah? Then, "There's another development on the other side of downtown, called the Distillery District, it's renovated old factories, cobblestone streets, art galleries, restaurants. There's some condos going in there I thought I'd check out."

Richard said, oh yeah.

"We filmed there a couple of times. I'm a film producer?" Like a question, like Leah was talking. Richard figured it was her way of acting young, of flirting. He said the movie business sounded interesting and listened while she told him about it, what made the Canadian movie business so challenging, and he wondered how long it would take her to ask if he ever considered getting into that business. She said something about tax advantages and he knew she was close.

He said, "Hey, if there's decent restaurants at this distillery place, maybe we could have lunch, look at some condos after," and she said that sounded like a great idea.

They didn't wait for Leah to come back, they just walked out to the parking lot and Richard said he'd follow across town.

Kristina, getting into her Volvo SUV, said, "I'll drive slow," and Richard said he'd be okay.

Driving across town on Lake Shore, underneath the expressway, Richard was thinking this whole Toronto thing is going to be okay. There was still a lot of work to do, Angelo and Danny Trahn would get on board, that was huge, and the stragglers had to be taken care of and the cops had to be brought in line. The Homicide guys hanging around Sharon were a problem, but Richard and his boys had enough inside contacts to know what was coming. The cop situation would be fine. They'd get Sharon, her sailor would get taken care of, and Richard would land on top.

He was thinking maybe he would look into the movie business, could be fun.

CHAPTER **18**

SERGEANT SAGAR LOOKED AT the guy's face, covered in blood, his stringy long hair all over the place, and said, yeah, that's him. "Charles Davidson. Chuck, or Chucky."

Price said there wasn't much left of his face, was she sure?

Looked like he was shot in the back of the head, close range, and then maybe once more when he hit the floor.

Sagar said, "Yeah, that's him. He was with one of the small gangs, got patched over, had to start again as a hangaround."

"Doesn't look like it worked out too well for him."

The crime scene guys were waiting to get going, standing out front smoking. It was cold, they could all see their breath, standing all over the front lawn, the house like every other one on the street in quiet Scarborough. Except inside, it was filled with a hundred pot plants and a dead body.

The sun was just barely coming up when a guy, Karim Singhdal, and his son, delivering papers to the house next door, saw the front door was open a couple of inches. The guy, still standing by the first cop car that arrived, wanted to just keep going, they could tell, but the kid, probably ten years old, he went right up to the door and saw Chuck. He made his old man call it in. Something for show and tell.

McKeon said, "They didn't even take anything."

Sagar said, no.

There was no furniture in the house at all. The whole place was covered in poly, the floor, the walls, the windows, everything. The front windows had plywood boxes built around them with lights inside and curtains, fitted right over the windows. Timers turning them on and off. The walls were covered in tin foil and the whole room was filled with plywood tables stacked two high like bunk beds, with four-hundred-watt lights on tracks to move them back and forth across the room like the sun.

And every inch of table was covered with marijuana plants— a thick, verdant jungle.

McKeon said, "Looks like a good job." She looked at Sagar.

Sagar glanced at Loewen and he nodded, so she looked back at McKeon and said, "Probably Danny Trahn. He's got hundreds of these houses. Practically sells the setup as a franchise."

She poked at a hose running from a plastic garbage can filled with sixty litres of nutrient to the upper beds, where it hooked into a Little Giant underwater pump. "The big-box hardware stores are perfect for this."

Price said, "Yeah, and garden centres. I heard there was one, not too far from here, guy could place an order for a four-hundred-square-foot grow room and the store would put everything together you need."

"I'm surprised," Sagar said, "they didn't deliver."

In the upper corner of the ceiling there was a large squirrel-cage exhaust connected to ducts running the length of the room and out into the hall through jigsawed holes in the walls.

"And still," Loewen said, "none of the neighbours noticed."

Sagar said it wasn't as bad as you'd think. "They come and go in the night. The place looks normal from the outside."

"Yeah," Price said, "and if you see something and make a call to us, everybody knows where you live."

Sagar said it used to be they blew through a house like this in six months. "Pretty much destroyed it inside, mould, water damage, all kinds of shit. Now, they're taking better care, getting more crops."

"Unless they miss a payment."

Sagar looked at McKeon and said, "Maybe. We're hearing rumours about Chuck's bosses, but there wasn't any trouble with Danny Trahn."

Loewen said, "You sure this is one of his?"

"Pretty sure."

"So," Price said, "we're going to have a war."

Sagar stepped closer to the door to get some air, it was stinking hot in the place, and said, "Seems like it."

McKeon said, "It could be personal though, or internal business."

"Doubt it," Sagar said. "Don't usually find those bodies, do we?"

"Shit."

They stepped out of the house onto the front lawn and the crime scene guys went in, one of them saying, "Who's counting the plants?" Price thanked Sagar for coming out to ID the body, and she said, no problem. Price looked at Loewen and said, "You didn't have to come out," and Loewen shrugged, not much to say.

Price said, "It's good we've got this interdepartmental co-operation."

Sagar said, "Yeah, well, you wait till you see the Mountie you have to sleep with," and McKeon said, "Do I get Lafleur? He's hot."

The coffees showed up and they leaned against the car, watching the crime scene guys going in and out. McKeon's phone rang and after she said something to her husband about the baby, she stepped away for a little privacy.

Price asked Sagar how she was doing and she said, "Shit, does everybody know?"

"Not everybody. Not anybody really."

Sagar nodded, said, yeah, but she was pissed. A huge investigation, going after the bikers for over a year, made some decent arrests and then their best witness, hell, their only witness, kills herself while she's at a safe house. Sagar's witness.

Price said, "You sure nobody else was there?"

"Pretty sure. No signs to indicate. She was depressed."

"Convenient though."

Yeah, Sagar thought, but also for me. If something had happened to the witness, Sagar would look like the obvious leak. Suicide was a lot better.

Loewen said, "How come you didn't catch it, aren't you and Bergeron the suicide kings?"

Price looked at him, knowing he was just trying to deflect the flak away from his girlfriend, and decided not to ride him. He said, "Rahim and Lou got it. No reason to think it's anything else." Then he said, "Unless the lab report has something," and he looked right at Loewen.

Loewen said, no, didn't look like it. Shit.

Then Price just couldn't help it, he said, "Shouldn't narco be all over this?"

Loewen said there were only a few thousand grow ops in the GTA, the Greater Toronto Area, and who knows in the suburbs past that. "We can't cover them all."

Price said, "No, yeah, I understand. Lucky for the shooter you weren't covering this one."

And let that hang there for a minute. Lucky.

Loewen looked at the ground and kicked the dirt.

Price said, "It's okay, Loewen."

But it was getting to them all.

McKeon came back putting her phone away. She looked at Sagar and said, "Have you got any kids?"

"No. Not yet." She glanced at Loewen, but he found something to do over by the forensics van, and Price walked back to the house.

"This working and having kids is tough."

Now it was just Sagar and McKeon leaning on the car, sipping coffee.

Sagar asked if it was the shifts, maybe it would be better straight days, McKeon could get transferred to something like that.

"Maybe. I think it might just be the job. Any job. You know, for a while there we never even considered the job."

Sagar said, "What do you mean?"

McKeon said something about how they fought for so long

for the right to work, you know, "And just to get the jobs. And I don't think anyone ever put the jobs themselves under the microscope before, you know, never compared them to anything."

"To what?"

"That's just it. We always just thought a career was good. Any career was good, but we never thought about choices."

"Who's we?"

"Women."

Sagar said, "Oh, right." Then, "You want to stay home with a baby?"

"I don't know, I just think we never thought about it, you know? Like we always just thought no matter what the job was, it was the top goal. My husband, he's been home with the baby six months and he hasn't even looked into daycare."

"So?"

"I don't know, he says maybe he'd rather stay home and babysit his own kid, than go to work and babysit a whole movie crew."

"Yeah, well, if you can afford it."

"It just seems weird, it's just usually we always think our careers are the most important things."

And Sagar thought, yeah, well, as long as they're going good. If her witness did get thrown off the balcony and this war heated up, she'd likely find herself riding a Ski-Doo in June someplace north of the treeline.

Price came back, saying, "She talking about jobs again?"

McKeon said, "Nathaniel's throwing up again," and Price rolled his eyes.

He said, "Look, Maureen, babies throw up, it's not always a big deal. MoGib can handle it."

"I'd like to be there."

"Yeah," Price said, "you'd like to be there or you wish MoGib wasn't."

"What's that supposed to mean?"

Price just stared at her and she said, what?

"What? What do you think?"

"Yeah, what?"

"You think he's a man without a job."

"So?"

He looked at her, raised his eyebrows.

McKeon said, "Oh, that's such bullshit, Andre. I still think he's a man."

"Without a job."

Sagar said, "Look. You don't have a job like his, you're not babysitting movie stars. You're going to find out who killed Chucky, put him in jail. But you can understand your husband would rather take a few years off, raise his kids. He can go back to work later. It's not such a big deal for him, men didn't have to have movements and marches so they could get the jobs."

Price said, "That's what I've been saying," and McKeon said, "No, it's not."

"Well, it's what I meant."

Loewen had been standing by, listening, and now he said, "Who did kill Chucky?"

Sagar, glad to be back to business, said, "One of Danny Trahn's guys, I guess. One of his not very bright guys, I'd say, left the body right here."

Loewen said, "You don't think someone dumped him here so we'd think that?"

"They don't give a shit what we think. They only care what the boys from Montreal think. Letting them know they aren't rolling over."

Price said, "This is going to be fun."

And Sagar looked at McKeon and said, "Wouldn't miss it for the world," and McKeon smiled a little.

Sagar thinking, no one feels guilt like a mother.

SHARON STARTED TO CLIMB on top, turning her back to him and saying, "You like the reverse?" and Ray said, not as much, so she turned back around and lowered herself down. She was thinking she'd just heard Jerry Hall shilling for some Viagra rip-off, saying she'd been with older men and younger men, and with the older ones the problem they had could be treated medically, but the younger ones wanted you to listen to Coldplay and there was no treatment for that.

And here was Sharon moving back and forth on top of a guy in his late forties, didn't need any treatments and he liked Gretchen Wilson. And he stroked the inside of her thighs, moved his rough hands up and down slow from her knees to her pubes, driving her crazy.

It started out, she just wanted to put him in a good mood, but by the time they were finished she was feeling pretty good too.

She said, "You want a beer?" and he said, "I love it when a woman says that."

"That's what you love about me?"

He was lying back, his head on the pillow, his eyes half-closed, and he said, "Among other things."

She got up and went to the fridge, coming back with two bottles of Steam Whistle, saying they were the only beers left, you need an opener. She put one bottle on the table beside the bed, rested the cap of the other on the edge, and gave it a smack.

Ray said, "That's getting me hard again."

She handed him the bottle and said, "The way to a man's heart."

He sat up, took a long drink, and said, "You know, for most women that's just a stop on the way to the wallet."

Sharon smacked the top off the other bottle and said, "If I was most women, you wouldn't be here."

True enough.

She sat on the edge of the bed and put a hand on his thigh. She noticed he wasn't kidding. She thought, Jerry Hall should see this.

He said, "But we should talk about it."

She thought, yeah, now we're in the mood. "It's a good deal, Ray. The thing is, people want to know where you get your supply."

"Who cares?"

"Well, with no supply you're just some guy with a boat."

"But I've got the supply. I showed you."

She kept stroking his thigh and she said, "But you can see where, you know, you just show up out of nowhere. You didn't start out dealing, small time, working your ass off, servicing customers, getting a couple of suppliers, working harder, getting bigger and bigger."

He said, "We talking about me or you?"

She squeezed his leg. "People want to know."

"But they understand I can't tell them."

She went back to stroking. She was amazed he could carry on a conversation, his dick bobbing up and down like that. Most guys she knew, in that state, a naked woman rubbing their leg, could only think one thing.

She said, "What if the supply was part of the deal?"

"What do you mean?"

"What if," she put her beer on the table and put both hands on his thigh, "someone wanted to buy out your whole operation."

He kept looking at her and she was sure he was still thinking business. Bastard. But she was starting to really like him. She'd have to watch out about that.

She said, "What if someone made an offer to buy your boat, and the legit contracts you've got, and the contacts you've got for the dope? Take over the whole thing."

She was looking him right in the eye, waiting for him to blink, but he didn't. He just looked like he was thinking about it and he said, "It would have to be a pretty good offer," and she thought, all right.

Then she thought, that was quick, though.

But it was the right answer.

"A really good offer. A year's worth of income. You were talking four hundred grand a month, twelve months a year, that's nearly five million bucks."

He said, "It's not twelve months a year, there's the winter lay-up. It's eight or nine months."

"Still, let's call it five million bucks."

"Yeah, let's."

She pulled her legs up on the bed and curled them under her ass, sitting right beside him, by his chest. She put her hands on his pecs.

"Say you get half upfront."

"Okay."

"And the other half after the first successful delivery."

"Do they want me to deliver?"

"I don't think so, I think they can get their own guy."

"Certified captain?"

"I think so."

Ray nodded, like it wasn't the best idea he'd ever heard, but it could work. He said, "And they get all the ownership—the tug, and the barge, and the contracts."

"And the supplier."

"And I get two and a half million bucks. American."

She said, yeah, honey, "It's always American dollars."

"Okay."

"And," she said, "you get two and a half more when it works."

He said, you think I can get that in writing? And she said, what about honour among thieves, and he smiled and said, "You're so cute."

She thought, okay, good. She still couldn't figure this guy— at all—but she was glad he wasn't so stupid he thought he'd be getting the rest of the money. Still, two and a half million bucks was pretty good.

She said, "What are you going to do with it?"

"With what?"

"The money."

"I don't know, I don't have it yet."

"But you must have some idea."

He said, yeah, I guess. "I've had some ideas." He sat up, leaning on his elbow and looked at her. "This guy you're dealing with, he has a boat, right?"

"One of them does," thinking Nugs's big sailboat.

"You know how big it is?"

"I know they've had some big parties on it, couple dozen people."

"It's in good shape."

"I guess, yeah. Couple of years ago he let some rich kids, wanted to be tough guys, sail it to Cuba."

Ray said that sounded good.

Sharon remembered those kids, four of them, three guys and a chick, they were going to bring back cocaine. They came back with nothing and Nugs took their brand-new cars their parents had bought them. She said, "Good for what?"

"Maybe make it part of the deal, maybe trade boats."

"On top of the money?"

Ray nodded, said, "The two and a half million and the boat."

Sharon said she had no idea how much the boat was worth but she thought Nugs was getting tired of it. "He doesn't use it as much anymore, said it has a bad vibe." And she knew Nugs was going to trial in a couple of months. He might want to get rid of the boat before he lost it in some kind of proceeds-of-crime thing.

Ray said, "It's too late in the season to sail south like that, but you could get to Kingston or Montreal. Maybe Halifax or something. I don't really know that part of the country."

Sharon said, "I do."

He looked at her and she thought about saying that sounded good, the two of them taking off, but she wasn't sure it was an offer.

She wanted it to be, though.

And then she had to get that idea out of her head. There was no way these guys would watch him and their money sail off into the sunset. With Sharon on board, too.

Ray said, "So, you think you can work this out?"

"Yeah, I think so."

"And you can just take your cut from the second half, the money we get on delivery."

She said, ha ha, you're funny.

And she saw he was still making Jerry Hall proud. She wrapped her long fingers around his dick and said, "You and I will work out my cut together."

And as she spread out beside him she felt like she really liked him, she liked being with him, this wasn't just negotiation.

She'd have to make sure that didn't affect her judgement.

CHAPTER **19**

Nugs was saying they should just take him out, just kill him.

Richard said, yeah, they could do that. "But do we really need to?"

And it was driving J.T. nuts. He'd thought Nugs was the one going soft, always worried about cops and other shit they'd taken care of, afraid to really step up. J.T. had thought Richard was the man, he was getting shit done, but now he wasn't so sure.

Nugs saying, "They pop one of our guys like this, no reason, we've gotta do something," and Richard saying, yeah, of course, but they had to be professional.

Richard saying, "What was Chuck doing there to begin with?"

Nugs—good for him, J.T. thought—started right away with, who gives a shit, no reason to take him out, none at all, and Richard didn't have much to say to that.

They were in a hotel room in a place up on Highway 7. When

J.T. was a kid, the place was two-lane blacktop north of Toronto. Now it was like downtown Chinatown, all kinds of office buildings and buffet restaurants, and the whole place pretty much Chink. Chink writing on the buildings, the storefronts in the malls, hell, J.T. could only tell what banks they were by the logos and the colours.

It looked like, if this bullshit went on much longer, he'd have to tell them he shot Chuck. Tell them he was putting together some cash, thinking about starting his own grow ops and that Chuck had said Danny Trahn was the man to see, could put the whole thing together, and J.T., like always, wanted to do it right fucking now, and Chuck, like always, had a million reasons not to get up off his fat ass.

Finally J.T. convinced him, just show me a house, show me the setup so I know what I'm talking about, and by the time they got there, Chuck, whining all the way, J.T. couldn't take it anymore. He was going to suck it up, just let it go, but when they actually got inside, Chuck not shutting up for a second, J.T.'d had all he could take.

Besides, he figured, if they were going to go to war with somebody, Danny Trahn, or the Italians, or these bikers out in Sarnia who weren't in line, or whatever, he didn't want to be standing beside a guy didn't have the balls for it. That was one thing J.T. learned in Afghanistan—the enemy's only half your problem, if that.

And now J.T. couldn't really tell how much of Nugs was an act. Richard seemed to get him calmed down and the other guys in the room, couple guys from the Brampton chapter, were ready to move on to other business.

Good enough, J.T. figured, we've got business. He was at the meeting to run the scanner that blocked any bugs or microphones. These guys had way better equipment than he'd ever seen in the Army.

Richard was saying, "The price increase is the beginning, we also have to change some territories."

The Brampton guys—they still looked a little like old-time bikers, big bellies and jeans, but they were working on it, one of them wearing a golf shirt—were on board. They were saying they had the manpower ready.

"That's good," Richard said.

Then one of the Brampton guys said, "But we didn't get the word this was national."

Richard said, "You're getting it now."

"From you?"

"Yeah, from me."

J.T. watched the room get tense again. There were a lot of things about the setup of this organization he really liked. You had a lot of independence, that was for sure. Once you were a full patch, as long as you kicked up your percentage, it was a great franchise. The thing was, though, the independence made it tricky to give orders from the top. Like the Army, he figured, the guys who thought they were in charge, working in offices ten thousand miles away, had very little say over what went down on the ground.

But these guys, Richard and the guys from Montreal, they'd built an organization that worked. They had chapters all over the world, and in Canada they had almost no competition. J.T. was impressed.

He was also impressed the way Richard was saying, "It's going to increase your territory at the wholesale level. You get access to more meth labs, more ports, even more manpower if you need it."

And J.T. knew the Brampton guys were all show. They wanted it too. They wanted it bad.

"Okay," Richard said. "We've got some work to do."

Everybody was on board and J.T. really liked that.

IT WAS A HUNTER MARINE 44 Deck Salon. A nice boat. Ray said with two people you could sail it anywhere in the world and Sharon said, "Okay, let's do it."

They were sitting in Bobbi's Mini in what looked like a gravel parking lot off a shipping channel down by the docks. The boat wasn't moored in a yacht club or the public area by the Lions Club. Sharon said Nugs and his boys owned a bunch of acres of the port lands they got through their crooked politicians and developers, hoping to score on the Olympics that never came. Now they were working on a world's fair or an expo, something like that.

"Besides," she said, "they had some parties, weren't exactly yacht club approved."

Ray said, "I bet."

"Nugs got this boat from someone owed him money. He took over the mortgage. I didn't know you could mortgage a boat."

"Oh yeah, you can do all kinds of things, if you can make the payments."

"So, if it's the offer they made, plus they throw this in, it's a deal?"

"Well, we can't very well just take their first offer, they won't respect us."

She looked at him sideways to see if he was joking and she couldn't tell. She said, "Uh-huh," and asked him, did he want to see the inside?

He said, "It's okay, I'm sure it's fine. Stainless steel appliances, Corian countertops, two bedrooms, and big plasma TV."

Sharon said, yeah, that's pretty much it. "Nugs had a new stereo put in, got these giant speakers. No MP3, though."

"How exactly is this going to work?"

Sharon tapped the wheel and nodded. Now she had that awful song, "Sailing," in her head. What was the guy's name, Christopher Cooper? Something like that, something about finding tranquility. She said, "You're getting the paperwork done on the sale of your boat, right? It's all legit. You're going to leave that in your pilothouse, that's what it's called?"

"Yeah."

"Okay, and the first load, four hundred pounds. Then they'll leave the money on this boat."

"You already planned it out?"

"Took some negotiating."

"You were pretty sure I'd like this boat."

She watched him looking at Nugs's boat, Four Stroke written on the side of it, the whole thing clean and shiny, brass rail running around the side, little cabin on deck with windows all around and said, "What's not to like?"

Ray said, "Yeah."

"They're going to like that the boat is the supply even better."

"You think?"

She said, oh yeah, sure. "Once they see how it works, they'll fit out a bunch more boats. They'll probably have container ships going to China and Europe fitted out next year."

Ray said, water the plants with salt water, and Sharon said, they'd work it out.

"Okay," Ray said, "we can get to Montreal or Halifax this year, spend the winter, and in the spring go south. Florida, or Barbados, or something."

"Sounds good."

She glanced at him, trying not to stare. She still couldn't figure him. This was exactly the deal she wanted but he took it so easy. Richard got everything he wanted, she got everything she wanted. She couldn't believe it would actually work out, there's really no such thing as win-win.

But it looked so good.

Christopher Cross, that was the guy's name. "Sailing." Something about a dream and the wind to carry me and soon I'll be free.

Soon.

RICHARD SAID, THAT'S GREAT, everything's great, a terrific deal. "Except, you don't get the money."

Sharon said, "What?"

"You can have the boat, but you don't get the money."

"What good's the boat without the money?"

Richard said, "You get to sail off into the sunset."

"You're the one," she said, "told me it was all business. What kind of business is this?"

"It's the kind we do."

She stared at him.

The music was loud and thumping, the chick onstage bored, and there was almost no one else in the place, Jackie's, a strip club on Queen Street East. It was done up outside to look like a western, cowboy boots and six-shooters, but it'd been a long time since anyone kept it up.

Sharon thought about saying, does your movie producer girlfriend know you come here for nooners, but she knew better than to push it. She knew better than to try to negotiate with him too. This was the deal. She had no idea how much the boat was worth, but it might be worth it just to get out of this stinking town. What did that song say? Everybody knows this is nowhere. Something about back home being cool and breezy. Well, hell, she didn't know about back home, but maybe Ray was right, sail that boat down to the Bahamas, he seemed to know what he was doing. Could be okay for a while. Sharon never did plan ahead very well.

So she said, "We get the boat."

"And you get a few bucks, come on, we're old friends. What you do," Richard said, "is you get two bags the same. We put the money in one, we put some counterfeit in the other. Some real bills across the top. You show your boy one bag, then you take the other."

She said, "What is this, a movie?"

"Does it feel like a movie?"

And she thought, no, it feels like me holding the fucking bag again while you get everything you want, but she just said, "No."

"And when you sail off into the wild blue, you tell him whatever you want. You open the bag and you see the phone books, or newspapers, or whatever shit, and you're shocked."

"How much across the top?"

"Real bills? I don't know, five, ten grand."

"Could it be twenty?"

Richard shook his head and said, sure, Shar, for you. "It can be twenty."

Sharon said, okay.

She leaned back in her chair and so did Richard. That was the deal, what choice did she have? Meeting over.

A stripper walked up to the table and put her hand on Richard's shoulder. She said, "You want to come upstairs now?" He looked at Sharon and the stripper said, "If you both want to come, I should get Lorraine." She looked at Sharon and said, "She's really good with chicks."

Sharon said that was okay, she was just leaving, and Richard said, you sure?

"Yeah, thanks anyway."

Walking out the door, Sharon was pissed off how guys like Richard could never grow up and it was still okay, they could still get to the top. She'd always be left holding the fucking bag.

On Queen, she lit a smoke and tried to think. There must be another way.

BURROUGHS WALKED INTO the station house, Sawchuck right behind him, saw Loewen talking to Sagar and said, "Hey, Loewen, she giving you heads . . . up," and laughed.

Sagar said, "You haven't heard?"

Burroughs stopped, shrugged, like if he hadn't heard it couldn't be important. "What?"

"We picked up Mon Oncle Bouchard ten minutes ago."

Even Burroughs couldn't be cool about that. He said, "Holy shit." Then he said, "Just him?"

"Five more in Montreal."

"They really think they have enough to make something stick?" He motioned to the command office down the hall.

Sagar was already walking that way, saying, "Come on, look at the warrant."

Burroughs said, "Holy shit" again, and looked at Loewen. Then he went into the command office.

And Loewen thought, yeah, you ugly shit, see what they got.

CHAPTER **20**

IT WAS THEIR THIRD DATE and she'd suggested staying in, said she'd gone on a cooking vacation to Tuscany, at the Villa Pantanio near a place called Siena and she wanted to try making something. Bergeron said that would be fine.

Really, Ruth was thinking that she liked this guy, and she wanted to find out if they actually got along. So far they'd been to a couple of restaurants, he had to leave early the first time to arrest the "torso killer," and the second time they had a little awkward moment when she was getting into her car until she kissed him. He'd said maybe they should go to a movie, but she wanted to find out how they got along with no distractions.

They got along good.

He told her about his wife and kids, and she told him about her kids—two girls, both still in high school—and she said her husband left her. Sometimes she told people her marriage ended, like it was a vacation or something and its time was up, but with Bergeron she said, "Harvey and I got together in university. It was good, you know, for a while, but he started seeing someone. Someone a lot younger."

Bergeron said, "He a lawyer?"

"How'd you know?"

"Just a guess."

She'd told him dinner could wait for an hour and took him upstairs.

They were back in the living room, then, finished dinner, which was great, better than any restaurant he'd ever been in, he said, and she believed him, and he said, "Best appetizer too," and she'd laughed and said it was the house specialty, but not many people got to try it. They finished the second bottle of wine, the one he brought, and she was feeling good, relaxed, at ease with this guy nothing like any of the men she knew.

If she asked him questions about his work, he answered her, but he didn't go on and on about it. She thought most of the guys she knew, if they did what he did, she'd never be able to shut them up. He said things like, "Yeah, a couple of times," when she'd asked if he ever had to use his gun and just "No," if he'd ever killed anyone.

He asked her a lot of questions, and he laughed when she said she felt like she was being interrogated. "I'm not really," she'd said, "I just thought I was supposed to say that."

"Don't worry, if you ever get interrogated, you'll know it."

He was barefoot with his Dockers back on and his shirt unbuttoned. She'd put on what he thought was a man's shirt till she told him it was lounging pyjamas for women, costs more than you want to know.

"I'm sure of that."

He looked around the house and she could tell it was a lot bigger than he was used to. So big four people could live in it and never have to see each other—like they did until Harvey left and she started insisting the girls eat dinner with her four nights a week. She thought they probably did out of pity, but if that's how they had to get it started, so be it. She didn't feel sorry for herself and they'd realized that soon enough.

Now Ruth and her policeman boyfriend, Detective, she called him, were sitting on the couch in the living room, the gas fireplace warming it up nice, talking about Neil Young.

Bergeron saying, "It must have been '68 or '69, place in town called the Riverboat. Buffalo Springfield had just broken up, he was playing solo. He played a song called 'Everybody Knows This Is Nowhere.' Said he was trying it out. I bought the album a couple years later when it came out, it was the title track."

"Never heard of it." She leaned against him, her head honest to God on his shoulder.

" 'Cinammon Girl' was the big hit off the album, almost the only one you hear these days. But that 'Everybody Knows,' it really hit me hard. Neil singing about when he thinks about home it's cool and breezy. When I thought about home it was suffocating."

"What do you think of as home now?"

"Oh, Toronto for sure." He had his arm around her and she liked it. "I've been here a long time. You?"

"I grew up here. You know the story, my grandparents came from some village in Russia, lived in Kensington Market, ran a fruit stand, my parents went to university, and bought a place at Bathurst and Eglinton."

"And you bought at Bayview and Lawrence."

"The houses keep getting bigger," she said, "but we're all nostalgic for Bubbie's two rooms upstairs from the store."

He just held her. She liked it, she liked this guy. If he had anything to prove he'd already done it. He didn't have answers for everything or try to fix everything. She could tell he knew that some things just were.

She sat up and asked if he'd like a glass of Scotch.

"Sure."

"I've got a bottle Heather Gelb gave me, one of the Divorced Women's Drinking Club members." She went to a cupboard in the dining room and came out with a bottle and two glasses. "We don't really drink, but Heather kept it when her husband moved out, said it cost eight hundred dollars. Let's see if it's really any better than eighty-dollar Scotch."

Bergeron was smiling. "Okay, let's."

She handed him a glass, realizing that after the two bottles of wine and now the Scotch, he'd be spending the night. There hadn't been a man who spent the night since Harvey left, but she liked the idea with Bergeron. She was just about to pour when the front door of the house opened and she said, "Shit."

Bergeron was on his feet. "What?"

"That's gotta be Harvey. I told him a hundred times he can't just walk in here anymore."

She watched Bergeron put the empty glass down on the coffee table and walk to the front door. He'd said the entrance hall was bigger than his whole living room when he'd arrived and now Ruth followed him, hanging back. She heard him say, "That's far enough," and heard Harvey say, "Who the hell are you?"

Bergeron said, "You can't just walk in this house."

"The hell I can't, this is my house."

"Not anymore."

Ruth was in the entrance hall then, standing in the doorway

to the living room. Harvey looked at her and said, "What the hell's going on, Ruth? Who's this idiot?"

"He's my date, Harvey."

"The girls aren't home, are they?"

She noticed Bergeron had a hand on Harvey's arm and was moving back out the front door. She said, "No, Harvey, the girls aren't home," and watched how easily Bergeron moved him outside.

The two men stood in the driveway, Harvey waving his arms and Bergeron calm. Calm but forceful, walking Harvey to his car, yet another Porsche, Ruth noticed, and standing there while Harvey opened the door. He had a few more things to say and Ruth had the feeling if he went on much longer Bergeron would help him into the car.

Finally Harvey backed down the driveway and drove away. Ruth couldn't help but smile as he left. She knew if she'd been home alone Harvey would have had some lame excuse for stopping by, he would have stayed for hours telling her how his relationship, like he'd ever called it that with her, wasn't working out right, how he missed the girls, and then begged to spend the night. In their bed.

But now she watched Detective Gord Bergeron come back up the driveway in his bare feet and she knew he'd never begged for anything in his life. He said, "We were going to try some Scotch, right?"

This time while she was pouring, his phone rang, quick little beeps, and he said he had to get it.

She watched him say, "Yeah," a few times and then, "Holy shit," and "Motherfucker," and then, "Yeah, good, thanks for calling. I'll see you in the morning," and hang up. She thought if he said he'd have to go she'd be understanding, but she wouldn't like it.

He said, "Wow, this is gonna be big."

"What is?" She didn't really expect him to answer. She figured if he said something like he couldn't tell her, she'd still be understanding, but if he said something like you don't want to know, that might be it for this.

He said, "That was Armstrong. The RCMP just arrested eight of our guys. Narcotics mostly, a couple of G&G, that's the Guns and Gangs unit. Shit, they got Burroughs. Raided our lab. Picked up Mon Oncle Bouchard in Montreal, some other bikers and a bunch of cops there. Oh man, the shit's really going to hit the fan now. This is huge. We're drinking this Scotch here, right?"

He held out his glass and Ruth didn't know what to think.

She poured them each a double.

RICHARD WAS ONLY half listening, looking at his watch, knowing what was coming, and anxious for it. But he was also interested in what this guy, Garry, was saying, telling them his theory about movies.

About sequels.

"It's not the sequels that are the problem," he was claiming. "That's what people always say, but some of the best movies ever were sequels. *Empire Strikes Back*, that's the best *Star Wars* movie."

Kristina drank some of her Scotch—no ice, no water, Richard noticed—and said, *"Godfather Two."*

Richard agreed with that, it was a great movie.

Garry agreed too. "Darker, more serious, the second ones always are. It's three, that's where they fall apart."

Richard was mostly watching Garry and Kristina talk, sitting in the lounge of the Westin Harbour Castle Hotel. They were down a couple of steps from the lobby, but it still felt wide open, even with the guy playing soft jazz on the grand piano, like they were sitting in a hotel lobby.

Kristina introduced Garry as the guy who was going to direct the movie she was producing. It was going to be a sequel, but Garry said don't call it that, say it has some of the same characters. He said, "A sequel sounds like you're cashing in," and Kristina said, "Aren't we?" and Garry sighed, and shook his head.

Richard thought that must be what real artists did. Before they came down from their room to meet with the guy— Kristina saying she just couldn't get out of the meeting and Richard could hang out in the room if he wanted—she had said the movie was a sequel to *Swing*. In the elevator, she told him it was the one, the lifestyle movie, and he'd said, oh right, the swingers, the wife swappers. And as the elevator doors opened, he'd said, "They go to that resort in Jamaica, what is it, Hedonism? And one couple brings back some coke. Yeah, all your movies are about smuggling dope."

Kristina had said, "You got a problem with that?" and Richard had said, no, he liked it.

"How do you feel about fags?"

Richard said he had no problem.

"Good. All the best directors are." They were in the lobby then, looking for a table in the lounge. "The thing about the swinging in the movie, it would only work if women were into it."

"In the movie?"

"No. Well, yeah, in the movie, but also the audience. A bunch of guys won't get together and go see a movie about swapping wives."

"No?"

Kristina said, no. "They'll joke about it, they might watch it on cable if it was porn, but if it's going to work as a movie, a real movie, women have to be into it. And women's movies are directed by fags."

They sat in the lounge and Richard started checking his watch. Kristina told him all about *Gone with the Wind* and all these other big Hollywood movies, how they were all about the chicks and all made by fags. Richard said, yeah, but that was a long time ago, why didn't she just get chicks to make them now, but then Garry showed up, and pretty much took over the conversation.

When Richard's phone rang, he looked disappointed and said he had to take this. Then he walked to an empty corner of the lounge.

On the phone, Nugs was calm. He said, "Hey." Then he said, "There's been some action in Montreal. Can you talk?"

And Richard thought, on a fucking cellphone? Shit. "It's okay, I know."

"I don't think so, it just happened. It's big."

Richard said, that's okay. "It was planned."

Silence on the phone for a few seconds, then Nugs said, "Motherfucker." Then he said it again, "Motherfucker."

Richard said, "Yeah." He waited a second, silence on the other end, good, and said, "Don't do anything now. Put something on the web page, we don't know anything about it, blah, blah, blah, let Diana handle it. We'll have a meeting tomorrow."

Nugs said, "Fuck. Planned?"

Richard could tell he needed to talk about it. Shit, the top guy for twenty-five years, Mon Oncle Bouchard taken down, some top guys in Quebec, and a whole bunch of cops—Mounties, Montreal cops, and practically the whole narco division in Toronto. All Nugs's contacts, his whole payroll. Yeah, he wanted to talk.

Richard said, "It's okay, Frantisek," using Nugs's real name. "Looks like head office is moving to Toronto. I just needed to make sure everything was okay here."

Nugs didn't say anything right away, and Richard thought, good, we're really coming along here. This'll work, this'll be good. Then Nugs said, "Yeah, let's have a meeting," and they set it up for noon the next day. Guys were going to need to sleep on this.

Richard flipped his phone shut and looked around the hotel lobby. There was some kind of festival going on in town, some kind of book thing. It was like the film festival without the actresses, just the nerds who make them. Chicks in glasses, middle-aged guys in shitty suits. But they all had money. This town was all about the money.

He was thinking, if this really was one of that guy's movies, this scene wouldn't be here, it would be in that restaurant on top of the Tower, the 360. Richard would look out over the lights of Toronto stretching off in three directions as far as he could see. He'd look south to New York state, right there, and he'd say something like, "I own this town."

But he walked back to the table where Kristina was still listening to Garry and he thought this was pretty good too. This was okay. Now Garry was talking about how it depended on whether they knew going in there were going to be more movies. "*Lord of the Rings*, you know there's three, you know the middle one is the middle."

Kristina said, what about *The Hobbit*, and Garry said, don't be silly, we're serious here. He said, "But, like *Saw*, if it does enough box office, they just keep making more until it flames out, *Saw Seven: Bifocals*."

Richard didn't see the problem with that. You make your money and you move on. He'd gotten all he could out of Montreal and Mon Oncle, and now he'd moved on to Toronto. He'd need a new national president, someone for the cops to focus on and Nugs sure seemed like the guy. Richard settled back in the big leather lounge chair and drank some of the Scotch. When Kristina had ordered it, Laphroaig, saying it some way he never would have got from the spelling, he'd said sure, he'd try it too. Turns out she was right, it was good, nothing like that blended crap he'd tried a couple times before.

Garry was saying, "It's all about the characters. The storyline isn't such a big deal, but these characters are good. And you promise me Ainsley Riordan is coming back, don't you? Don't you?"

"She'll be back."

Garry said, okay. "This is going to be great then, better than the first one, bigger."

And Richard thought, yeah, like Toronto's going to be bigger than Montreal. This is like the sequel, the next one. They're not fat guys on motorcycles anymore, they're businessmen in a business town. The cops taking over narco in Toronto, Barb Roxon and an inspector named Jurevich, and the Mounties coming in to clean up the mess were already on Richard's payroll. He watched Kristina joke with Garry, put her hand on his forearm, say something about Ainsley Riordan's boots, and he watched Garry pretend to be sick, and then they both laughed.

Richard thought, yeah, this was what he'd been working for, this was where he belonged.

CHAPTER **21**

"IT'S LIKE *American Idol* in there," Armstrong said. "He's singing so bad."

Bergeron said, shit, eight guys.

"You notice Barb Roxon didn't get picked up."

Bergeron looked at Loewen and said, "Or you."

Loewen said, come on, fuck.

They were having breakfast at the Golden Griddle on Carlton, across from the old Maple Leaf Gardens, place still empty since the new ACC went up.

Price came back to the table, his plate loaded with scrambled eggs and covered with huevo sauce, hash browns, and sausages.

McKeon said, "Jesus, Andre, you trying for disability leave?"

"Haven't eaten in days, this cholesterol diet." He looked at McKeon's bowl of yogurt and granola, and said, "You lost all the pregnancy weight, what are you doing? You're still breast feeding, the kid's going to starve."

She said, "Where's Sagar?"

Loewen said she was already in a task force meeting. "It's such a mess."

"They been working this over a year." Armstrong shook his head. "Goes back five at least, since Burroughs took over narco."

"Really since Anderson made inspector."

"I notice he's not charged."

McKeon said to Loewen, "And you didn't know?"

"She didn't tell me a thing. Said she didn't even know."

"She didn't know she was looking into cops?"

Loewen said, "She wasn't." They were all looking at him, Price, McKeon, Bergeron, and Armstrong. He said, "She's in enough shit. Lost her witness, those bikers'll never see the inside of a courtroom, the ones they picked up were all in Montreal."

They all ate.

Bergeron said, "Man, the work those guys will have to go over again."

"What guys?"

Bergeron said, yeah, what guys? "Who is going to take over? We're so short staffed now."

Loewen said, "Well, like you said, Barb Roxon is still here."

"Yeah, because she's clean, or they didn't have enough evidence?"

McKeon said, "Andre."

He said, "Well."

Armstrong said, "Looks like Whyte or Jurevich."

"At least Internal Affairs will be busy for years."

"Not that we give a shit about that," Armstrong said. "But then there's all the cases they worked, all that shit'll have to be opened up again. Five years' worth."

"Fuck."

"Well, Loewen, looks like you'll be busy. Might even get that promotion."

Loewen said, great. "Just what I wanted."

But he was thinking, I'll take it, though.

ARMSTRONG PARKED in front of the strip mall and said, "At least we can close this one now."

"At least."

In reception the East Indian chick with the thick, curly black hair was sitting on the couch reading a magazine. This time her T said, "They're real and they're spectacular."

Armstrong said, "Isn't that false advertising?"

She flipped a page in the magazine saying, "Cost you a hundred bucks to find out."

"You're still pissed," Armstrong said, "we didn't want to bang you last time."

She looked up and said, "You want to now?"

Bergeron said, "We're looking for Zahra Nekounam."

"Nobody here by that name."

"What is she here," Armstrong said, "Jasmine?"

The Indian chick, Sunitha, looked right at him and said, "What do you want her for?"

"We just want to talk."

Sunitha laughed, saying, shit, I never heard that before. Then, "She's with a customer. Been in five minutes, he's probably almost done."

"We can wait."

Sunitha looked at Bergeron, surprised they didn't just barge in and throw the guy out. But no, they waited.

A couple minutes later a guy in a suit, no more than thirty years old, came waltzing down the hall looking happy and relaxed—another satisfied customer—till he saw Armstrong and Bergeron. He knew what they were right away and looked like he was going to shit himself.

Bergeron said, "Get going," and the guy was Ben Johnson going out the door.

Sunitha smirked and laughed a little, flipping the page of the magazine.

As they walked down the hall, Bergeron said to her, "It feels good, you know. You should look into it, minority chick, you got a good chance of getting on the force," and she started to say something but stopped. It wasn't the stupidest idea she'd ever heard, becoming a cop.

ZAHRA WAS WASHING her hands in the sink in the corner of the little room, looked like a doctor's exam room. She said, "Wait in reception, I come out," and Armstrong said, "That's okay, we're here already."

She turned around, drying off her hands, and said, "No discount for double, you both pay."

Armstrong said, "We look like customers to you?" and she shrugged. Why not?

She was wearing some kind of loose pants, looked like silk, with an elastic waistband pulled low, low over her hips and a tube top over her breasts. And sandals, Bergeron noticed, that looked expensive and comfortable. Massage parlour, he figured, on her feet all day. She said, "What you want? You want to watch?"

Armstrong said, no. "We want to talk to you about your husband. Kumar."

She looked sad. "You police?"

"Yeah."

She asked if she could get her smokes, so they went to the tiny lounge room. Zahra got her cigarettes, then opened the back door of the place, and stepped out.

Armstrong and Bergeron stood outside the door and Zahra sat on an old chair. Behind the mall were the loading docks and garbage bins for all the stores. She lit her smoke and inhaled deeply. Up close like this, in the sunshine, Bergeron could see she was older than he had thought, into her thirties anyway.

He said, "You didn't report it."

"Report what?"

"Your husband getting killed."

She shrugged and smoked, flicking ash. "Nothing to report, we are not here, we don't exist."

Bergeron looked at Armstrong, then back to Zahra. He said, "What happened?"

"You know already, don't you?"

Her accent was heavy but her English was okay. Bergeron couldn't figure her at all. He said, "Did you push him or did Sharon MacDonald?"

Zahra shook her head and said, "Sure, you want to put someone in jail."

"We just want to know what happened."

She inhaled on her cigarette and blew smoke at the sky. It was cold out and she wrapped her arms around her naked midriff. "What happen?"

They waited, giving her some time. She looked like she wanted to tell someone, might as well be these guys. After a minute she said, "He hated here." She looked up at them and shrugged. "He wanted to go back."

"To Iran?"

"Shiraz. Is beautiful."

Armstrong said, yeah. "I've heard that."

She looked at him like she didn't believe him, but then she shrugged, she didn't really care. "We were in England, then we came here. He was artist, you know?"

"We heard."

"You hear about Mahmoud?"

"Yeah."

Now she really didn't believe them. "Pig. Scum. Kumar was very good artist. Very good."

"But."

She smoked and shook her head. "But he thought like artist. Lived like artist. No money. Mahmoud, he wanted money."

"An extortion racket? That why you're here?"

She said, "I give him nothing. I do what I want."

Bergeron and Armstrong both watched her. They believed her.

She said, "Kumar hated it here, wanted to go back. I say no way. I love it here." There was a lot of sarcasm in her voice, but it wasn't total. "You know why people love Toronto?"

"Why?"

"People come here to make money. No other reason. Make good money."

"But he wanted to go back home."

"Home." She took a final drag, and flicked her cigarette towards the garbage bin. "What is home?"

The two cops looked at her and Zahra tilted her head back, closed her eyes. "He was depressed, he was sad. He gave up. I would not go with him, I would not move again." She looked right at Bergeron and said, "When he jumped, I almost jumped with him."

"He jumped?"

She stood up, took half a step so she was almost touching Bergeron. "He jumped."

She walked back into the massage parlour.

Armstrong looked around the loading docks and garbage bins, and said, "You know something."

"What?"

"I believe her."

"Well, we got no evidence either way, now." Then, "You know what's funny."

"What?"

"If we had just interviewed her to begin with, talked to her and Sharon MacDonald, we would have written it up as suicide."

"Yeah, even with Sharon MacDonald's print on the back of the guy's jacket? And her history with him?"

"Sure. I mean, what could we have done with that? Imagine Angie DeRosa, that's all we bring her? She never would have pressed charges."

"But Burroughs had to go and get involved, try to protect his buddies."

"Guy's problem, he has ambition."

"It'll get you every time."

They walked back through the massage parlour to their car.

IN THE ROOM AT the Westin Harbour Castle, Kristina had binoculars and she was standing at the window looking out. There were a lot of sailboats tied up to docks all along the water and a couple of ferries making the ten-minute trip out to the islands. And there were even some freighters. Off to the left, the big cement company silos were right beside the Docks nightclub, and off to the right was the Island airport, small planes taking off and landing all day. She said, "After *Dead Calm*, you remember that one? With Nicole Kidman and Sam Neill?"

Richard was lying back on the bed, his head on a couple of pillows. He said, yeah, the one on the boat, with the crazy guy.

"That's the one. After that, we made one on a plane, the whole thing took place on a Cessna."

"The whole thing?"

She put the binoculars down and turned around. She was wearing the white robe the hotel left out in the bathroom, Richard didn't think he'd ever seen anyone put one of those on before. "Yeah, it's almost real time, the movie. Starts out in Colombia, they load the plane with coke, it's got extra fuel tanks, and they start flying north. It's a couple, like on the boat, a guy and his wife, but they're not getting over the death of their kid, they're entrepeneurs."

Richard said, "They started a business in Florida, sightseeing, or something, sunk their whole lives into it, every cent they had. Then, when they were going bankrupt, they met this guy."

"Something like that. They were the all-American couple, blonde, fresh-faced."

"They were just going to do this once, pay off some bills."

Kristina smiled and said, "What business did you say you were in?"

"So what happens to them, the all-American couple?"

She walked the few steps from the window and sat on the edge of the bed. Richard, his hands behind his head, a little hair on his chest, his dick still damp, looked right at her.

"There's some flashbacks, we see them getting in deeper and deeper. Anyway, when the picture starts, they're loading the dope and the Colombian guy asks them to take a passenger, some guy they've never met."

"And they do."

"And as they fly, they get more and more paranoid."

"As you do," Richard said, "when your sightseeing Cessna is full of cocaine, your flight plan says you started in Bohunk, Tennessee, and a guy you don't know is there to kill you or bust you when you land in Florida."

"So you have seen it."

"Something like it."

"Well, it sounded easy," Kristina said, "shooting on a plane. Build a set, get a little second unit stuff in the sky, and it's all controlled."

She ran her hand up and down his leg, from his ankle to his knee and back. "It was one of my first as PM, production manager. Sort of between the producers and the crew. Tough job." She ran her hand a little higher and watched him twitch.

"But you could do it."

"It would have been easier if it was prop coke instead of the real thing."

"A little."

Now she was rubbing his thigh.

"It played some festivals, did okay, went to cable, video. This was back in the day. Came out on DVD a little while ago."

Richard said, "You're proud of your work."

She kept rubbing his thigh, but she didn't look at him. It had been a couple of days since they met at the condo building, but it wasn't the first time they'd been to bed.

She said, "Can I tell you something?"

"Sure."

She still didn't look at him. "I got too far in with somebody and I didn't tell them," she said. "Then when it came up, it was a big deal, but I don't think it has to be a big deal."

"No?"

"There are a lot of people in the movie business who are posers, you know?"

"Yeah."

"You know, they want to make these tough-guy movies and hang out with tough guys, but really they all went to private schools, and the Ivy League, and all that."

Richard had no idea where she was going with this, but he knew if she kept rubbing his thigh with her long red nails, they'd have to stop talking and go again.

"And I didn't. I mean, I did, I went to private school and everything, but I'm not from old money."

"No?"

"No. And you don't seem like you are either."

"No?" Now he could see where she was going with this, but he was just going to let her. What she really wanted to find out, he was pretty sure, was where he got his money. She might even want him to invest in a movie. He wasn't sure what he thought of that.

"But I figure, you know, I'm making a new start here, new city. I've got a new deal with a bigger American company, things are going well."

"So, what's the problem?"

She said, "Have you noticed something about my movies? I told you about a few of them."

He was going to string her along, but he liked the feel of her hand on his thigh, and he liked the way her robe was falling open, the sides of her perky little tits peeking out at him. He said, "Yeah, they're all about dope."

"Or smuggling," she said. "We do a lot about smuggling. I get the feeling I can tell you this, you seem like a cool guy. I started out in the business. I wanted to make it on my own, you know, do everything myself."

"Like in the movies," Richard said, and she nodded, like she understood he meant that was the only place it works like that.

"Yeah. But my dad's a little famous and people who knew him, or wanted to know him, were willing to help me." Her hand stopped and she looked at him. "You ever heard of Ronnie Northup?"

Richard laughed. He said, shit, I thought this was going to be serious, some big criminal thing or something. "Ronnie Northup, the king of pot? Yeah, I've heard of him."

"And what do you think?"

"What do you mean?" Richard still didn't know about her, but if she was Ronnie's daughter, this was going to be better than he thought. In the early sixties, Ronald Northup, a scholarship kid from Wales, started importing hash into the U.K. By the seventies, he was probably the biggest importer in Europe and he moved into North America. Back then a lot of it came through Montreal, and when Richard was a kid, he probably unloaded tons of the stuff. Ronnie Northup was a legend. He shipped it in rock band equipment. Richard remembered one of those big seventies bands, Pink Floyd or ELP or Supertramp, they did a tour with a whole orchestra, started it in Montreal—hundreds of crates full of equipment were actually pound after pound of Afghan hash and Thai stick.

Kristina said, "I got a lot of meetings because people wanted to hear stories about my dad and I got a lot of scripts that had to do with that stuff, but I really did make it on my own. The meeting is only the beginning, I still had to close the deals, make the movies."

"Sure."

"So what about you? What's your deep, dark secret?"

Richard said, me? "I don't have any secrets."

Kristina started to say, sure you do, everyone does, but there was a loud bang, like fireworks going off right outside the window. She jumped up, and looked out, and said, "Holy shit," walking to the window, and picking up the binoculars.

Richard stood up and walked over, stood right behind her. She said, "That's no special effect."

The huge fireball was burning out and the giant plume of black smoke was rising.

Richard said, "No."

Kristina said, "No. Something blew up."

Richard put his hands on her shoulders, and his lips close to her ear, and said, "Looks like a boat, some kind of accident," and she said, you think?

She took his hands and pulled them down to her breasts and bent over a little, grinding her ass into his dick. She said, "I don't know, look, there's nothing left, that wasn't a freighter. Fuck."

Richard said, yeah, that's a good idea, come on, and started to pull away, but she held his hands and kept grinding into him.

"Don't go anywhere." She moved against him, the robe sliding off, and said, "Right here, okay," and Richard thought, okay, standing here looking out the window at the fire and the boats going to check it out, if that's what she wants. Like a movie.

———

J.T. STEPPED ONTO THE BOAT carrying two plastic bags from Swiss Chalet and a six-pack of Corona. He walked into the pilothouse of the tug.

Nugs got up from one of the high swivel chairs, looked like a barstool, and said, "You get the rib combo?"

"I thought you said just ribs."

"Shit."

Nugs moved past him and J.T. followed to the mess, Nugs saying, "How'd it go?" and J.T. said, good, man, good.

"Lit up the harbour."

Nugs took the round plastic container out of the bag and pulled off the lid. He said, "Oh good, there is sauce," and poured most of it over his fries.

J.T. looked through the tray of knives and forks on the table for an opener, Corona still not using twist tops, and said, "Must be tough, see that boat go."

"I was finished with it." Nugs dipped a rib in sauce and ate off most of the meat.

J.T. watched him, surprised he didn't get that sauce all over his beard and mustache. J.T. was sticking with the clean-shaven Army haircut he'd had pretty much his whole life.

"Still, man, it was a beautiful boat."

"Had to be done."

J.T. nodded, thinking, yeah, that's way you've got to be in this business, not sentimental. It was just a boat, you can always get another one. Shit, look at all the chicks Nugs's been through since that Amber.

"You see the plans?"

J.T. said, yeah, and picked up the papers. Ten pages of drawings, looked pretty good, guy did them with a ruler at least, and two pages of supplies listed at the back.

Nugs said, "We're gonna make some changes. Guy says do it with plywood and two-by-fours, we're going to go with metal supports, weld it together."

"It's a big space," J.T. said. "Take a lot of work."

"You don't work, you don't get paid. Plenty of guys looking for work."

"You got a captain? Someone to, what do they say, pilot it?"

Nugs said, yeah. "Great thing about this tug-and-barge system, you only need, like, six guys for the crew. Plus, we can leave it one place for a long time."

J.T. looked out the small windows of the boat, staring at the Stelco plant, the big coke ovens, but imagining the open sea. Or at least the Great Lakes. He said, "You ever hear that song, Gordon Lightfoot? About the boat?"

" 'Wreck of the *Edmund Fitzgerald*'? Sure." Then it was in J.T.'s head, Lightfoot's voice, almost talking, a deep monotone, but getting higher at the end of every line. Nugs said, "I like that one, something about, creeping 'round my back door."

J.T. said, "They all kind of sound the same to me."

"Man's got a style."

J.T. figured, yeah, sure. You get something unique, something people hear and right away go, oh yeah, that's Lightfoot, you stick with that. He said, "So, they really didn't have anything on here?"

"Couple of plants on the other boat, the barge, whatever they call it."

"But we can fit out the whole cargo space?"

"Not the whole thing, some of it. Still have to move some cargo. But there's so much space on here. I'm thinking about putting a lab where they had their plants."

J.T. thought, shit, yeah, a floating meth lab, keep it moving, getting supplies from different cities, that'd be great. He said, "I've got a contact in Detroit could move a lot of this shit."

Nugs said, "Yeah? We've got contacts."

"Always good to have more."

Nugs said, yeah.

"I met this guy in Afghanistan, Army sergeant from Detroit, was with Young Boys as a kid, delivering on bicycles since he was, like, ten. Could do amazing math in his head. Set up a decent network, that war is like a pipeline for dope."

Nugs finished off his ribs and tore open the little damp napkin thing. "What was that like, Afghanistan?"

J.T. smiled and drank some beer. "Great, man. Fucking Boy Scouts with guns. Sleeping under the stars and blowing shit up all day. It's like a game for those ragheads. They've been doing it for hundreds of years, fighting off everybody. What else have they got to do?"

"But the chicks all covered up?"

"Oh man, they got some whores, you wouldn't believe. They start them young, train them. Not like here, these chicks have no attitude."

Nugs laughed and said, you're getting all nostalgic.

J.T. said, yeah. "But you can't do it forever, you know."

"You ready for some real work now?"

J.T. looked at Nugs and saw a guy, for the first time, looked like he was serious. "Whole new game, isn't it?"

Nugs said, "It's time Toronto started running this country."

J.T. said, yeah. It was good, a real chance, like they said, in on the ground floor. Nugs was stepping up big-time. This Richard Tremblay, he was the real deal. No one could get in their way now.

Nugs said, "Speaking of whores, you want a party?"

"In Hamilton?"

"Hey, man, Steeltown, the city that works. Some quality working girls."

J.T. said, yeah, sure.

They walked off the huge empty boat, J.T. thinking that Ray, poor bastard trying to unload the hunk of junk, actually had a good idea. And balls of steel, but he was a loose end.

Had to be done.

SHARON SAID, "How did you know there was a bomb on board?"

"Like you said, they weren't just going to let us sail off into the sunset."

"I thought they'd give us the boat at least," she said, thinking, after they wouldn't give us the money.

Ray paddled the little inflatable raft towards the beach at Ashbridges Bay, around the point from the smoking debris of the sailboat and said, "I saw the one with the short hair, looks like he's in the Army, doing something."

"He could have just been getting Nugs's stuff."

"Well, that and I figured once they found out my boat was empty."

"What? Empty?"

He shrugged. "It could be a giant floating grow op, like we said. Eddie worked out all the details, the power, the generator, solar panels, windmills, scaffolding for the beds, everything."

"And it worked?" She couldn't believe this guy.

"It could work." He paddled hard towards the beach. It was a cold October day, with one of those low, hanging grey skies. "Pretty sure it could."

"Pretty sure, holy shit." She shook her head. She'd had a

paddle in her hand since they jumped off the sailboat, but she hadn't stuck it in the water.

"Come on," Ray said, "what did they spend fitting out that brewery, a million bucks? I told you, I'm broke."

"And insane. They're still going to kill you."

"They think they just did." Ray stopped paddling and looked at her. "We left them the plans, like a business plan. They're businessmen. You said yourself, once they get it up and running, they'll fit out more boats, they'll take them on the high seas into international waters, they'll fit out container ships. It'll work easy."

"Easy?"

They got to the shore and Ray got out, pulling the raft the final few feet. Sharon stepped out, not even getting her boots wet. She said, "But now we've got nothing."

"Maybe," Ray said. He started letting the air out of the raft and said, "But you stole their money."

Sharon stared at him, stepping on the raft, getting the air out of it, and said, "What?"

He didn't even look up, he just kept pushing on the rubber, the whooshing of the air coming out about the only sound around them. "You were supposed to switch bags, give me phone books, or newspapers, or something, and give them back the money. But you didn't." He stopped and looked up at her. "You switched it again."

She said, "You think I'd take a chance like that?"

"Once you had that money in your hands, you'd never give it up."

"You have no idea what you're doing."

"Maybe not." He looked right at her and she thought, yeah,

but maybe. Then he nodded at something behind her, and she turned around and saw Bobbi and Eddie walking along the boardwalk.

She said, "You think they'll just let us go? They might think we're dead now, but the minute we start using credit cards or passports, they'll find us. They have connections, you know."

"What was your plan, taking the money? Give it to your daughter. Didn't you think they'd go after her?"

Sharon didn't say anything. She hadn't thought that far ahead, still her biggest problem, jumping into something without thinking it through. She saw a way to grab that money, so she did. Bobbi was supposed to meet her in Kingston and she was going to jump off the boat and leave Ray there.

Except she really did like him.

Bobbi and Eddie walked up and Sharon noticed they were holding hands. She wasn't too surprised.

Ray said, "Did you get it?" and Eddie said, of course, and dropped a canvas bag on the beach.

Sharon recognized it, but couldn't place it. She said, "Was that in my apartment?"

Eddie said, the cops aren't watching it anymore. "They've got their own problems."

Ray unzipped it and said, "Your buddy, Ku, he was an artist, did you know that?"

"No. How did you?"

"His wife told me. You know what else she told me?"

"What?"

"That guy who came looking for him, the guy in your bathtub?"

"Yeah?"

"He wanted these." Ray opened the bag and Sharon looked in. It was filled with passports, Canadian, American, European. Driver's licenses, birth certificates.

Sharon picked some up. There were no pictures. They were perfect fakes. She said, "Holy shit."

"Guy was a pretty good artist. And a hell of a forger."

Sharon said, poor guy.

Bobbi said, "The money's still in the car, it worked great."

Sharon's plan. She bought three bags the same instead of two. Showed Ray the money on the dock by the sailboat. He carried the bag of phone books on board himself. She left the other bag, the one with the money, in the trunk of the Mini. When they sailed off, J.T. came back and got it. Except he got another bag of phone books and Bobbi got the one with the money.

"So," Sharon said, "What do we do now?"

Ray said, "You said you liked to drive. Just take off, go to Vancouver, down the coast to L.A., maybe Mexico."

She said that sounded good.

Bobbi said, cool, and held up a set of keys. "Take the Mini. We'll get something else. Meet up with you."

Ray said, "The Mini?"

They walked to the parking lot, two couples, out for a stroll.

Sharon squeezed Ray's hand and said, "You know, not all deals work out like this."

"We'll see."

And she thought, but maybe.